FIFTY FEET DOWN

Sophie Tanen

This is a work of fiction. Names, characters, places, and incidents either are the product of the author's imagination or are used fictitiously. Any resemblance to actual persons, living or dead, events, or locales is entirely coincidental.

FIFTY FEET DOWN. Copyright 2023 © Sophie Tanen. All rights reserved. No part of this book may be used or reproduced in any manner whatsoever without written permission except in the case of brief quotations embodied in critical articles and reviews. For more information visit www.hansenhousebooks.com.

Cover design by Elizabeth Jeannel

ISBN 978-1-956037-25-8 (hardcover)

ISBN 978-1-956037-24-1 (paperback)

ISBN 978-1-956037-23-4 (eBook)

First Edition

First Edition: September 2023

This Hardcover edition first published in 2023

Published by Hansen House

www.hansenhousebooks.com

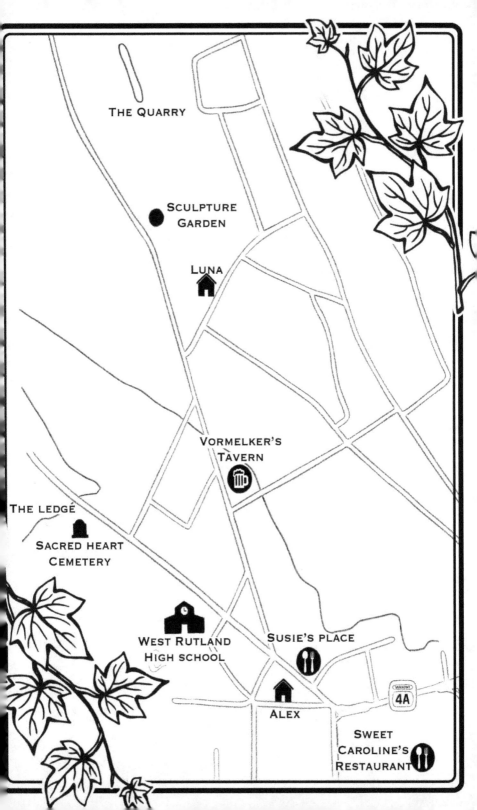

For Mom and Dad,

Vermont will always be home, because that's where you are

Chapter One

I HAVE NO CHOICE but to actually leave the apartment today, because the peeling green wallpaper I've been staring at isn't hiding the secrets I need to discover about this new town. Today is a day for exploring, for digging. Not that there's an overwhelming amount of exploring to do, but, well, it's better than unpacking for the third day in a row.

It's easy to forget in the mid-morning haze that I no longer live alone, and my toes snag on the cramped kitchen table as I maneuver around the space. Of all the recent changes in my life, the one that breaks me might just be this half broken espresso machine. I'm trying to figure out which button to press, desperate to fill my empty coffee mug.

I slide the cup away from me, leaning forward until my forehead presses against the cool counter, exhaling in frustration. Everything seems to be a million times harder lately, taking more effort and energy than I have left in my reserves. My eyes blink up, gazing at the rustic red mug I'd brought with me when I "moved." It has a black outline of the Brooklyn bridge, and I reach a delicate finger out, tracing it. Even with the pad of my finger pressed right up against the ceramic, everything feels too far away to handle.

As I stand up again to wrestle with the grinder, the door on the other side of the living room creaks open. Reyna steps out, rubbing her eyes, the long black hair that nears her belly button a complete mess. I can't see past her fingers, but I think she might be glaring at me.

"Still waging war against the coffee maker?" she grumbles, pulling a green mug from the cupboard.

I deliberately don't look away from the coffee grounds I've spilt over the slab of marble beneath me. "Yep. Still losing, too."

"Your ability to turn every inch of this apartment into your own personal enemy is *baffling* to me. I finally woke up after you rammed into the couch for the third time."

"It's eleven in the morning on a Tuesday, I refuse to feel bad about that. Besides, I needed you out here so you could make my coffee for me out of pity."

"You better learn quick." She pushes past me, and I step out of the way, knowing she'll make her cappuccino well before I figure out which button to press. "Here in Vermont, we actually have to make our own coffee. There's not a Starbucks on every corner."

I resist the urge to point out that there's not a Starbucks on *any* corner. Or anywhere, for that matter. "Who says I go to Starbucks?"

She looks over her shoulder, a flicker of humor in her brow. "We don't have a Dunkin Donuts, either."

Glancing at the ceiling, I push further away, resigning myself to one of the granola bars I have tucked under my bed. I open my mouth to ask something else, to try to break the ice of a new living situation, but my phone blares out from where I tossed it on the couch. Taking the out, I rush over to it, smiling tightly as I retreat back into my room. I glance at the screen, only remembering that I haven't put on my glasses when the name flashing at me is blurry and illegible. I don't bother looking for my glasses just yet, because there's only one person that ever calls me, so I press the green *accept* button anyway.

"Alex!" a bright voice chimes through the speaker, confirming my suspicions. Elise, my sort of boss but mostly friend, has probably been at our office for hours, waiting until an appropriate time to call. I'd warned her that if I had to actually work on this *expedition*, or whatever she wants to call it, I would at least get to sleep in on some days. She decided that was a fair tradeoff.

I pull aside the curtains I managed to get up yesterday after several failed attempts, peering out the window. The street below is mostly deserted, since it's mid morning on a workday in a town with a population of less than two thousand residents. I bet if I looked outside at the busiest part of the day, though, I'd still see nobody.

"Good morning," I mumble, collapsing back onto my bed. At least I'd been able to find a decent mattress for my shitty apartment.

"*Is* it good?" she asks hopefully.

"It's decent," I cave in, because I hate the guilt seeping into her voice. It wasn't her fault that I'd already used up too much time off this year, that I couldn't afford my own personal investigation.

Elise and I work together for a small, but not tiny, online newspaper in New York City. She's not my *boss* boss, but she's technically my higher up, and she somehow convinced my *actual* boss, Tom (the one good thing about this is getting away from that asshole), to let her be the one to check up on me and take reports.

There's a small creak from her side of the line, and I can imagine her leaning back in her old desk chair, propping a foot up on our shared trash can. "How are you getting settled?"

I look around my tiny space, feeling like I'm in a dorm room for the first time in nearly five years. I hadn't expected much more than a dingy, shared apartment, but it's still sort of a letdown to realize I won't get to sleep in my *actual* bed for at least a few more weeks. Or months.

Oh, *God*, what if it's months? There's too much to do, too much to find out, too much-

"It could be worse," I finally say.

She sighs, the sound crackling through the speaker. "I know. This is always the problem with out of state projects, we have to find the cheapest lodging possible. You're lucky you're not in a hotel."

"A hotel would be nicer, probably."

The unspoken words echo between us. *You're lucky you found a way for us to pay for it.* But she can't say that out loud, not in the office. Instead, she says, "There are no hotels in the actual confines of West Rutland. I'm pretty sure you have to live there to put on a convincing investigation."

"Oh, God, *please* don't call it an investigation. I'm not a freaking cop, what if someone hears you?"

Visualizing Elise's grin through her voice, she says, "Sorry, I just had to get you smiling. You've been pouting ever since you found out you had to actually move."

"It's not moving," I point out. "I'm being *temporarily dislodged.*" What had initially been a plan to go on vacation, to look for my own answers, had been converted into so much more for the sole sake of money, and not losing my job.

"Is the town at least nice? What is it..." she trails off, rustling as she looks through her notes, "West Rutland? That's totally a town where a bad director would set a shitty movie, don't you think?"

"I *feel* like I'm in a shitty movie," I mumble. "And I don't know, I've barely left my place other than to go to the Walmart in the city next to us. Did you know that the Walmart in Rutland- not to be confused with *West Rutland*, I guess they're two completely different places- is the lowest performing Walmart in the *country*? Someone sitting half passed out on the ground outside the store told me that."

Elise laughs incredulously. "Wait, so they just named an entirely separate town, outside of Rutland, *West Rutland?*"

"There's also a Rutland Town, if you're interested. I guess people in Vermont aren't super creative."

"Guess not," she hums. I sense the mood shift before she speaks. "Hey, um, what did you tell Rachel?"

I freeze in my tracks, fingers and breath going still. "I didn't tell Rachel jack shit."

Elise clears her throat, recognizing her misstep at the same time as she realizes she can't go backward. "Oh. Well, I just figured-"

"Well, stop it. And if she asks, you can tell her to fuck right off."

A sigh. "Alex-"

I hold up a finger, even though she can't see me. "Or, better yet, if she stops by the office, tell her I ran off to Vermont of my *very own* volition, just to get away from her." I pause. "No, actually, don't. She doesn't need the ego boost."

"I don't think she's feeling at all egotistical at the moment-"

"Good," I spit, even as I sink further into my bed, memories plaguing me from only months ago. Questions and no answers. "If she tries to call you, don't answer."

After a moment, Elise sighs and obediently changes the subject. "Okay, well, what about… him?"

Him. That's almost worse. "I'm working up to it."

"You've been working up to it for several months."

"And I think that's understandable, given the circumstances."

Elise doesn't press the subject. She remembers quite well when I showed up at the door of her apartment, my father's will in hand, tears streaming down my cheeks. "Are you going out today?"

"Yeah," I say, pulling on my shoes and nearly dropping my phone in the process. "I was just about to go find someplace to get lunch, see if I can't talk to a few of the locals. There's not that many bars, though, which sort of puts a wrench in my plan of '*sit next to random people while they drink and get them to talk.*'"

"I'm sure you'll figure something out," Elise teases, and I roll my eyes at the sheer unhelpfulness of it all. "In the meantime, while you go prancing around a small town in the suburbs-"

"I don't think Vermont has suburbs."

"-I have my own work to do. Call me with an update sometime soon, work related or otherwise." The word *otherwise* has too much meaning behind it, and I flinch.

"Don't expect much," I choke out, but she's already hung up.

Huffing, I gather everything I might need to explore for at least a couple hours. Slinging my bag across my shoulder, I double and triple check that it has my notebook, wallet, and at least three pens in case I lose one, or it runs out of ink. After a moment, I open my wallet to make sure I have cash. Will most places here be cash only because they're small businesses? I don't really know how it works. I've gotten way too used to using Apple Pay.

I grew up in New York City, in the Bronx before moving to Brooklyn, and remained there even in the recent loss of my parents. It felt wrong to leave, even though I was never particularly close to either of them. That's the trouble with growing up in the city; it moves so fast paced, so... merciless. Jobs take up every ounce of your time because everything is so competitive. I've never minded, given that I'm single and I work with my best friend, but if you have a family... I don't know, it's easy to get distracted.

And in no time, you continue to get distracted, every day, until time runs out.

Even so, the city was all I ever knew. No vacations, no business trips, no field trips. Crossing the state line between upstate New York and Vermont was officially the first time I left the state. But when I crossed it, I felt... absolutely nothing. Maybe because the one person who meant most to me is now dead to me, and the other two are actually dead.

I glance warily out the window once more, where I can see my neighbor two houses down come outside to check the mail. Who would have thought I'd be nervous to go out and meet a bunch of strangers from redneck Vermont?

Despite the fact that it's mid-June, I grab a flannel in case I stay out into the evening. I wrap it tightly around my waist, covering the inch of skin exposed between my short sleeve button down and black shorts. I hesitate at the door to my bedroom, fingers lingering over the rusty doorknob.

Moving into a new apartment is always so weird, especially since Reyna has already lived here for several years. I know she's always had a roommate, and I'm just replacing someone else, but I still feel like I'm intruding on her home.

This place certainly doesn't feel like mine.

Mentally smacking myself, I wrench open the door to find Reyna sitting at the tiny table squeezed into the kitchen. Her bedroom is across the way from mine, and in between is a single room that functions as both kitchen and living room. The stove and fridge are pushed against the back window, the TV stand so close to my door that I can't open it all the way. The first couple days, I tripped over the leg when bolting from my room, but today I cautiously veer past it.

"I'm heading out," I say as I pass Reyna.

She only grunts, hunched over her laptop and clearly immersed in work as she eats a bowl of cereal.

After a moment's delay, I plunge forward. "I'm going to grab an early lunch. Any recommendations?" I don't bother asking her to join me because one, she's eating literally right now, and two, I don't really have the desire to spend any more time with her than necessary.

When she doesn't respond immediately, I move to leave, but then she mutters over the bowl, "You should go to Suzie's."

I turn back, seeing that she still hasn't bothered to look up. "Suzie's?"

She nods, swallowing a spoonful of oats. "Suzie's Place, it's just down the road. Not a bad diner to go for some decent hash browns."

I don't mention that basically everything in this town is "just down the road," considering it's made up of one road, and instead murmur a simple, "Thanks," before swinging the door open.

We live on the second floor of an apartment complex just off the main street in town, and the metal stairs clang and creak as I descend them carefully. The building looks so old, I don't really trust them to hold my weight yet, and I breathe a sigh of relief when my sneakers make contact with the sidewalk below. I look around to gain my bearings. The whole place smells of pine and maple, smoke drifting over the trees from one of the nearby factories. There are a few places that look like stores or restaurants, and I march forward, hoping I'm heading in the direction of Suzie's Place.

Wrapping the top part of my short, auburn hair into a tight knot, I take in the quiet of the neighborhood, the closed front doors and windows. There's nothing protecting me from standing out, no big crowd to hide in, no tall buildings to duck into. I walk on, fiddling with the bottom button of my shirt, searching for something to do with my hands in this foreign place. They fall to my side when I see the large, wooden sign reading *Suzie's Place* in large, blue block letters. It's weather worn, the paint peeling so much that the letter S in *Suzie* is nearly illegible.

A little bell rings when I push the creaking door open, revealing a clearly old, half-filled restaurant. Not old as in gross, but old in style, and the whole place is shrouded in the scent of maple syrup. A woman in an apron and about four different kinds of denim, maybe in her mid thirties, leans against the counter, chatting to an older woman who's eating a large stack of pancakes. Glancing between the completely full booths and the counter, I slide onto a stool two seats away from them.

The server notices me, holding up a finger to the other customer and coming over to me. "Well, you certainly look new. Driving through?"

Hm. They probably get those a lot. West Rutland doesn't exactly seem like the place people move to voluntarily, not unless they have some sort of link to it. Too small, too obscure. A smudge on the map nestled between Rutland and Castleton Corners that no one notices unless it's pointed out. "Um, no. Just moved here."

Her face brightens up, and to my surprise, the customer the waitress had been talking to slides her stuff over, moving so she's sitting next to me. "You hear that, Lucia? She just moved here." The waitress turns back to me. "It's not every day new folk move here. It's always a little bit exciting."

"I'm Lucia," the woman next to me says, extending her hand. She peers down at me from a pair of thin glasses, eyes blank and so skeptical that I recoil. Hesitantly I take it, looking at her clothes to see it's covered with... is it paint? But there's no colors, it's all white and gray. "That's Joanna, she owns this place."

"I'm Alex." I turn to Joanna. "If you're Joanna, who's Suzie?"

Joanna smiles widely. "Call me Jo. Suzie was my grandmother. She and my grandpa opened this place up when they were young, and we've managed to keep it running."

"It's popular," Lucia says, taking another bite of her pancakes. "Businesses with sentimental value tend to be that way."

"Ah, Lucia," Jo teases. "Are you saying I hold sentimental value to you?"

"I'm saying your food is the best part of this town," Lucia says, fond. "And you're pretty nice to have around, too."

"Especially when you needed a babysitter."

I follow along blankly, feeling a little overwhelmed. If I went to a random restaurant in the city, absolutely no one would talk to me. The waitress would come over, take my order, and I'd eat the rest of my meal in silence.

And that's the way I preferred it, to be honest.

Sensing my discomfort, Jo changes courses. "What can I get you?"

Jumping, I look frantically at the menu, and when I can't read it because I forgot my glasses (it's one of my main flaws, nine out of ten days I just can't see) I say instead, "What do you recommend?"

"Get the maple pancakes," Lucia advises before Jo can respond, and as she says it, I remember how big maple syrup is in Vermont. "I promise they'll be the best you've ever tried."

I'm a fan of everything maple, so I flip my menu shut. "Sounds like a plan. Maple pancakes it is. Some coffee, too, please."

Grinning, Jo takes the menu. "Coming right up." In a flash, she disappears through a door that must lead to the kitchen, her long blonde braid swaying between her shoulder blades, and I wonder whether there's another cook back there. There's no way she's the only waitress *and* the only cook.

"So," Lucia says, with that distinct air that makes me feel like I'm getting interviewed. "Where did you move from? Nearby?"

I swallow a large gulp of water. "New York City."

Lucia hums. "Gets more expensive there everyday, doesn't it?"

I nod, and I take another sip of water. There's no good way to start these conversations. *Hey, can you tell me everything you know about the local murders? Well,* are *they murders? Have any of your friends been acting strange or bloodthirsty recently?*

Jo comes back out of the kitchen, and I track her as she delivers a plate of scrambled eggs to an older couple. Lucia nudges forward, watching. "She's got more help on the weekends and at night. A few of the kids who just graduated get some good hours in here to save up for college. But she saves a lot of money by working the place herself during the day."

"Wow. That's a lot of work."

"It's a good thing she likes it," Lucia says, sipping on her coffee, still giving me that harsh stare. "So, tell me. When'd you move here?"

"A few days ago," I answer honestly, the words spouting out of me as if she might reprimand me if I lied. I already feel a little on edge about the possibility of having to use my cover story. "I've been getting settled in, haven't really had a chance to explore."

To my relief, Lucia's eyes brighten a bit at this, as if talking about West Rutland is her favorite pastime. "Well, we may look small, but you can find a lot of good places if you're looking."

"Any recommendations?" I push.

She leans against the counter, shoving aside her now empty plate with a rough elbow. "Well, there's some other restaurants, but I imagine you won't need that after you eat, will you? There's the marsh, the lookout, the quarry-"

The word *quarry* sticks out from my notes, from the case, from the theories, and I stop her. "Quarry? What's that?"

Her voice dies in her throat, a weird sort of confusion melting across her face. As if she's surprised she said it. She nods, in a trancelike state, and I can't tell whether she loves or hates the place. Maybe a mix of both. "Yeah. Yeah, they're great basins towards the edge of town where they used to mine marble. They're filled with water now, retired, but they all connect to one another with this… cave system." The words taper off, and she stares at a spot over my shoulder.

I shiver. "Cave system? Seems creepy." And dangerous.

She seems to jerk out of the stupor, shaking her head. "You have no idea. But we're a big marble town, there's a lot of businesses that come out of it."

"Like what?"

She lifts an arm, suddenly looking tired as she rubs a hand across her lips. It was like she had an instinct to be excited about the quarry, but then something dark and conflicting overtook her thoughts. I squint, trying not to look too scrutinizing in the way she'd scrutinized me only moments before, even as I try and fail to read the woman's expression. "Me and my husband own the sculpture center down that way, off Marble Street."

"Seriously? It's called *Marble Street*?"

"Like I said," she says dryly. "Marble town. You should check it out, though, some of the sculptures are rather beautiful. Tourists tend to like it."

I glance again at what I had originally thought was paint but is probably actually marble dust, or maybe paste? "Are you an artist? Did you make any of the sculptures?"

She smiles, and that sincerity is back, the serene glow. "Yes, that's part of why we opened it. My husband's very much the business man, and we buy from a lot of artists all over the state. We operate as a museum during the summer, and then we sell during the winter."

"I'll definitely check it out."

She digs through her purse, pulling out a twenty and leaving it on the counter. "Just head down the street, and you'll see a gravel road off to the left with a sign. You'll find us there." She pauses, looking me up and down before coming to some sort of decision, nodding her head. "Okay. Tell Jo I said bye, will you?"

I watch Lucia slip from her stool, looking even older now that she's standing and no longer smiling. She disappears through the door, and I anxiously await my food, itching for my notebook, waiting for the moment I can head toward that quarry and actually write something down.

Chapter Two

FOUR DISAPPEARANCES IN THE past month; not enough time to presume anyone dead, but steadily getting there. That's all the information they gave me when they shipped me off to this tiny town, because that's all anyone knows.

In only three and a half weeks, four teenagers from West Rutland High have been dropping like flies, one by one since the start of summer. Normally, my office would never have caught wind of something so discreet, but I'd been… researching. Taking the name and address found in my dad's will and absorbing all the information I could about the town since I couldn't yet find the nerve to look deeper into the person. Elise and I found the articles pretty quickly. I guess big news can travel fast in a small town.

As I walk down the silent street, I scan through everything I know about the case from my lined journal for what feels like the dozenth time, picking apart where the hell to start. Four separate incidents, with no indication of cause, about a week apart from one another. West Rutland's tiny police station is doing what they can to investigate, but they don't really have the manpower for potential murders. It's easier just to go with the "runaway" theory. Small town stations aren't designed for stuff like this.

The weirdest part isn't even the fact that this tiny, insignificant little town had a sudden spike of questionable occurrences. The *weird* part is that *nobody is talking about it*. Minimal news coverage, no backup in the investigation from outside cities. I suppose that's because nobody's survived... whatever this is. No bodies have turned up, no evidence left behind. No notes, no odd behavior. They're just gone.

I read over these small facts from my notebook, over and over, trying to consider possibilities or explanations for something like this. Payback? Serial killer? Or could it be as simple as four boys running away during the summer after their senior year?

But, then, why wouldn't they go all at once? Why one at a time?

My thoughts are cut off by my phone buzzing in my pocket, and I dig for it, figuring it must be Elise. But when I squint to read, I immediately decline. It's not a contact, just a set of ten digits flashing across the screen, but it doesn't matter. I recognize it anyway. I deleted it only three months ago.

Shaking my head, I shove both my phone and notepad back into my bag, zipping it with a rough tug. I focus instead on following Lucia's directions, peering to my left so I don't miss the entrance she'd described. Once again, I kick myself for leaving my glasses on my nightstand, but if there's a sign, I shouldn't miss it.

I must walk nearly half a mile by the time a road appears, leaving the main part of town and entering a cluster of wilderness. I squint, making out the letters on the small sign swinging from a wooden post just to the right of the gravel. I'm pretty sure I can make out the word *sculpture*, and that's good enough for me. Hoisting my bag higher onto my back, I veer onto the road, pacing in between tall stalks of grass and various plants, tiny white flowers blossoming around rocks and broken bottles. Looking back where I came, I can't even see the buildings I left behind, and I walk a little faster, hoping I hadn't misread the sign.

I hadn't. After a few meters, a clearing comes into view, along with an array of sculptures scattered across the grounds. Some stand on classic pedestals, new and bright like they'd just been chiseled yesterday. But others are embedded into the ground, extending beneath the tree roots, making a home in the dense foliage. A few lighter ones hang from branches like windchimes, and another is so densely covered in vines I momentarily think it's just a bush. They stretch back as far as I can see, small paths veering deeper into the woods, presumably with more artwork to admire. The shine of the white marble hurts my eyes, the shapes ranging from people and animals, to more abstract work that curves into every shape and size imaginable. I gape at the garden, flowers blooming at the feet of statues.

And beyond those woods, a quarry waits with a basin full of questions, beckoning me farther.

"Looking to buy a ticket?"

I nearly jump out of my shoes, pressing a hand to my chest as I whip around to see a small shack with a window off to the right. A woman about my age leans out of it, arms folded along the window sill. A silk scarf ties golden brown curls to the back of her head, a pencil tucked behind her ear, and I realize this must be Lucia's daughter, or niece, or something like that.

"Yes," I stutter out, digging through my bag for my wallet. I eye the *cash only* sign, internally thanking my past self for thinking ahead.

Just as I've managed to pull a five dollar bill out, she narrows her eyes at me, and I shiver under the intense stare. "Oh, wait, are you Alex?"

Dumbfounded, I just nod.

She grins, disappearing for a moment, only to reappear through a door at the side of the building. Wearing a green tank top and tan cargo shorts, she walks toward me with hand extended. "My mom told me the new girl in town would be coming. I'm Luna."

I grip her hand, and her skin is rough with callouses, but warm to the touch. Her fingers feel like individual rays of sun, and cold shoots up my arm the moment she lets go. "Alex," I say, even though she knows that.

"First visit's on us," she says, shooing away my money.

Reluctantly, I tuck the bill into my pocket, making a mental note to leave a tip on my way out. "Thank you."

She shrugs. "What can I say, you made a good impression on my mom. Besides, the good money comes when we sell a bunch of pieces in the offseason. Did you like the maple pancakes?"

Eyes widening, I nod, still stuffed from the meal. "Delicious, I'm thinking of stopping back on my way home for some more."

Luna grins, leaning back on her heels and shoving her hands into the pockets of her shorts. "Not a bad idea, Suzie's is sort of addicting."

"I'm glad I live so close to it, then."

She only snorts. "If you live in West Rutland, you live close to everything. I hope you didn't bother bringing a car."

"I did, but I already owned one, so I think I get a pass."

"Excellent, that was a trick question. I've been in the market for a friend to drive me places."

I bark out a surprised laugh. "I knew it. The free ticket was just a bribe."

"Now you're getting it. West Rutland is actually stuck in the eighteenth century, bartering will get you everywhere."

"Okay," I pretend to consider thoughtfully, tapping a finger against my chin. "If it's bartering we're working with, you better have some interesting places for me to drive you to. Right now, my destinations consist of the grocery store, Walmart, and… that's it."

"I'm afraid there's not much else, unless you're really into trees and birds." Lifting her eyes back to me, she folds her arms across her chest. "What brings you here, then? Alex," she adds after a moment, the name rolling off her tongue.

I look around, covering my eyes so as not to look directly into the sun. The sky is crystal blue, not a cloud in sight. "The museum, or Vermont?"

When I glance back, she's staring at me. "Both?"

I sigh, sort of distracted by how golden her eyes are turning now that she's directly under the light. I take a small step back.

"Well, I came to the museum to look at some cool sculptures. Mission accomplished. I don't even know where to start."

"You haven't seen the half of it," she promises me. Jogging back to her ticket booth, she grabs a folded map from a display. "This'll make sure you don't get lost, there are a lot of trails all through the woods that'll take you through all the exhibits. Keep a look out for the plaques at the bottom of the piece. My mom's are the best."

Before I can say anything else, a man surfaces through a cluster of trees, knocking aside a branch before coming up to Luna's side. He brushes dirt from his jeans, tucking what looks to be a duster into his back pocket. "Hey, honey. Lunch break?"

"Oh, no. This is Alex. She just moved here."

The man, who must be Luna's Dad, raises his thick eyebrows. "Did you? How interesting."

Awkwardly, I glance between the two, hugging my arms around my body. "It... certainly is."

"Well." He extends his hand, "I'm Roger Morgan, Luna's Dad. This your first time at the sculpture garden?"

"It is," I say, feeling meek and small under his powerful gaze. *It's pretty much my first time anywhere in this town.* "Very... very beautiful."

"Indeed. Welcome, Alex," he says, and although he doesn't smile, I can tell he means it. Without another word, he stalks off towards a group of sculptures on the other side of the clearing.

"Sorry about that," Luna mutters when I don't say anything, but doesn't elaborate. She just watches her father until he stops at one of the statues, scrubbing away some wet moss.

I shrug it off, moving to examine a nearby sculpture. It appears to be a figure eight, the rough marble reaching towards the sky. It's amazing, really, how something like this doesn't fall. That despite the holes, and the marble that's been chipped away, it's still strong.

Searching for something to say, I ask, "Did your parents grow up here?"

Luna wrinkles her nose. "Oh, no. Mom grew up in Boston, and Dad's from Maine. They didn't come here until they got married."

I watch as Mr. Morgan shifts a piece of marble, wincing and rubbing his back when he stands up. "What made them move here?"

"You sound so surprised, as if you didn't choose to move here, too."

"Maybe I'm just looking for kindred spirits. Maybe they came for the same reasons I did."

Luna lifts a shoulder, leaning against one of the statues. It wobbles from side to side under her weight, but she doesn't seem bothered. "Hell if I know. Maybe for some goddamn peace of mind."

Her dad bends over once more, gritting his teeth. "Did it work?"

"What? Moving here?"

"Yeah," I say as he stands and disappears behind a wall of marble covered in ivy. "Did they get the peace of mind they were looking for?"

Luna looks around, the sun lighting every curl of her hair of fire, igniting each strand. It's as though the light is drawn to her, every curve of her face and body. "I don't know. I'd like to think so. Initially, I guess."

"West Rutland seems to only be peaceful in theory," I admit, thinking about the bustle of the diner, of the four missing kids that everyone seems to be ignoring. "That tends to be the case with small towns, they only seem simple until you're a part of them."

"I think it's because nothing's actually simple once you look too close."

I gnaw on the inside of my cheek, nodding towards the nook of trees obscuring the quarry from my view. "Maybe not towns as a whole, but I'd like to think you can find sections. As far as I can imagine, the quarry seems pretty damn peaceful. If you go by yourself and take away all the mindless noise. I'm sort of excited to visit, I've never seen one in real life."

My gaze shifts toward Luna, just in time to see her own eyes darken. Even in the brightness of midday, shadows overtake her entire face, and she lowers her head, fingers running over the smooth marble. "Now I *really* know you're new here."

I flick my brows up, but she doesn't elaborate more. She just pushes away from the statue, straightening her shirt.

"I should get back to work," she mumbles, not quite looking me in the eye.

I press my lips together, not sure what I said wrong. "Okay. Nice to meet you."

She doesn't respond, and stalks off toward the single, tiny building on the property, disappearing inside.

AGAINST MY BETTER JUDGMENT, I go to the quarry.

I figure out, from Luna's map, that you can access two of the quarries directly from the sculpture center. I cut through the indicated paths, admiring the hunks of marble as I pass. They come in a range of color, a few pinks and greens scattered around, but mostly white and onyx. Signs hang from the branches above, describing whether each piece of art is for sale or a permanent fixture of the botanical gardens. I brush my fingers along one of the pieces, the marble smooth and textureless under my touch.

Trying to distract myself, I read every plaque, getting up close so I can make out the letters through my blurry vision; every title, every artist, every description, but none of it works. My mind is too caught on how Luna's entire demeanor has shifted at the mention of the quarry. How the light shrouding her had suddenly veered directions. The scene plays itself over and over in my mind, like a record scratch, freeze frame moment in a movie.

Then I remember her mom. It'd been an achingly similar reaction. The darkening of the eyes, lowering of the face. Nearly identical, but I can't quite put my finger on what either of them were trying to say.

I break through the trees, stumbling across stone, and for the first time since seeing Luna, my mind goes empty.

Fifty Feet Down

I don't know what I'd been imagining. I'd read up on quarries when I saw there were a few in town, even saw a few pictures, but I hadn't expected it to be quite so... big. The vast cliffs stretch out before me, creating a giant pit that drops off at the edge of the path. Sharp points and ridges border every inch of rock, insidious and beckoning at the same time, telling me *danger lies here*.

Creeping forward, I peer over the edge, slightly disappointed when I can't see the bottom. It makes sense, really. It must be filled with rainwater since no one bothered to drain it when they stopped digging. Fingers gripping the railings that line the quarry, I stare at the still, near-black water. I can't tell whether the darkness comes from the marble reflection, the dirt, or the sheer depth of the eldritch basin. I think I'd rather not know the answer.

Feeling slightly put off, and a little bit frightened of the whole thing, I back away slowly. Wherever my research takes me, I hope it's not back here.

Chapter Three

IT'S AS THOUGH REYNA remained stuck in time all day, because when I return home (is it weird to refer to this new, temporary place as *home*?) she's back at the table, but on the other side, this time watching a video on her laptop. Not wanting to get pulled into conversation, I slap my phone to my cheek, pretending to be talking with someone. She gives me a small nod before returning to her computer, clearly not feeling the need to talk to me either. I slip silently into my bedroom, where I actually dial Elise.

She answers immediately, not bothering with a greeting. "Did you find anything?"

I groan, sitting back in my desk chair and propping my feet up on the heater. "It's been six hours since you last asked, what could I possibly have found?"

"You said you were exploring!" Elise exclaims, and I hear the clink of what sounds like a wine glass. "Did you meet the townspeople? Did they suck?"

"I met a few," I respond, drumming my fingers against the packet of notes I'd just finished looking through on my walk back. As if I hadn't read through them a million times already. "And don't call them townspeople, this isn't the seventeen hundreds."

"Sorry," Elise says sarcastically. "Did the 'people of West Rutland, Vermont' suck?"

"They seem nice enough," I sigh, because it's true for all of the people I met. "There's a killer restaurant down the road from me, so at least there's that."

"Small mercies. But nothing interesting?"

I spin in my chair, hopping to my feet. "I'm playing the long game. Make friends first, ask questions later. They always spill more to people they're comfortable with."

Elise grunts. "Don't take too long, though. I'm already floundering here without you."

I grin. "Bored?"

"I just got home from work," she pouts. "And it's *Tuesday*. Finn's was calling my name, but it felt wrong to go without you."

"And it totally would have been. Shouldn't be longer than a few weeks, if there's even anything to find out."

She scoffs. "Four disappearances? One a week, for four weeks straight? I'm gonna say something's going on."

"Yeah. Towns like these have a habit of keeping their secrets close to their chests, though. I saw a little bit of that today."

"Oh, yeah?"

I lean against the windowsill, fiddling with the curtains. "Especially with newcomers."

Hesitating for a moment, contemplating her words, Elise finally says, "It would be helpful if you actually knew what he looked like."

Stiffening, my eyes flutter shut. "I thought we were talking about the disappearances."

"Does your father's mistress fleeing to West Rutland with your half brother nineteen years ago count as a disappearance?"

Sucking in a breath, I nearly pass out at the bluntness of her question. Since showing up at her apartment that day, throwing the will down on her kitchen table and downing half a bottle of wine, we'd been dancing around the topic, communicating mostly in meaningful glances and code. After I had a breakdown about it, I think I went into the denial phase, even as I orchestrated a business trip to a nothing-town specifically so I could find him.

So I could find… the only *sort of* family I had left.

Clearing my throat, I say, "No, no it doesn't count. And I don't want to talk about him. I want to talk about the case."

"Alex-"

I open my mouth to respond, but movement catches my eye outside my window. The sun has just dipped behind the mountains, and only a soft, blue glow remains across the street below. There's just enough visibility to see Luna, the girl from the sculpture place, pass under a streetlight, reading a book as she walks.

"I have to go," I say into the speaker.

"Wha-"

The sound cuts off, replaced by dead silence as I shove my phone into my pocket, flying toward the door. The metal of the staircase clangs beneath my feet as I take the stairs two at a time, rounding the corner of the house just in time to see Luna passing in front of me, unaware of all the noise I'm making. I hurry to catch up, fingers dragging tentatively against the siding as I peek out into the street.

"Hey," I say breathlessly from a few feet behind her, and she whips around to look at me.

Calming down when she recognizes me, she flips her book shut with a snap, hugging it close to her chest. "Hey. Alex, right?"

"Yeah," I say slowly, realizing that I don't really have a plan. Sometimes following instinct can be stupid. "Um…" I trail off, mouth dry, distracted by the soft planes of her face now that she steps back into the circle of light of the streetlamp.

Gazing warily at my gaping mouth, she rocks back and forth from heel to toe, tucking a strand of hair behind her ear. She must have taken the hair scarf off when the sun set, because it's now tied to her belt loop. "Can I, um, help you?"

I shake myself, blinking rapidly. "Um, yeah. I just wanted to apologize."

At that, her features harden, some emotionless mask overtaking her. "For what?"

I shrug, scratching at an invisible itch at the back of my neck, shifting uncomfortably from foot to foot, thinking this might have been a mistake. "You know. Whatever I said to offend you earlier. I didn't mean anything by it."

Pursing her lips, she looks away, casting her face into shadows. "I'm sure you didn't."

Speechless, I try again. "I mean, obviously I'm new here, I made *that* clear enough with whatever I said. The last thing I want is to immediately make, like, enemies."

I mean it as a joke, and though she doesn't look quite *annoyed*, she remains stiff, as though she'd rather be anywhere else. "I don't have the time to be your enemy."

The point is clear enough. *I don't want to be your friend, either.*

Lifting my hands, I say, "Fair enough. I just wanted to apologize, for... well, whatever."

Her movements stutter at that, eyes softening and flickering with something I can't describe, but it falls away as fast as it came. "So that's all, then?"

I think on it, and despite the hardness in Luna's eyes, they're the same as Lucia's. Only I hadn't seen the same malice, or downright annoyance, in Luna's mother's that I see now. I decide on, "I'm willing to barter with free rides for your forgiveness. But in the meantime, tell your mom I say hello."

Rolling her eyes with a huff, she turns on her heel as the last of the sun rays completely disappear. To my surprise, she murmurs, "I will," before disappearing into the night.

MY PHONE VIBRATES ALL the way back up to my room, and I yank it from my pocket to see about a dozen messages from Elise. She's never been a fan of not getting the last word.

Elise: *Did you just hang up on me?*
Elise: *Helloooo.*
Elise: *Alex, you bitch.*
Elise: *Answer me, or I'm never talking to you again*
Elise: *I will not hesitate to abandon you in rural Vermont.*

I roll my eyes, because I would just drive back on my own and sit on her front stoop consistently ringing the doorbell until she relents. I open the messages up, quickly typing back, longing to just get in bed for the rest of the night.

Alex: *I'm investigating like the journalist-turned-cop I am. Job comes first.*

Elise: *I AM the job!*

Alex: *Go to Finn's. Get a drink for me, god knows I need it.*

Elise: *No bars in bumfuck nowhere?*

Alex: *There's no anything, but I'm sure I'll find something eventually. Night xoxo*

Silencing my phone as I shut the front door behind me, Reyna asks, "Did a bomb go off?"

Distracted, I nearly stumble over the TV stand. Out of breath, I ask, "What?"

She nods to the door. "You ran out pretty fast."

I pass my phone from one hand to the other, inching closer and closer to my bedroom. "Yeah, sorry, saw someone I needed to talk to."

Reyna only shrugs with a chuckle. "Hey, whatever, doesn't bother me. I just didn't realize you knew anyone besides, well, me. Goodnight."

"Yeah, goodnight." Moving as quickly as I can without looking crazy, I firmly shut and lock my bedroom door behind me, flinging myself on the bed.

For such a small town, I have no idea where to start.

Chapter Four

JASON KNOLLS.
    Henry Bradford.
    Xavier Martin.
    Kyle Jenkins.
    I pace in circles around my room, treading trenches into the carpet and compiling my research in my journal.
    All four of them just finished their senior year at West Rutland High, the majority born and raised in Vermont. Only Kyle moved down from a city a few hours away when he turned eleven. I can't claim to know about the West Rutland teenage hierarchy, but from the looks of their yearbook, they're part of the "cool" crowd. Three baseball players, one lacrosse player. Jason and Xavier played basketball in the winter while the other two played hockey. Three of them played on the West Rutland High soccer team, and two were in band. Looking up their social media accounts, there's a little bit of a crossover; they clearly know each other well, their friend groups mingle, but they're not *best friends*. There's not a single photo that I can find of all four of them. It's

always only two or three, with someone I don't know sprinkled into the mix.

With every photo I observe, every stranger I take in, I wonder if it's him. I look for myself, for my father, in each feature, convincing myself each time that we share a nose or face shape.

I spend my morning scrolling through Vermont news, searching for scraps of articles already published. There's a few here and there, but it boils down to this: no one knows where the boys disappeared to, no bodies have been found, nobody knows who or why, and nobody knows for a fact that they're even connected. Part of the problem might be that West Rutland doesn't actually have a newspaper, or magazine, or any sort of news station. I guess it all rolls over into Rutland City news, but that also means it's not as much of a priority. Everything seems to be glossed over, forgotten, or minimized if it happens outside the Rutland City borders.

I push away from my laptop, already frustrated. Only managing to fill up a page or two of information in my notebook, I flip it closed and lean against my desk, rubbing my forehead. Sure, no one *technically* knows they're connected, but how could they not be?

Stretching my neck, trying to massage the stiffness that comes with crouching over a screen for three hours, I check again that the school is, in fact, closed for the summer. A lot of schools offer summer programs, but the town is so small that it's not really worth it. Any kid that wants it can go to the school programs in Rutland, so visiting the school is a bust, unless I want to stick it out here until September.

I shudder at the thought, even more motivated to pull on my shoes and go back into town.

My stomach rumbles as I glance at the time. I consider for a moment whether I should try someplace new, find more people, make myself a little more known. But on the other hand, I might as well build on what I've got, so I veer into the parking lot of Suzie's Place.

"You're still here!"

Jo's voice startles me from my vague daze the moment I've fully entered the diner, the door swinging closed behind me and boxing me into the relieving air conditioning. The place is a lot less crowded than yesterday, lunch hour already come and gone, and Jo leans against the counter alone, chin on her fingers.

"What?" I ask. "Did you think I'd up and move away after less than a week?" A twinge of guilt spreads through my stomach as I speak, because that's exactly what I'll end up doing.

Jo sighs, motioning towards one of the stools. "You'd be surprised."

Without even having to ask, she pours me a cup of coffee. Do I look that bad? Adjusting into the soft bubble of the stool, I wrap my fingers around the mug. "Do people move away often?"

"Depends. A lot of people who were born here stay. But on the rare occasion someone moves here, they usually don't last long."

I tilt my head, surveying her. It's a sad thought, really, that this place isn't good enough for the people who aren't stuck here. "Why?"

She shrugs, looking around fondly. "Hell if I know, I've been here all my life. Never wanted to leave. It's home, you know?"

I nod my head, trying to find a place to slip in a question, or a comment about what I'm really here for. Part of me figured the whole situation would be the talk of the town, but even when I strained to overhear conversations yesterday, nobody offered anything.

"Well," I say after a moment of silence. "If you get me another plate of those maple pancakes, I might just stay for a while."

Grinning, she takes the menu I hadn't even bothered to open, and I notice the wrinkles and calluses of her hands, aged far more than her forty or so years. "Five minutes, Alex."

I give a wave, pulling out my notebook but leaving my pencil behind since I don't have anything new to add. I need to figure out where to visit next, if there's any places the boys might have frequented-

"You seem to be good at making friends."

I jump in my seat, nearly tumbling off the side of the stool. Catching myself against the counter, I swivel around to see Luna reclined in one of the booths. She pulls her legs up toward her chest, a yellow sundress flowing down and brushing the surface of the leather. Papers spread out across the table, an empty plate covered with syrup pushed aside.

Turning completely, I lean back until my spine presses against the counter. The cool metal makes me shiver, but I just shift so I can rest my elbows on the counter, too. "And I didn't even have to offer up anything in return, but I can't really count it. Pretty sure it's her job to be nice to me."

"I'll bet you tip well," Luna muses, twirling a pencil through her fingers. "City girl, you know."

"That must be it."

We fall silent, and I adjust my glasses as I peer closer at the papers covering her table. After a moment, I realize they're actually pieces torn from a sketchbook, discarded in frustration while she works on another attempt in the notepad.

"Are you allowed to convert a restaurant into your own personal art studio?" I ask, thankful the rest of the room is empty so I don't have to shout. The vast expanse of space between us stretches, cold and empty.

Chuckling, she tosses her pencil aside. "Only during the off hours. Once it gets busy Jo'll kick me out on my ass."

"I sure will," Jo affirms as she backs out of the double kitchen doors, plate stacked high with pancakes and sausage. She slides it across the counter to me, refilling my cup as she does. Steam curls up, and I add a packet of sugar.

Wiping her hands on a dishrag, Jo nods to Luna, who still lounges in her booth. "I see you met Luna?"

Shifting uncomfortably, I mutter, "Sort of."

She glances between us, then claps her hands together. "Well, I'll be in the back. Call me if you need anything."

She disappears, and the doors flutter shut behind her. I debate for a moment if I should turn back to Luna or let the conversation fizzle out. I douse my pancakes with syrup, stabbing a few pieces with my fork.

"Too engrossed in your food to talk?" Luna taunts me, and I turn back, swallowing.

"It *can* be distracting," I confirm, taking another heaping bite. "Priorities, you know? Besides, I didn't think you'd want to talk to me. What was it you said? *You don't have time for enemies or friends or anything in between* or something of that dramatic variety?"

Sighing, Luna leans forward to rub at her temples. "Yeah, I'm sorry about that. I was having... not a very good day."

"Because of me?"

"No. Well, technically yes, but I know it wasn't intentional."

Confused, I say, "Um. Okay. So..."

"What I *should* have said," she goes on, sounding tired, "is that though I sometimes feel like I don't have the mental headspace to talk to people, I really need as many friends as I can get. And from the looks of it, so can you."

"Well, you're not wrong about that," I say hesitantly, trying to gauge her, to figure out her emotional mood swings. I suppose I can't fault her too much, even though she won't explain what exactly I'd said wrong, or *why* her instinct was to not talk to me.

Breaking the awkwardness, Luna nods to my half eaten, forgotten plate of pancakes. "You're making me want to place another order."

Thinking that Jo could use the break, I switch topics to the paper once again poised beneath her fingertips. It's not regular printer paper, I realize, but rather thick and rugged, bigger than usual. I'm not super familiar with art supplies, but it looks like paper that thick might be meant for paint, not just pencil sketching. "What are you working on?"

Looking surprised I asked, she glances down at her work before looking back at me. "Portraits," she answers, holding up the sheet of paper to display an extremely detailed picture of a woman lounging on her back, weeds and flowers poking up around her, crowning her face. Eyes closed, fingers brushing her cheek, the woman dozes in a meadow, and it baffles me how Luna manages to make something on a sheet of paper feel so calm.

"Who is it?" I ask, holding my glasses still as I peer closer. My foot twitches, wanting to take my body across the room to her booth, but I stop myself, hooking my ankle around the leg of the stool instead.

She shrugs, letting the paper flutter back down to the table. "No one in particular, I just draw whoever comes to mind. I don't like drawing real people because they never come out quite realistic."

My eyes widen. "That looks realistic to me."

She shifts, slinging an arm around the back of the booth. The strap of the dress falls from her shoulder, revealing smooth, dark skin, but she doesn't bother fixing it. "I guess realistic isn't the right word. They always come out good, but there's always something *wrong* if I try to replicate someone exactly, you know? There's just something that I can't quite capture. I guess because I'm so familiar with the people I'm trying to draw, maybe I'm too nitpicky."

"I bet you are," I say. "I doubt anyone else would notice."

She sighs, beginning to scoop up the crumpled up papers, dumping them into her backpack. "Well, you know what they say.

You're your own worst critic. Especially when your mother's an award winning artist."

I hum, remembering my pancakes and that it probably looks weird if I don't eat them. After taking a few bites and swallowing, I ask, "She does sculpture, right? Does she draw too?"

Luna shrugs. "Every artist usually starts out drawing in one way or another, so she *can*, but she doesn't like to. She says, and I quote," she rolls her eyes, lifting her fingers to make air quotes, "*'two dimensional art doesn't capture what I'm trying to say.'*"

I snort. I'm not an artist by any means, but even *I* know that sounds pretentious. "I've always been a fan of paintings more, but I think that's because I like color more than anything else."

Luna's brows shoot up. "Do you paint or anything?"

Huffing, I exclaim, "God, no. You know the term tone deaf, for horrible singing? I'm whatever the art equivalent to that is."

Luna laughs, slipping what looks to be a protective sheet over her drawing (probably so the charcoal doesn't smudge) before flipping the book shut. "Well, what do you do?" She pauses, eyes looking at the ceiling. "I haven't asked you that already, have I?"

I shake my head. When would she have asked me? During the two conversations she snubbed me?

"Good," she sighs. "My memory is shit. That's why I'm an artist instead of, like, a biologist."

"I'm definitely not a biologist," I say, shuddering at the thought of science. The word *journalist* sits at the tip of my tongue, where it always tries to escape, but I swallow it back down. "I work from home," I lie through my teeth, swirling a piece of sausage in syrup. "Customer service."

Luna's mouth falls open. "No kidding?"

I grimace, then shrug. "Alas, not kidding. Tech support. It's pretty lame, I know, but it pays the bills."

Leaning forward with her elbows poking into the table, she holds up a finger. "Hold on. So you work from home. Does that mean you could go *anywhere?*"

Cringing at the direction this is going, and thinking on my feet as fast as my muddled mind will let me, I nod. "Yeah, I guess so."

She guffaws. "So, you're telling me, the country is your oyster, and you chose to come *here.*"

I shift uncomfortably, surprised. I know *I* wasn't super excited about the prospect of coming to rural Vermont, but I hadn't expected her to be quite so... self-aware. "I mean, technically it's best to stay on the East Coast, just for time zone's sake..." I stutter. "But..."

Incredulous, she slaps the table with a shake of her head. "Amazing. A girl leaves the big apple for the tiniest town in the world. I just can't wrap my head around it."

I almost say it then. Not that I'm a journalist, not that I'm searching through her town's dirty laundry, but what I'm *really* looking for. Her wide, amused eyes seem to pull the words out of me, like a thread connected to my sternum, but I swallow them down. Instead, I set my fork down on my now empty plate, fully swiveling my stool to face her. "Tell that to my bank account. Vermont's a lot cheaper, I'll tell you that." I pause. "Would you want to go?"

"Go where?"

"To New York? Since you seem to think it's so much better."

It's not that I *don't* love New York. I do, it's an amazing city, with some amazing opportunities. I saw that first hand my entire life. I guess I feel about the city the way Luna seems to feel about Vermont, like nothing is special once you've experienced it.

Seaming her lips together, she drums her fingers against her thigh, over the bare skin exposed where her dress ends. "I don't even know anymore. I haven't thought about it in... a while."

Something overtakes her voice with her words, similar to how she'd reacted when I first met her. She looks remarkably small, her shoulders caving in on themselves as she rolls her pencil back and forth between her thumb and index fingers. The booth swallows her whole, towering over her hunched form.

Desperate to will away whatever cloud settled over her, I say, "If it makes you feel better, it's not all it's cracked up to be. I'm here instead of there, aren't I?"

She looks up at me through her lashes, smooth strands of hair falling across her face. "Oh, yeah, and you look so thrilled about that."

I curse myself, wondering how miserable I might have looked when she saw me walk in. "It's an adjustment," I mumble, ducking down towards my cup of coffee. The liquid's gone cold since I last took a sip, but I choke it down, if just for something to do. I feel a little guilty, making her think that I just *chose* to come here. Because, really, I never would have, under ordinary circumstances.

And it seems, by the way she's acting, that maybe she wouldn't be here under different circumstances, either.

"IS THERE A BAR around here?"

Luna jerks up, letting the door swing shut behind us, giving one last wave goodbye to Jo. Glancing at her phone, she flashes the screen in my face. "You do realize it's only two in the afternoon, right?"

I roll my eyes. "Not for *now*, what do you take me for?"

She shrugs. "A woman leaving the big city for a shitty, empty town, with her loner job? Probably an alcoholic."

Scowling, I resist the urge to blurt out the truth, that I'm not as weird as I have to pretend to be. "I'm not an alcoholic, you assuming prick. As you so astutely pointed out, I'm trying to make some friends in, how did you phrase it?" I look at her pointedly. "'This shitty, empty town?'"

Kicking at the rocks lining the road, she grips her backpack straps tighter. "Okay, I sort of set myself up for that one."

"Is that a yes?" I ask, slowing to a stop at the corner of the road, where we'll have to part ways. "You can recommend a bar or two?"

She stares at me, biting her lip, as though fighting an internal war. Caving in, she drags a hand down her face. "Tell you what. Are you busy Friday night?"

"We covered this, I have no friends. I'm never busy."

Amused, she looks up to the sky. "Fine, then. Meet me outside Suzie's around nine? I can show you a few places."

I breathe a sigh of relief at having someone to introduce me to some other people in town, but I'll have to be *really* careful about the questions I ask with Luna right next to me. "Yeah?"

Lifting yet another shoulder, she murmurs, "What are friends for?"

"Are we friends?"

"Not if you're gonna be a jackass about it."

Grinning, and feeling only slightly nauseous, I nod. "Fair enough."

Giving me a peace sign, she turns on her heel and marches off in the direction where we came from, head bowed. My stomach flips over, thinking about Luna uttering the word *friend*. Really, I hadn't come here to make friends; I came to get a job done. But if I had to pretend for a while to make any headway, I suppose that's a sacrifice I'm willing to make.

Even still, casting a backward glance at Luna as she glides away, rounding a corner toward the sculpture center, guilt echoes in my skull at the thought of taking her down with me in the process.

Chapter Five

FRIDAY IS STILL THREE days away by the time I get home from the diner, and I have no idea what to do with my time until then. It's pathetic, really. I've never been one to sit in my bedroom twiddling my thumbs, distracting myself with bad TV, but that's all I can do for at least thirty six hours.

Normally itching to go out and investigate, I can't bring myself to think of a plan. Instead I try to prepare questions that won't sound too suspicious to Luna. But I can only spend so much time procrastinating before my mind catches up to me.

I wish I'd been able to come here on my own terms, to go at my own pace. Standing, I settle down at my desk, fingers hovering over my keyboard, going so far as to type in *p...a...* before frantically hitting the delete button, groaning as I lower my forehead onto the space bar.

"Hey-"

I hop to my feet, slamming my laptop closed as I go. Somehow feeling caught, I turn to see Reyna leaning wide eyed against my door frame, hand half raised in greeting. I fold my hands in my lap, swiveling my chair. "Um. Hey." In my limited time living here, Reyna's never come in unannounced.

She flicks her brows up, glancing to my now closed computer. "You're not doing anything creepy, are you? Because I would've appreciated a heads up on any weird hobbies before you signed the lease."

"Would it have been a dealbreaker?"

She pauses. "No. Did my desperation for a new roommate come through that bad?"

"Yes." I push away from my desk and lean down against my knees as I come up with a lie. "And it's not creepy, it's just something confidential."

"Ah, yes, the privileged and restricted life of tech support."

"Did you need something?" I ask pointedly.

"Kind of wanted to see if you were still alive. You've been cloistered away for like two days now."

"It's nice that you care."

She huffs, the corners of her lips twitching upward. "And your laundry's done. Has been since yesterday." She steps back, closing the door behind her with a snap.

I slump in my chair, dragging a hand roughly over my face. Taking deep and steadying breaths, I open my laptop again, surprised when I go to try again, but my fingers shake so hard that I accidentally hit the *o* key instead of the *p*, and then I close the search window altogether.

Jason, Xavier, Kyle, Henry… The names of the missing boys haunt me, swirling into my thoughts and dreams, but a completely unrelated name stands at the forefront. A father, and a son.

My dad never claimed to be the best father in the world. He was distant and annoyed at the best of times, and away for weeks without a word at his worst. But he provided for me my entire life, and he said he loved me even though he never showed it, and that had sort of been enough for twenty two years.

But shortly after my twenty third birthday, and eighteen months into dating the girl I thought I would marry, he had a stroke. A … bad one, leaving him completely paralyzed on his left side, and only two months to live. The world fell apart from every angle imaginable. It tore into my family, my relationship, my childhood. Into everything I once thought to be true.

Maybe that's why I feel so sick about going to meet Luna later, about all the lying I would have to do just to make it through the night, let alone my entire investigation.

"I'm going on an extended vacation," I said to Elise one morning at work, after staying up the entire night unable to stop the thoughts and tears and anxiety. Two months since I'd opened that will and found a second descendant to my father that I never knew about, and I still couldn't think of anything else. Even after everything with Rachel… It's like… if I couldn't have her, I could at least have this. I *needed* this.

Elise had jerked up in surprise, upending a stack of papers in the process. Cursing, she bent to scoop them up, but I didn't help her as I normally would have. I just stood there, too hardwired to focus on anything else. I needed to get through this conversation.

"You- what?"

But before I could respond, Tom's voice sounded from his nearby office. I hadn't noticed his propped open door, and he leaned back in his chair with pursed lips. *"Are you, now?"*

Clearing my throat, I glanced at Elise before moving over to his doorway, trembling hands curled into fists. *"Yes, sir. I need three weeks off."*

He exhaled roughly, like he was actually thinking about it, before he said, *"You and I both know you don't have any more vacation time."* I wished he'd called it *paid time off* rather than vacation time, because the days I'd missed to plan my fathers funeral and grieve the loss of the life I'd once had didn't exactly feel like a vacation.

"I know, but-"

"Nor would it be appropriate for you to miss that much work. We'd have no choice but to replace you."

Tears welled behind my eyes, and I wanted to punch something, preferably him. I didn't have anything anymore, and I needed this. Seeing Rachel yesterday in passing, for the first time since we ended things, at the cafe where we'd met each other two years ago, almost sent me into catatonic shock.

I needed to find something new. I needed something, something, something-

"I'm sorry," Tom said, in a way that made it seem like he wasn't sorry at all. He definitely wasn't. *"We need you here too much."*

"What if I just quit?" I asked maniacally before I could stop myself, finding that I hardly regretted it.

Tom's nostrils flared. *"I think that-"*

"*Vacation wasn't the right word,*" Elise scrambled to say, suddenly right next to me. Too wrapped up in my own emotions, I hadn't noticed her get up to join me. "*She was just joking about quitting. What she really wants is clearance for an out of state investigation.*" She glanced at me. "*That even just getting out of the state would feel like a vacation, and she could focus on her work better.*"

Elise has a way of twisting things that makes her such a good writer, and apparently, she'd done as much research into West Rutland as I had.

Closing my eyes now, I shut my laptop, unable to look into him any further. I don't know what exactly I'm afraid of. Whether it was that I'd see my dad in his face, or that I wouldn't. Or maybe I wouldn't see even a hint of myself in him, and that would mean I really was alone in this world. That when I'd fallen into my own mind, abandoning Rachel in the process, I would have done it for nothing.

I set my jaw. The thought of coming into this town and leaving empty handed makes me want to throw my computer out the window, so I get up to search for something else.

Passing Reyna on the way out, I grab my keys from the hook and swing the door open before I can lose my nerve.

She calls after me from the table. "Wait, your laundry-"

I'm outside and down the stairs before she can finish.

I avoid Suzie's, and I avoid the sculpture garden. I know better than to put all my eggs in one basket, and the probability that the people I've met have *nothing at all* to do with the disappearances is way too high. As small as the town is, a few out of several hundreds isn't that many.

And I don't want to risk running into Luna and saying something stupid before Friday.

Instead, I head to the high school, even though I know I'll find it deserted. Made of marble on the main street, right across from Town Hall, it stands small and simple, the white stone faded. Clearly decades have passed since the last renovations, and nobody seems to want anything to do with it during the summer.

The only activity takes place on the soccer field around the back, fenced off with the gate locked. The group of boys must have jumped the barrier, tossing the ball around and shooting through cones set up on the goal lines. A collection of girls lounge against the fence, a few with books and a pair passing a softball back and forth.

I see it before the impact comes. One of the guys kicks the soccer ball, attempting for a goal, but with *horrendous* aim. The ball soars over the fence, way to the left of where the goal would have been, and I don't have time to duck before it collides with my head.

A collection of gasps and a fair amount of laughs make it past the ringing in my ears, and I'm pleased to notice that I hadn't toppled over. Getting taken out by a seventeen year old would have been enough to send me back to New York.

I get a hold of my bearings in time to see two of the girls scrambling over the fence, their softball mitts abandoned. One of the boys shouts at me, "Sorry," and another just yells, "Hey! Throw us the ball!"

I pick up the soccer ball from where it rolled a few feet away, tossing it from hand to hand as the girls stop in front of me. They both have dark hair, but one has it cut above her ears, and the other's long locks are wrapped in a bandana.

The girl with brown skin and a bandana smiles sheepishly. "Sorry about your head."

"Luckily he's not that good of a kicker," I say, handing it to them. "You should've made them get their own damn ball."

"Hey, Cassidy!" one of the boys yells with a smirk that makes me want to chuck the ball at his head. "Gonna just stand there?"

Short haired girl (Cassidy, apparently) rolls her eyes, and shouts back, "This is your punishment for sucking at soccer."

The boy flushes deeply as his buddies holler, and Cassidy turns back with the ball resting on her hip. "Dude needs an ego check, Anthony got named captain for next year and suddenly he thinks he's God's gift to soccer."

"He's always thought that

I whistle. "Man, I do *not* miss high school drama."

Bandana girl elbows Cassidy with wide eyes, a silent conversation passing between the two of them, and Cassidy seems to collect herself, clearing her throat. "Anyway, we should-"

"Hold on," I say quickly, trying not to sound too eager, because high school girls were the best way to get information about high school boys. "Don't give it back to him so quick. I don't like his tone."

"No one likes his tone except his girlfriend and his mother," Bandana girl says flatly. "Who are you, anyway? Do you know Anthony?"

"Thankfully no," I say. "I don't really know anyone."

"Oh, *newbie*," Cassidy realizes with a grin. "Right on. Are you here to see a sick relative?" Bandana girl elbows her again, hard.

I just snort. "Nah, I moved from New York City."

Now *that* gets their attention. Cassidy's eyes go wide, and Bandana girl shuffles closer with an excited smile. "No shit. I'm dying to move there for school. Wait, are you a new teacher? Is that why you're at the school?"

"I'm at the school..." I say with a breathy laugh, "...because I have to walk by it to get pretty much anywhere, and then your friend nearly gave me a concussion."

Cassidy held up her finger. "One, he's not my friend, and two, he's definitely not strong enough to give anyone any kind of injury."

"Okay," I huff, because clearly they hate this guy. "If he sucks so bad, why did he get named captain?"

Cassidy rolls her eyes for what must be the fourth time. "Because he's the only rising senior on the team. Doesn't mean much if your only opponent is yourself."

"Besides," Bandana girl says, "we're gonna be *terrible* this year since-" Catching herself, she trails off with a sigh. "Nevermind."

She came so close, I can tell. Every time someone gets close to the subject of the disappearances, they back off just as fast, like saying the words would poison the town further.

"How do you do it?" I ask gently.

They just stare at me.

I breathe out slowly. "I mean, I've been here for two weeks and I already feel the creepy crawlies whenever I think about those disappearances. How are you guys just… hanging out, playing a game of pick up soccer?"

A muscle feathers in Bandana girl's jaw, but Cassidy just scrunches her face up like she wants to scream. "I know you're new, but I wouldn't devote too much worry to that conspiracy theory."

"*Cassidy*," Bandana girl hisses.

Cassidy just brushes her friend off. "Sorry, sorry, I know you can't speak ill of the dead, but I have no problem with speaking ill of assholes who *fake* their deaths. Hell of a Senior prank, don't you think? My bet is they'll come back a week before they're supposed to start college, laughing their asses off."

I click my tongue in genuine surprise and tilt my head. "*Oh?*"

The boy (Anthony, the girls had called him) doesn't give me a chance to elaborate, to ask more questions, because he's hopped the fence on his own and jogged over.

"Ladies," he drawls, throwing his arms over their shoulders, and I want to punch him in the head even though he's a child. "I know softball's slower than soccer, but even you know how to throw a ball five yards over a fence. We're trying to have a game here."

Cassidy wrenches herself from under his grip. "I just didn't want to embarrass you when you saw I could throw further than you can kick."

Completely forgetting about my existence, the girls begin to follow Anthony back to the field, the boy long gone and back over the fence to resume the game. They only make it a few steps before Bandana Girl grabs Cassidy's wrist, pulling her back. She technically whispers, but she's doing a pretty bad job of it. "Cassidy. You need to stop spreading that bullshit. What if that girl had been one of their cousins, coming to visit the grieving parents?"

"Why is everyone assuming they're dead? In case you've forgotten, nobody's found the bodies."

"Why would they pretend to die?"

"Because they're *assholes*," Cassidy exclaims, no longer trying to hide what they say. "Come on, you *know* they are. " She turns to me. "Okay, hear me out, tell me if I'm way off base here. Did you know Jason once ran away for two weeks when we were fourteen? Just for fun, and because he'd gotten into a fight with a friend and wanted payback. He's the *epitome* of an attention seeking narcissist, this is right up his alley. Kyle, too, didn't he get kicked off the soccer team for getting into fights on the field? Henry got put into detention so many times for harassing girls that I wouldn't be surprised if he's rotting in some New Hampshire prison for rape. And then there's Xavier, whose parents *suck*, he couldn't wait to get away from them! I hear he actually has a boyfriend, that they were going to run away together-"

"Alternatively," Bandana Girl says angrily, "Xavier might have been hate crimed in our ridiculously ignorant town and thrown in the quarry."

"Have you seen the other three? The straightest, whitest, most boring guys you've ever seen? Yeah, forgive me if I don't think homophobia has anything to do with this."

Bandana girl just huffs. "Sorry about her."

I lift my hands. "Hey, maybe she's right. We can hope, at least."

Her mask of calm seems to break, devastation peeking through to just how rattled she is. "Yeah. We can hope."

They head back to the soccer game, and I walk away as casually as possible until I'm out of sight. Rounding the corner toward the street, I tear my notebook from my purse, scribbling furiously. Because those girls just gave me something to work with.

Four reasons the people in this town might hate those boys.

Four motives.

One for each of them.

"YOU LOOK LIKE YOU'RE going out."

Reyna stops me as I head toward the door, fifteen minutes before I'm supposed to meet Luna. She's sitting mostly in the dark, curled up on the couch with the dim light of her computer illuminating her face. I think her bedroom is even smaller than mine, and that's why she's always out here instead. Doesn't make it any less off-putting, though.

"Sort of," I say, adjusting my top. "Don't sound so surprised."

Reyna actually smiles. "Not surprised. Well, I am, considering there's so few people our age around here."

"I've noticed," I say slowly, leaning over to click on the lamp in the corner. "Why is that?"

Reyna sits up a little bit, stretching before pressing back into the arm of the couch. "It's the circle of the small town. Kids and teenagers get stuck growing up here, they leave for college and their mid twenties to *explore the country*, or whatever, before they inevitably end up back here, where they have their own wretched kids, and the cycle continues. You and I happen to be of the age where no one wants to live here."

Before I can stop myself, I ask, "So why are you here?"

She laughs grimly. "Unavoidable, unfortunate circumstances involving family. You'll find that's probably the case for every other twenty four year old here."

I think about Luna, about her mood swings and the darkening of her eyes, and consider whether Reyna might be onto something.

"So, who is it?" Reyna rips me from my thoughts, seeming genuinely interested.

"Her name's Luna?" I say tentatively.

Reyna stills, and even with the shadows swallowing her face, I can see something flicker there, an unreadable emotion. "Luna Morgan?"

Stomach dropping at the implications of her monotone voice, I confirm, "That's the one."

Reyna heaves a heavy sigh, shifting so her chin is resting on her fist. So heavy that it makes me want to run back to my room and stay there for the rest of the night.

"...should I be worried?" I ask after a moment.

The look on Reyna's face dissipates as fast as it appeared, and she waves her hands. "No! No, of course not, I'm sorry, I-"

"Do you know her?"

Reyna snorts. "First off, that's a stupid question, because I know everyone whether I want to or not."

"You're not making me feel any better."

"We went to school together," she explains, lifting her body to tuck her legs beneath her, pulling the couch blanket over her. "She graduated the year beneath me, but we took art together."

I shuffle back and forth, trying to gauge the situation. "Um… Did you not get along?"

Reyna slaps her forehead. "No, God, just ignore me. She's great, super nice, a bit cold sometimes but that's to be expected considering… well, anyway."

I think about asking her to elaborate, but she looks so suddenly uncomfortable that I decide I'd better just let it go. "Okay. Well, should I tell her you said hello?"

Remaining quiet for a moment, she finally answers, "Probably not."

Chapter Six

LUNA'S TEN MINUTES LATE.

I pass back and forth in front of the diner, which is filled to bursting on a busy Friday night. People, mostly teenagers, flow in and out of the place in a constant stream, laughing and falling over each other. A group of boys pass me, and I dig my heels deeper into the dirt, resisting the urge to put on my interviewer voice and see what information I might get from a few tipsy high schoolers. Did they know the kids that disappeared? What were the dynamics like in school? Were they all actually friends, or was there something else going on?

The opportunity passes, and I slump further against the tall *Suzie's Place* sign, crossing my arms tightly around my chest. In the time that I've waited, I've watched the sun descend fully behind the mountains, plunging me into darkness. Pursing my lips, I check the time again, thinking I must have been set up. Is this because of whatever I said on that day I first met her? Is it payback? Not for the first time, I run the conversation through my head again, but it all becomes blurry after a while, unfocused.

My mind then flies back to Reyna and whatever the hell that brief conversation had been. Maybe I should have pressed for more details, Reyna's discomfort be damned.

I adjust the plain shirt I've tucked into loose pants, fiddling with the piece of fabric acting as a sort of belt. I went with what I usually wear, although I probably spent more time picking out an outfit than I'd *ever* care to admit.

Sighing, and trying not to feel too disappointed– why am I disappointed? I'll just go myself and shamelessly work people for information– I push away from the sign, shoving my phone roughly into my pocket. I don't even know why I keep checking, she doesn't have my number.

The sound of rough footsteps startles me, and I turn to come face to face with Luna as she skids to a stop in front of me. I hold my hands out against her shoulders to catch both her and myself as we wobble to the side.

"Whoa," I yelp. "Are you being chased?"

Luna lurches back, leaning forward onto her knees. She doesn't respond, only holds up a finger to tell me to shut up as she gasps. Sweat shimmers across her forehead, and I wonder how far she'd run. Wonder *why* she had to run.

"Did you somehow get lost in the four streets that make up this town?" I ask dryly, folding my arms across my chest. Even as I do, I tug at my shirt to adjust it, making sure it's fully tucked in.

She finally stands up straight with a glare and rolls her eyes. "Oh, ha-ha."

I squint, peering closer at her rattled features, the blood drained from her face. "Is everything okay? Where were you?"

She gives me a pointed look, as if to say *you're lucky I came at all*, and the withering expression makes me shrink back. "Does it matter?"

"Sort of."

She sighs in frustration. "Nowhere important. Do you want to go out or not?"

"Yeah," I say slowly. "After standing here for twenty minutes alone, I'm in *desperate* need of a drink."

Unfazed, Luna nods. "Good, then. Vormelker's?"

My eyes burst out of my head. "*Excuse* me?"

She laughs, and it eases my little bubble of anxiety. "Vormelker's Tavern, it's down the road. They've got some mean wings."

Baffled, I ask, "Who names a bar *Vormelker's*?"

She leads the way down the dark road. "Victor Vormelker, actually. Family business, same as most places here."

"Victor Vormelker," I muse. "What an unfortunate name."

"I know, right? I feel like people had the worst names in the early 1900s, never less than four syllables with twelve vowels."

Laughing, I say, "If I had a last name like that, I would name my bar probably *anything* else. Usually, I'm annoyed at how bland my last name is, but now I'm just thankful."

"What is it?"

"Hmm?"

"Your last name. You only introduced yourself as Alex."

Hesitating, thinking that the odds of her looking me up are slim to none, I answer honestly. "Brown."

She snorts. "Brown?"

"Well, it's better than Vormelker's."

"I'm not sure that it is, Alex Brown, CEO of the simplest name possible."

"Technically, my name is Alexandra," I point out, even as the name feels uncomfortable on my tongue. I haven't gone by the long version of my name in nearly fifteen years. "That adds a little bit of spice, don't you think?"

Pausing in her stride, Luna turns to squint at me through the dark. "No. You're much more of an Alex than an Alexandra."

"Pretty sure I'm both."

"False. The two names give off *very* different vibes."

"They mean the same thing, though," I say once we're walking again, and I can breathe easier now that she's looking ahead again instead of at me. "*Defender of mankind*, apparently. We did a project on our names in middle school."

"Defender of mankind," she murmurs into the night. We round a corner and leave behind the light of the diner in favor of a darker, much louder street. "That's my point. Alexandra is a very poetic name, so that totally fits. Alex? Not so much."

"Are you saying I'm not poetic?"

"Not as much as an Alexandra should be."

"Well, I don't need to ask what Luna means." I point up at the clear sky to the small, white crescent winking down at us.

Luna smiles tightly. "If it makes you feel any better, I don't think I quite live up to that beautiful definition, either."

I open my mouth to respond, to tell her that she just might, but music and chatter grows louder the further we walk down the street. People mull about from building to building, gathering in small groups with drinks in the outdoor patios. Lights are strung up on the utility poles, crisscrossing over the street and illuminating more people than I've seen in this town so far.

"There's nothing to do during the day," Luna leans over to tell me, as if reading my mind. "But we make do during the evenings in our little downtown."

"This isn't a downtown," I argue, momentarily distracted from the sight and noise. "Only cities can have downtowns, because you could theoretically fit multiple towns into the size of a city. This is a *street*."

"It's a downtown that's proportional to the size of the town," she insists. "It makes us feel better to call it that."

I keep a look out for the signs telling me what's what. There are a few restaurants and shops that have closed for the night, but the rest of the buildings (a grand total of four) are the bars, plus what looks to be a dessert place.

"Which one is..." I trail off. "I've already forgotten what it's called."

Luna snorts, nodding to the one at the end of the street that's less crowded than the others. There seems to be a band playing in the one closest to us, so that's probably why. We pass by the flashing lights and loud conversations, the doors wide open and beckoning.

"Why not here?" I ask, nodding along to the tune that sounds vaguely country.

Luna wrinkles her nose, scrunching her whole face up in shadows. "Too crowded, it's everyone's favorite."

"You're too cool for what's *clearly* the best bar?" I tease with a grin.

She gives me a harsh sideways glance and corrects, "Too tired."

Flinching at the moderately scary flash in her eyes, I snap my mouth shut and shuffle a few inches away from her.

All at once, Luna deflates, shoulders slumping as she wrings her fingers together. "Sorry. This is the first time I've gone out in... a *while*," she admits as we walk, growing further away from the noise.

"I can't say I'm surprised, if you bite off everyone else's heads, too."

She rolls her eyes, but doesn't say anything, which leads me to believe that I might be onto something. But the action is so pitiful that I decide to firmly push away whatever warning Reyna's words might have been.

Vormelker's Tavern is calmer and emptier than the rest of the street, and I understand what Luna meant when I breathe a sigh of relief at the quiet. She leads me inside, motioning to a table in the corner.

"I'll grab the drinks," she murmurs as we separate. "Better not to get caught in conversation with Barry. If he lays his sights on you, we'll be stuck at the bar for hours."

My lips curve, taking a leap. "You could just say you don't want to share me."

Luna lets out a startled laugh. "Trust me, I'm trying to save you. You're fresh meat, he'll *definitely* try to take you home."

Part of me thinks I might take my chances. There's almost no one better at giving information than a tipsy man who wants to get in your pants. But with a quick glance toward the mildly sleazy guy in his mid-thirties wiping down the bar, I figure it's best not to argue.

"Just a beer for me, then."

The bar is made pretty much entirely of old fashioned wood: the tables, floor, walls, chairs, it's all made of that dark, musty wood that looks about a thousand years old. How old is this place? Decades, probably. Something about this town feels old, weathered. Maybe it's the deep, decades old quarries.

Or maybe it's just the dust.

Two drinks clunk down against the table, echoing sharply around the bar. It's not that it's completely empty, but the music and conversation remain a gentle lull, people for the most part staying in their own bubbles.

"For you," Luna says, sliding my drink across the wood as she lowers herself into her seat with a jug of moonshine.

I accept, clinking my nails along the glass. "Thanks."

We fall into a relatively awkward silence, and for a moment I wish that we'd gone to the more crowded place, or at least sat at the bar. I got so used to being in the same place, I haven't had to meet new people in years. I never bothered.

Luna peers at me over glass. "When was the last time *you* went out?"

"Two weeks ago," I answer honestly. It'd just been in New York.

"You look uncomfortable."

"It's not the bar."

Luna snorts, leaning back. "Yeah, me too. I've sort of been... not socializing a lot. Lately."

"Why?" I ask, intrigued, wondering whether it has anything to do with the string of disappearances. Not for the first time, I consider the possibility that *she* is somehow looped into it all. It seems unlikely, but then again, small towns... They tend to be surprising.

Taking a sip and lowering her glass, she says, "Can't say I've wanted to. Home felt... better. Safer."

It certainly does.

When I don't respond, she says, "You miss New York." It's not a question, but a statement. And only a semi accurate one.

"I guess," I say, shoulders caving in on myself. I'm a pretty good journalist, decent investigator, but I'm a crap actress. That's why I try to go with a story that's as close to the truth as possible. "It was sort of a spur of the moment decision, moving here. I had this... other job there, for a long time, but it was a lot of pressure you know? Pretty intense work, and I thought having a more casual, less demanding job would be... good for me. Remote, you know? And like I said, New York's expensive. I couldn't swing it anymore."

Luna pauses, gazing at me, before eventually drawling, "And...?"

I stare at her. "And... what?"

"Who'd you leave behind?" she asks, words delicate and surprisingly gentle.

I gnaw on my lip, but quickly stop myself in favor of sipping on my drink, teeth clanking against the glass instead. "No one good."

She sits back. "So you moved to get away from him?"

Without missing a beat, I murmur, "Her, actually." I glance up just in time to catch Luna nodding, not a muscle out of place. "But yeah, that might have been part of it." The way it all went down, the way I caught her. The way it was all my fault, the way I hadn't been able to focus fully on her even as I broke up with her.

Luna pushes her drink around in front of her, dragging a wet ring behind it. The water from the condensation makes the wood shine under the dim, orange light. "How's that working out for you?"

I crack a grin. "Mediocre at best."

Luna laughs. "You already look better than you did a few days ago. Less ragged."

"I wish I felt that way."

We're interrupted by two older women approaching, one of them holding a tray of mozzarella sticks, and my stomach grumbles.

"Luna!" the first woman exclaims, leaning forward to envelop her in a hug. Luna sputters in surprise, having been halfway through swallowing, but smiles nonetheless.

"Hey, Ruth." She nods to the other woman. "Leah."

Ruth is smiling so wide, they must know each other well. They look about Lucia's age; maybe they're friends with her mom. "It's been quite some time, how are you?"

Luna lifts her glass to give an invisible *cheers*, even though neither of the women have drinks. "Not bad."

Ruth smiles wider when she turns to look at me, a question in her eyes that I can't quite read. "Who's your friend?"

"This is Alex." Luna introduces me with a lazy wave of her hand, as if they should know this already, as if I'd been here for longer than ten days.

"I don't think I've seen you before."

"I'm new here," I say, then cringe inwardly at my choice of words. What am I, the new kid in middle school?

Even though that's sort of how it feels.

"Oh!" Ruth exclaims. "Well, welcome." And this new information must be why Ruth speaks so lowly next, in an inconspicuous whisper to Luna. "How is he?"

Mouth opening ever so slightly, Luna shifts a little in her seat, shoulders slumping discreetly. As I watch on curiously, some of the light reflecting in her eyes gutters out. Glancing quickly toward me, she gives a curt nod. "The same."

He. *Boyfriend?* I think to myself. *Ex-boyfriend?* I try not to feel too disappointed. Moreover, I try not to think about *why* I'm disappointed.

Another thought occurs to me then. Maybe this... person... is just a friend who knows one of the boys who disappeared? Yeah, that would make sense. Maybe a family member, brother or something. I know Luna isn't related to any of them, but...

Ruth straightens once more, mouth seaming into a straight line. "Oh, well, I'm sorry to hear that. Tell your mother we say hello, and that she has to come back to margarita night, yeah?"

Luna gives them a wobbling thumbs up, and then they've disappeared across the room, claiming a table an appropriate distance away. I breathe a sigh of relief, not for myself, but for Luna. I hadn't even realized how nervous I was that they'd stay.

Her eyes follow them as they go, but I keep mine on her, observing every movement. She turns back to me with a heavy sigh, downing the rest of her drink.

"Who is...?" I trail off hesitantly. I avoid making direct eye contact, scared of the question, but it's impossible to miss the way she stiffens, looks away.

"He's... gone." There's a pause while she swallows and wills a smile onto her face. She stands. "Another round, then? I'm going to run to the bathroom, so this one's on you."

She's gone before I can respond, head ducked and face hidden as she hops down the wooden steps toward the narrow hallway in the back corner. She pushes through the swinging door, and I stare long after she's disappeared from sight before I remember that I have to get the drinks.

No one sits at the bar as I approach, only a few nearby tables occupied, and I slide onto one of the rusted metal stools. The bartender doesn't notice me at first, and I drum my fingers along the faded wood, clearing my throat.

He turns, brows high on his forehead and a slow smile spreading over his face. "Hey, there. I don't think I've seen you around here before."

Ugh. I try my best not to wrinkle my nose. "Makes sense, considering I've never been here before. Can I get a refill for whatever Luna ordered?"

He clicks his tongue. "Right to business, then. Another moonshine for the regular. And what about you, then? Anything interesting?"

I smile blandly. "Just your cheapest beer."

He huffs, and he still doesn't wipe what he thinks is a charming smirk from his face. "Might want to reconsider. I think our cheapest beer is gonna be water compared to whatever you get where you're from."

Frowning, I ask, "Is the city girl vibe really that obvious?"

"In this bar, it is. I'll get you something in the medium area." He doesn't have to go far, the selection behind him relatively small, and as he pours from a tap, he asks, "So what's your name?"

"Alex." I glance over my shoulder toward the still closed bathroom door, taking my chance as I wrack my brain for Luna's earlier words. "Barry, right?

His face split open into a toothy grin. "Luna talking to you about me?"

I lean forward. "Something like that. Tell me, Barry, this place doesn't seem like the kind of bar to ask for IDs."

He snorts. "Have you seen our clientele? Nah, we don't usually have to, not many young folks in our town."

"Sure, sure. But I mean, what about the younger kids? Do they ever come here?"

Barry narrows his eyes, pulling back. "What are you, an undercover cop?"

"No," I roll my eyes, and come up with a half lie. "Just an out of towner who's seeing if she can bust her little cousin for going to bars three years too soon."

Barry tips his head back and cackles, and yeah, he's definitely not sober, because that worked way too easily. "Yeah, we get the high schoolers in here sometimes. They have these horrible fake IDs, and I like to fuck with them by really scrutinizing them for like an entire minute. The panic on their faces consistently gets me through a ten hour shift." His expression sobers. "Haven't seen them much lately, though. They've been keeping to themselves."

I jump at the topic. "I don't really blame them. The whole town's on red alert, no sense adding illegal drinking to the list of horrible occurrences in this town."

Barry just exhales, finally sliding the beer and moonshine to me, and I pass him my card. As he slides it through the small machine on the counter, he responds, "Yeah, not exactly great for business. Can't say drinking is the worst those kids got up to. Your cousin included, probably."

I dig deeper, remembering the words of the high school girls from yesterday. "It can't be worse than what I got into in the city. We could do *anything* there."

He just shakes his head, returning my card and leaning on the counter with folded arms. "Sure, because you had things to do. Here, the kids have nothing better to do other than get into trouble. Those boys who went missing…" He trails off, shaking his head. "I've seen a few of them blacking out on more than one occasion. Fights, pranks, whatever to pass the time. A few got mixed up in drugs. This one time, I had to kick this kid Anthony out because he got dared to break a glass on his friend's head. Knocked him out cold for a few minutes and then tried to do it to himself just for kicks."

My jaw drops. "Seems oddly violent for a teenager."

"I swear, these kids will do anything to keep themselves entertained. I wouldn't be surprised if they got themselves killed in an adrenaline rush. Or just doing something... really stupid."

Doing stupid things can get you killed in more than one way. It can make people angry, too.

Elbows drop down beside me on the counter, and I turn in surprise to see that I hadn't noticed Luna slip back out, pulling her drink toward her. I jump off my stool, tipping my beer toward Barry. "Nice meeting you," I say before pulling Luna away, praying she hadn't heard too much of our conversation, that it didn't sound too weird.

My worries are put to rest when we sit down and Luna shoots a look in Barry's direction, who looks all too pleased that I talked to him for so long. "What were you talking about?"

I wave her off, my fingers shaking slightly. "Just keeping myself occupied since you abandoned me."

Luna laughs, looking lighter than she'd been a few minutes before. She hesitates a moment, and then settles back into her seat, like we might sit together all night. "At least I know you weren't flirting with him."

I tap my drink against hers. "I wouldn't have flirted with him even if I wasn't a lesbian."

Chapter Seven

A LITTLE HUNGOVER, AND more than a little angry that my body wakes me up before eight in the morning on a Saturday, I stomp out of my apartment. I go where my feet take me, figuring a small walk might make me tired (and less queasy) enough to crash for the rest of the day. I'm halfway past Suzie's Place when my stomach rumbles, and I turn on my heel and head back. There's no hangover cure quite like a good, greasy meal.

The diner is completely deserted when I take a seat, not another soul in sight besides a single waiter. The sight reminds me how Jo apparently gets help from the teenagers on the weekends. He leans against a foggy window, a baseball cap snug on his head, a smoking cigarette dangling from his lips. He turns his head as though through caramel when the bell rings to signal my entrance, looking about as dead on his feet as I feel.

Forcing energy into himself, he hollers to me across the room, "Morning!" I don't miss the way he hastens to snuff the cigarette in an ashtray behind him, waving the smoke out the window.

I laugh, hopping onto my usual seat. (Can I call it my usual yet?) "Don't worry, I won't tell."

Flustered and hurried, he takes my order, disappearing back into the kitchen. Is Jo here? I guess it would make sense that there's other cooks; she can't be here all the time. The woman has to sleep.

Bouncing my leg against the stool's footrest, I spend the next ten minutes or so waiting for my food and checking the door every three seconds. To get him to say anything at all, I need to be the only one in here. If experience serves me right, the less people around, the more likely people are to talk. Unless, of course, the place is filled to the brim with people and noise, that's when you can *really* get into the good information because it's so loud, they feel like they can't be overheard.

But a room with three or four people in it, on a quiet, gloomy morning? It's a lost cause.

When he at last brings me my food, I thank him in a hushed tone, allowing him to walk away. *Don't rush it, don't seem like you're desperate for information.* The problem is that I'm horrible at being nonchalant in my day to day life, but sometimes interviews require it. Particularly when someone doesn't know they're being interviewed.

He goes around to clean up a table that must have been used before I arrived, wiping away crumbs and water rings. Hunched over my plate and trying not to appear suspicious, I cut into my meal (eggs, this time. I can't have pancakes *every* day, my stomach can't take it). I'm halfway through the hashbrowns when he comes back into my vision, beginning to wipe down the opposite side of the counter. I remember this from my brief time working as a waitress: when in doubt, clean.

He makes his way down the slab of marble, eventually stopping in front of me to mop up where someone must have spilled some maple syrup beside me. Snatching my chance, I clear my throat.

"Hi," I say, folding my arms so I can lean forward. "Excuse me?"

"Yeah?" he says, slowing his rigorous scrubbing as he lifts his head. "Everything good?"

"Delicious." Wasting no time, I nod my head toward the street outside, as deserted as the restaurant this early on a Saturday. "Do you go to the high school here?" I ask delicately, inching around the topic. Oh god, what if he's friends with one of the missing kids and he bursts out crying or something? I would bolt out of here so fast, I'd probably give up on the case and move across the country.

"I did..." he trails off, raising his brows in questions.

I plunge forward, not wanting to weird him out. "Can I ask..." I say slowly, doing my best to play dumb, "... I read something in the papers, just after I moved here a week or so ago."

Something shifts in his face, his entire body stiffening, and I can tell he knows exactly where I'm headed. After a moment of examining his expression, it doesn't seem to be an overwhelming sense of sadness, or discomfort, just a mask of calm. It encourages me enough to continue. "What's with all the disappearances?"

Nerves tighten as I wait for a reaction, and I breathe a sigh of relief when he only looks down with a grunt, spraying the counter with cleaner and resuming his scrubbing. "It sucks, is what it is."

I press my lips together, trying not to roll my eyes at how unhelpful that is. "Horrible, I know, I couldn't believe it when I read it. Four in a month?"

He nods, swallowing, and I tilt my head as he refuses to look me in the eye. "Yeah, four dudes in the year below me."

One year apart. Good, he must have graduated last year, then.

"They say they have no idea who's doing it," I say tentatively.

He rubs at an eye with his index finger, tossing the rag aside and leaning against the wall behind the counter. Breathing in deeply, he tilts his head back towards the ceiling, squinting. His throat bobs. "It's… I don't know. How do four people just disappear into thin air?" The words get quieter and quieter as he says them, like he spoke more to himself than me.

"Were you close with them?"

He shakes his head, but a muscle in his neck twitches. "No, no not really. I knew them, of course. It's a tiny school, everyone knows everyone."

"Really? I went to a huge high school, I barely knew *anyone*."

"Not from here?"

"Nah. I've always wondered what it would be like to just have the same people in your classes every year. Must have gotten repetitive."

Shrugging, he says, "Can be good, can be bad."

"Sort of sucks in this situation."

He pauses, leaning further over the counter, back curling toward me, and he lifts a hand to his face, almost like he wipes his eyes. "They were good guys. Didn't run into them much at school or anything, but I saw them a lot at The Ledge."

Inching forward in my seat without my permission, I press, "The Ledge? That sounds sort of ominous."

He rolls his eyes, looking relieved that we seem to be moving into familiar territory for him, and he finally faces me again. "Hardly. It's just one of the quarries, the one closest to the school, where we have parties and shit. There's a sort of path out behind the football field, it goes all the way out."

"I thought you got to the quarries by Marble Street?"

"That, too," he agrees. "It's a bit of a shortcut. They nicknamed it The Ledge, like, years ago because people kept falling in when they were drunk." He shuffles his feet, face reddening, as though he's one of the many people to have fallen victim to *The Ledge*.

Chuckling, even as my mind runs a mile a minute, I nod. "Parties still held there? Even in summer?"

"Oh, yeah, look where you are. There's not a lot of other options."

I don't have anything else to ask, but I don't need to, because the sun peeks through the windows now, bringing in the morning rush. The waiter gives me a stiff nod when a couple walks through the door, going off to take their order. The knots in my shoulders release, and the muscles in my face relax as I lower my head back to my eggs, appetite suddenly gone.

I know where I'm going next.

THE PATH IS SURPRISINGLY easy to find.

You'd think they'd make it appear more inconspicuous. Wouldn't these kids want to hide the entrance to their base? Then again, I suppose there's another entrance, so it's a moot point.

Circling the edge of the football field, the gap in the treeline stands wide open for everyone to see. I duck under a branch, the only block in the opening, before being swallowed by foliage. The path is well worn, fresh footprints overlapping each other in the mud, probably from last night. Generations of high schoolers have probably walked down this path, drunk or high out of their mind. How comfortable do you have to be to walk past your own high school when you're plastered? It's almost admirable.

Taking it slow, I keep a lookout as I follow the footsteps, the ghosts of last night's party goers leading the way. I don't know what evidence I expect to find that the cops missed, but taking a notepad and pencil to the potential place of the crime can never hurt. If all else fails, it might send me somewhere else.

Could that have been it? Could this have all started with that first boy, Jason, falling into the quarry and not getting out? But what about the other three, could they have *all* been swallowed by those giant pits of water? It seems believable enough to me; the thought of the abyss still freaks me out.

Nothing strikes me as out of the ordinary for the entirety of my journey, aside from a few needles and bottles here and there. After nearly twenty minutes, the woods spit me out, and I'm so out of breath that I consider whether or not the kids might have just gotten lost in the forest, wandered off the path. I squash this idea as soon as it comes, because I know for a fact that they've done search parties in these very woods. Several of them.

Stumbling to a stop not just because of tiredness, I realize that I'm not alone. A few yards ahead, standing with her hands braced against the railings that guard the quarry, is Luna. She's leaning over, head pressed into her knuckles, foot kicking at the rocks beneath her.

"Luna?" I call out, and my voice is so startling against the silence, I feel like I've shaken the trees.

Luna yelps and I think about what the waiter had said, about how easy it is to fall into the water. I reach toward her, but she's steadied herself before I can even take a step, glaring at me.

"Sorry," I laugh at how frazzled she looks. "I didn't mean to scare you."

Taking a shaking breath, she blinks away the anger that bled into her face. "No, I... Jesus, I just wasn't expecting anyone."

"Likewise," I say. "What are you doing here so early?"

Adjusting the string of her sweatpants with one hand and dragging fingers through her hair with the other, she mumbles, "Couldn't sleep."

"So you came here?" I ask incredulously.

She lifts her head, and I have to squint to make out her face, the sun behind her bright and all consuming. It turns her into a mere silhouette. "What are *you* doing here?"

I hold up my hands in mock surrender, walking toward her. "Same as always, I'm still learning the town. I hear quarries are a pretty big thing here, I've only ever been to one other."

She lifts her brows just as I reach a safe distance away, slowing to a stop. "If you've seen one, you've seen them all."

Shifting my gaze back to the quarry, I seam my lips together. "I sort of get that now. I was just at Suzie's. The dude working was talking about how people always gather here. I thought they'd be more... interesting."

Luna tries for a laugh, but it comes out hollow. "This is about as interesting as West Rutland has. The poor kids are making do with what they've got."

I scoot closer to the edge. "They're sort of scary."

She knocks against the metal lining the edge. "That's why they added these trusty railings, as if a piece of metal can stop the people in this town from being stupid."

"There hasn't always been railings?"

"Not in the nineties and shit. People just didn't care back then. A lot more people used to use the quarries for swimming than they do now."

I wrinkle my nose at the thought of getting any closer to the probably disgusting water. It's probably not black because it's dirty, but rather because it's deep, but... still. I wouldn't want to swim in a pool that appears to be filled with onyx tar. "I see why they don't. I'm unnerved by swimming pools if I can't see the bottom."

Luna pulls her mouth into a tight line. "In reality, quarries aren't as big as they look. A couple hundred feet maybe. Others are bigger of course, but you can only go so deep. This one's actually pretty shallow compared to the others. You could swim down and touch the bottom if you tried."

"No way," I gape, peering down into the abyss. Never before have I felt more as though I'm looking into a ceaseless, soul sucking pit. That if I were to jump down, it would never spit me back up. "I guess it's the dirty water. Makes the whole thing look a hell of a lot more ominous than it is."

"Actually, I think it's the dead bodies that put people off nowadays."

Eyes bugging out of my face, figuring I must have misheard, I whip my head towards Luna, only to find her giving me a mischievous smile. "That better be a joke."

"Only partially," she says, a weird mix of bitterness mingling with her grin. "Theory and speculation. There's technically no way to prove there's dead bodies since, obviously, we can't see the bottom. We just sort of assume that some of the disappearances from the past few decades have ended up in one of these. There's definitely a fair number of junk cars, though."

I'm still caught on the whole "dead bodies" part. "Wouldn't the bodies rise to the top? Isn't that how it works?"

"Not if they're caught on something else. Like, for example, one of the many junk cars."

"And how exactly do we know for a fact that there's cars in there? We can't see them any more than we can see dead people."

"Was that a Sixth Sense reference?"

"Not intentionally."

Luna laughs, somehow having the courage to lean up against the railing. Flakes of rust flutter to the grass beneath at the brush of her arms. If the rails are already this rusty after only a few years of use, they must be pieces of shit, and I step even further away from them. "People used to drive them off the edge for sport." When my eyes widen, she waves me off. "No one in them, of course. If the engine still worked, they'd put a brick on the accelerator or something, or they'd just muscle the thing in if it stopped working entirely."

"...*why*...?"

"What can I say? They were bored. The time before technology was a scary place, they had nothing better to do than destroy shit."

I picture it, a group of high school students in the eighties, with their poofy hair and leg warmers, pushing a car off the edge of a cliff just for the fun of it. It's a hilarious image. "Now I sort of want to push a car off the edge. Just to see what happens."

"You'd be more entertained if you set it on fire, I promise you that," she says dryly. "Actually, they would do that, too. Sometimes, they'd set it on fire, and *then* drive it into the quarry. And then jump in after it."

"God, I wouldn't even want to swim in that thing in the daylight, but at *night*."

Luna is quiet for a moment. "Yeah. Really bad idea."

"Have you ever been swimming here?" I ask curiously.

Luna stares out in front of her, fingers intertwining together so aggressively it's almost as though she's thumb wrestling herself.

"Not in a long time. I used to, when I was young. I know better now."

I open my mouth to ask why, how, what makes it so dangerous. How exactly this place is so different from an ordinary swimming pool besides its depth and general griminess. But you're no more likely to drown in a fifty foot pool than a twelve foot deep end, so what, really, is the difference?

But I don't ask why. Something on her face tells me not to, that I probably shouldn't say anything at all about it. Instead, I just scoot a little bit closer to her, bumping the elbow she rests on the railing with mine. "I wouldn't want to go into that stuff anyway. It looks almost solid, like tar."

"Might as well be. Better the cars get stuck in there than us."

Chapter Eight

LUNA LEADS ME THROUGH a much quicker path back to civilization, and it spits us out at the sculpture garden instead of the high school. We stay silent for most of the walk, ducking under branches and around ferns, but it's comfortable. She has a calming air about her. I can only hope I give her something of the same, too.

"Are you working today?" I ask when we end up by that booth where I'd first met her.

"Yeah," she sighs. "It's why I stopped by the quarry on my way here, to get rid of the splitting headache."

I almost bring back something from our first conversation. *I thought you didn't find quarries peaceful, so why would visiting one cure your hangover?* but I immediately decide that's a bad idea.

"Here," I say, digging around in my pocket for some cash. "Mind if I take a look around?"

She flicks her brows up but takes the bills anyway. "Didn't you already go around last week?"

"I did," I say slowly. "But I was distracted." I very deliberately don't elaborate.

Luna stares at me, a small smile tugging at the corners of her lips. "Sorry about that."

"No, you're not. Clearly, it was just a scam for profit. I see right through you."

Grin spreading fully now, giving me some feeling of inner victory, Luna says, "You got me. This whole town's actually just one big conspiracy, didn't you know?"

I pull up short at the choice of words, even though I know she didn't mean anything by it, because isn't it though?

Clearing my throat, I push the thought away. "You know, I'm starting to realize that. Any secrets hidden here?"

Luna glances over her shoulder, light and mysterious, as she grips the doorknob to her ticket booth. "A few. If you know where to look."

I'M DISTRACTED ONCE MORE, but I do my best to actually take in the statues. They're beautiful and creative, all in different shapes and sizes and contortions. Most are made of marble, but surprisingly, there's quite a bit of metal in the mix. I guess metal lets the artist add color with spray paint. It would be wrong to paint the already exquisite, elegant marble.

I weave through the trails, sculpture after sculpture peppering the pathways. They spit me out into various clearings, and I'm overwhelmed by how big the place actually is. Last time, I just found a sign and took the quickest path to the quarry. I could probably walk in circles around here for hours and never see everything.

After about an hour, I start to feel thoroughly lost even though there's signs everywhere. I haven't been reading them, just following the tug towards various statues, all the stories being told through the trees.

I pause near the end of a trail to peer at a statue of a woman shrouded in vines. Her body is naked, curved and sculpted, so realistic you could almost imagine a real body encased in the marble. Propped between two trees, leaves meld clothes around her form. They fall from her fingertips in liquid green, as though she's reaching out toward me, beckoning me into the forest to join her. Obeying, I take another step off the path, squinting closer.

"Beautiful, huh?"

Startled, I stumble back onto the trail and into the sunlight. I turn my head around to see Lucia leaning around a tree and into the gap at the end of the trail. She's not quite smiling, but not exactly frowning either, and the thundering of my heart calms at the sight of familiarity as I glance back at the statue.

"She is. One of yours?"

She shakes her head, wiping her dirty hands on an apron. She must be carving, because a pair of safety goggles sit propped against her hairline, the rest of her clothes covered in dust. Or whatever you call marble dust. "I don't sculpt people, they take a certain eye that I've never had." She pauses before smiling. "Luna has it, though. She's always been about portraits."

"I saw," I say, thinking back to watching her sketch in the diner, fingers covered in charcoal.

"I hear you've befriended my daughter," she hums, walking back towards what looks to be her workstation. She's set up in an empty field, where the last of the sculptures on display have tapered off. Instead, the area is replaced by a variety of equipment and marble. Tentatively, I follow her.

"Um," I say. "Sort of."

Lucia chuckles in understanding. "The apple doesn't fall far from the tree with that one, and by the tree I mean her father. Both have walls with as many layers as a century old tree. The layers themselves are pretty soft, though." She hefts up a small saw. "If you have the right tools."

Laughing at the metaphor, I say, "I don't think a lethal saw is the best way to gain trust."

"Maybe not," she sighs. "You seem to be doing alright, regardless."

I'm not entirely sure what that means, so I stay silent. I instead choose to squint at the array of tools at her feet, before lifting my eyes back to the large chunk of marble towering over us. It's extremely daunting, even just looking at it. She's clearly just started, and I can't really tell what it is yet, but the cuts are smooth and soft, her practiced hands already beginning to bring rock to life.

Before I can comment on it, Lucia asks, "How is everything otherwise, hmm? You look a little more settled than when I last saw you."

Smiling, I nod. "Yeah, you caught me on moving week, and that's just no fun. Tiring, you know?"

"I do," she confirms, somehow having the courage to haphazardly lean against the marble. It stays steady, though, not cut thin enough to break. "When my husband and I first moved here, it was a little overwhelming. You wouldn't think such a tiny place would be, but they're staggering in a different way, if that makes sense."

I nod with rigor. "Oh, trust me, we're on the same page. I think the city somehow felt smaller than West Rutland."

"Seems like you miss it, though. Luna mentioned something about finances having to do with your move."

I nod, thankful that part of my cover story had gotten through. "Yeah, it's like those Brooklyn apartment prices go up every day."

"Well, even if you felt a bit forced to come here, I hope it gives you something back. It certainly did for us."

"So why'd *you* move here?"

"Well, I met my husband on a ski trip, actually," Lucia says. "Here in Vermont, at a mountain a few miles away. Killington, have you heard of it?"

I shake my head. "I've never been skiing in my life, and I plan to keep it that way."

"Probably just as well," she laughs. "Robert's the skier in our family, being from Maine and all. I never liked it, but my sisters skied competitively through school. They dragged me to one of their competitions, and, well… I guess it might be a little ironic that I'm the one who moved here, to the snow and cold, while they both went further south."

It is a bit ironic, actually. "So neither of you are from here?"

"No, but we both fell in love with it. It was sort of like meeting halfway, in a new state and new life."

New state, new life. It's a nice thought, in theory. I can almost pretend that's what I'm actually doing. Not for the first time, the overwhelming feeling of *fakeness* overtakes me. It's much easier to blend into a crowd of faceless city people, constantly moving, just as fake as me. Knowing their names makes lying a little harder.

Instead of responding, I return my attention to her work, trying to discern what she's making.

Reading my mind, Lucia knocks her knuckles against the marble a few times. "It doesn't look like anything yet, I can see you trying to figure it out. It's quite the process, takes a lot of small layers. If you go too deep too fast, you'll make a mistake, or the whole thing might fall apart."

"It's a precarious artform," I muse. "Seems stressful." Anything as permanent as cutting through stone makes my anxiety prickle.

"Not really. Not when you know what you're doing." She looks back and forth between her tools and my fascination. "Are you interested?" she asks, looking excited. I remember what Luna said about preferring drawing to sculpting. Lucia probably tried time and time again to pass her specific craft down to her daughter, but to no avail.

"Yeah," I admit. "It's a very unique way to make art, I've only attempted the two dimensional stuff. And I was crap at it."

"You don't need to be good at drawing to sculpt, they're astronomically different."

"Are they? Isn't sculpting just 3d drawing?"

"Hardly, but that's mostly because of the tools." Grinning, and hoisting the saw, she offers, "I could walk you through a few tricks? If you're not busy."

"I'm not," I say, nudging the smaller tools with my toes. "You probably shouldn't let me touch the power tools, though."

The even wider smile that she gives me makes her look suddenly twenty years younger. "We'll start small."

"YOU *CARVED MARBLE ALL day?*"

Exhausted from working on a small slab of marble with Lucia for the past several hours (who knew you could do so much with a four inch cube of marble?), I wipe sweat away from my forehead, still walking home in the blazing sun. I wish I'd brought my car, but most of the hike home was back through the sculpture center in the woods, anyway.

Defensive, I hold the phone away from my ear at Elise's shrill voice. "Don't think of it as sculpting. Think of it as building relationships with people who might have information."

"Sounds to me like you've built a relationship with exactly *one* family." She pauses, and I can hear the smirk edging into her voice. "One *girl* in particular, actually."

I kick at the stones littering the cracked street. Every single street in this town probably needs to be repaved, now that I think about it. "That's not what I called you to talk about."

"You're deflecting."

I pause, because I am. "She took me out to a bar last night. Can't I use one person to introduce me to everyone else?"

"*Did* she introduce you to anyone else last night?" Elise presses skeptically.

The actual answer is no. In fact, we'd stayed at Vormelker's the whole night, casually chatting over a few drinks in the corner of the room. I didn't speak to anyone else the entire night, aside from the bartender, and I was perfectly content.

I slap my forehead with my hand. I *am* getting distracted, but it's hard not to.

"It's weird," I finally say. "Everyone I've met, they all seem normal. Obviously, I don't know what their actual normal is, but... I guess I haven't met any friends or family of the people impacted."

"Probably not," Elise conceded. "They're probably pretty closed off right now. But don't let your guard down, yeah? You could very well have met the person doing it, they're probably really good at hiding their feelings, pretending."

"Yeah," I trail off. The thought of any of the lovely people I've met possibly murdering four people makes my stomach twist.

"So what's your next steps?" Elise asks, back to business. There's a tapping sound in the background, and I can tell she's tapping a pen against her notepad. She does it all the time, it used to annoy the crap out of me. "Like, actual steps."

"I'm going to the hospital tomorrow," I blurt out through gritted teeth, sorting all the things I need to do through my mind. Interviewing isn't as easy as it usually is, when I have to pretend that I'm *not* interviewing. But we know how small towns work, and people only give information up to friends, not professionals.

"Hospital? Why? They never found any bodies, remember?"

"I know," I groan. "It's worth a visit, though, isn't it?"

"Maybe, if you could check in any of the rooms. It's not like they'd lie about having the bodies, right?"

"Well, let me know if you have any better ideas," I snap, irritated.

Elise sighs through the speaker. "Sorry. I know this sucks."

The anger cools down slightly, and I pause on the side of the road, closing my eyes. "They're not making it any easier. There's barely anywhere to go, a few bars and restaurants but absolutely no stores. Everyone just goes to the mall in Rutland City, which also totally sucks, by the way. But going there would be way too confusing, I wouldn't be able to tell who's from where."

"So stay in town," Elise says professionally, encouragingly, just as I get home. I nearly weep at the thought of a hot shower and my bed. "Keep doing what you're doing. You're right, you have a good process. Get close to people, make relationships with everyone you can. Someone will let something slip."

Chapter Nine

WEST RUTLAND DOESN'T HAVE a hospital. I guess small towns don't; they wouldn't have enough business for it to be worthwhile (not that that's a bad thing).

But, isn't it though? The nearest hospital from any given point in West Rutland is over twenty minutes away, all the way on the other side of Rutland City. Let's say an accident happens in my town, it'd take fifteen minutes for the ambulance just to *get* here. And then *another* fifteen to get back to the hospital, not including any time it might take to treat the person on sight.

As I climb into the black Jeep I'd inherited from my dad when he passed, all I can think is that this seems like a flaw in the system. A five minute ambulance trip versus a fifteen minute one could be the difference between life and death.

Rutland City and West Rutland *technically* border each other, but there seems to be a little area of nothing in between. Main Street leads out of West Rutland, and slowly the assortment of businesses and homes trickle out, until there is only a long stretch of road of cemeteries and open land. Slowly, civilization picks up again, and although I wouldn't exactly call Rutland a *city* (I'm slowly learning that there are no real cities in Vermont, they're just considered cities relative to everything else), it's certainly bigger than the tiny town I'd just left.

I'd define Rutland as a "drive through town." It's one of those places you stop during long drives home, when you need a quick and easy bite to eat. The main road that cuts through the city is flush with fast food and cheap restaurants, with one small mall, but the rest of the place is pretty residential. I crawl through the winding roads, more people dotting the sidewalks the further into Rutland City I get. The houses get a little bigger, but they're just as run down, and I try to put my finger on what exactly makes the energy startlingly different from West Rutland.

The hospital sits at the top of a tall hill on the east side of town, and there's a weird roundabout road that leads to the parking lot. I pull into one of the spots, settling back into the leather seats to grab my phone and notebook.

No body, no evidence. In theory, there'd be no point at all in going to the hospital, not if none of the boys have passed through. There's no one to talk to, no one to interview, no one to give me anything.

Then again, no one in West Rutland's given me anything, either, so here we are.

Groaning, I kick the door open, and it creaks as the lock gives. The car is about fifteen years old, my dad's back up that mostly sat in a garage unless I needed to drive somewhere. It's gotten a lot more use since it officially became mine, though. Driving's not always necessary in the city, but it can sometimes be nice. If just to take a drive across the bridge and look at the skyline. It made it all feel a little smaller, less overwhelming.

More like how Vermont feels.

The hospital doors slide open easily, revealing a wide open hall of chairs, and a small registration window off to the left. Even at high noon, it's eerily dark, with only a few lamps lining the walls instead of overhead lights.

"Hi," I greet the plump, bored lady at the window, who leans over a crossword puzzle. When she doesn't budge, writing what looks like *acapella* into the tiny, waiting boxes, I clear my throat. "Excuse me?"

She glances up, throwing down her pencil and sliding her chair over to the computer. Hands poised at the keyboard, she asks in the most monotone voice, "Can I help you?"

Unfazed, I put on my best, winning journalist smiles. "Hi, yes. My name is Alex Brown, journalist with the Manhattan Herald." I bristle when the woman lets out a long suffering sigh, but I push forward. "I'm sure you're familiar with the string of disappearances plaguing the area of West Rutland?"

She narrows her eyes, pushing her glasses up the bridge of her nose. "Yes, although I'm not sure why that particular story has brought you here."

I press my lips together. "Yes, well, one has to cover all their bases, yes? Have you had any unknown or unnamed patients check in in the past couple of weeks?"

She gives me a look that screams *Are you kidding?* "We always get a few unnamed, homeless drug addicts overdosing here and there."

I flick my eyebrows up. "Are there a lot of drug problems here?"

The woman sighs, sitting further back into her chair since she clearly won't need her computer. "More than a lot, although I wouldn't say it reaches West Rutland quite as much. They're a whole other breed of crazy."

Bristling, and unsure why I'm so offended, I spread my palms across the ledge of her window. "I see. Well, back to these men that came in. Any teens? Around eighteen?"

Sighing again, and looking like I'm taking about twenty years off her life by my mere presence, she scoots once more towards her computer and types away. Exhaling through my nose, I fold my arms across my chest to wait, leaning my hip against the wall. I turn to survey the dark and empty waiting room.

Movement catches my eye, coming around the corner from the main hallway that extends off this one. They're a few meters away, but the footsteps resonate over the otherwise empty space, bouncing off the walls and echoing inside my chest. Thankful that I remembered my glasses, I push them further up my nose, squinting at the familiar form.

I'm proven right when she glances slightly to the side, revealing her side profile. She slows just enough to wipe a tear from her eyes with her sleeve, pinch between her eyebrows as if to get rid of a horrible headache, before shaking her body off.

She walks out the door on the opposite end, where another parking lot waits, not noticing me at all.

"Miss?"

I jump, turning away from where I'd been transfixed on Luna's back, wondering why she's here. Who she'd come to see.

"No teens in the past month," she informs me, picking her pencil to return to her crossword. "I'd say sorry, but I suppose that's a good thing."

I glance back toward where Luna has now long disappeared, the door sealed shut behind her. "Yes, I suppose so." Pushing away the distraction, I turn back to the woman, who seems to have gone back to ignoring me. "Thanks for your help."

"I didn't help. Now unless you're dying, or seeing someone else who's dying, get out of the hospital, will you?"

WHEN I RETURN TO the apartment, for the first time, there's more than just Reyna. I pause at the front door, hearing the hush of voices drift toward me through the crack I've opened.

"Stop it," Reyna is saying, in a voice that attempts to calm but comes out as a panicked wheeze. "You have nothing to worry about if you stay away from there."

"But what if-"

Not wanting to hear anymore, I announce myself by loudly pushing through the door and shutting it behind me. I peer into the kitchen, where Reyna and a younger boy sit, munching food from Chinese takeout containers. My first thought, actually, is not *who is this?* but rather *where did they get that Chinese food?*

"Hey," I say, because Reyna and I's relationship has developed to consistent greetings and brief conversations whenever we're in the same room.

"Oh, hey!" Reyna says through a mouth of fried rice, wiping the corner of her mouth with her knuckles. "I didn't think you'd be home, you're not usually around during lunchtime."

"Is that a subtle dig that I never cook for myself?"

"Yes."

Breathing out a small laugh, I toss my purse though my open doorway before striding toward the fridge. "You're about to eat your words, I have a ham and cheese sandwich just waiting to be made." I nod to the kid who continues to eat his food, hunched over the table. "Who's this?"

"Oh, right, this is Anthony. Little brother."

I squint, beginning to see the resemblance, although his hair is blond in contrast to her deep black. "Ah. Nice to meet you."

He only grunts, and it sounds eerily similar to the sound Reyna makes when she's working and doesn't have the energy to actually say hello. Reyna jabs his arm with the end of her chopstick, making him sputter.

"Sorry," he says through a mouthful of food, finally glancing up at me. "Hello. Take out has that effect on me."

I pause as I stare at him, rewinding to a few days ago before exclaiming, "Hey, no wait, I know you! You hit me in the head with a soccer ball!" He'd been the asshole treating those girls like his personal servants, with a too confident smirk and a weak instep kick.

Reyna's jaw drops open with a snicker, turning to her brother to smack him on the shoulder. "Anthony!"

Anthony squints, before his lips curve into that same mischievous smile I'd seen at the field. "That was you?"

"Yeah, man, you didn't hit me hard enough to warp my memory."

He just ducks his head again, returning to his food. "Sorry," he says again, not sounding all that sorry.

"No worries," I say, amused, glancing back at Reyna. "Big age gap."

She nods. "I've seen bigger gaps than six years, but yeah." She pokes his cheek. "He was an accident."

"Stop calling me that!"

Reyna laughs. "I'm not wrong!"

"So, you're still in high school?" I cut in, probably saving Reyna from a stupid sibling fight.

Swallowing, he mumbles, "Gonna be a senior." He doesn't sound all that excited about it.

Something dings in my head, but I push it away, instead merely saying, "Cool. Well, I'll leave you guys to your lunch." Taking my plate and a bag of chips, I disappear into my room, moving to my desk to do what I'd actually come home to do.

My fingers hover over the keyboard. Up until now, I've refrained from searching up anything related to Luna Morgan online. I didn't find her on social media, I didn't look her up, nothing. I can't decide whether I didn't out of respect for the one friend I've managed to make, or because I was scared I would find something,

It sort of feels like the latter, because I can't get my hands to move.

At last, I manage to type in her name, letter by letter, with *West Rutland* after it. My hands clench as the page loads, spouting out information. And it's-

Not much, actually. I scroll through the page, and there's no articles that reference her name at all besides information about the sculpture center. No, wait, there's one, but it's an ad about an art show she had at a gallery a few miles north. I spend a little too long scrolling through pictures of paintings, admiring the craftsmanship, the detail, the beauty.

I tear myself from the stupor, clicking out of the frame and getting back on track. The only social media she has is Facebook, but it's about as bare as it can get. Only a profile picture from probably four years ago, of her leaning through the ticket booth window with a smile. Her hair only sweeps down to her shoulders, and her smile is wider, less heavy.

I close down the picture just as fast, not sure where this aching feeling is coming from.

Is it a small town thing, the lack of social media? I know West Rutland is filled to the brim with hunters and people constantly wearing camouflage and cargo pants, but they all have smartphones, too. Maybe they just don't need it, because everyone they know is in a two mile radius.

Scrolling through more and more Google pages, the muscles in my shoulders begin to untense, and I settle back into my chair when the links start to branch off to irrelevant topics.

Nothing. There's nothing at all here about who might be in that hospital. It must not be a relative, because she clearly doesn't have any siblings at all, or any extended family who lives here. I remember Lucia commenting that she has two siblings, but they both live in the south. Maybe it's just a friend. Maybe the *"he"* Ruth referenced at the bar.

I try not to feel too relieved.

I'M STEADILY RUNNING OUT of places to go without seeming like a creepy stalker. Going back to the high school so quickly seems like a bad idea, so I settle for just walking around. I weave through the limited streets, peering at lit windows and perking my ears up whenever I pass a pair on the sidewalk. The sun brushes over the tops of the trees, signaling the end of the work day, but the sidewalks remain deserted. Too early to go to a bar or a restaurant for dinner, and too late to visit any businesses, I head toward the one place I know people always gather.

But the Ledge, too, is lonely when I reach it, slowing to a stop under the canopy of leaves. I sigh, leaning against a tree with my fist pressed into my hip, eyes fluttering closed. Breathing in the silence, I try to think of a plan, any sort of plan, but everything entering my mind involves Luna.

The crunching of dead leaves under feet interrupts the quiet, and I jerk up, leaning around the large maple tree just in time to see a figure burst out into the clearing. The boy's breathing heaves from his chest. He's clearly run here, and he slows to a jog, stopping completely just a few feet from the edge of the quarry. I almost step out of the trees to ask if he's okay, but he walks toward the railing, leaning over it with his fingers braced against the rust, like he wants to tear the metal right out of the ground.

And then he screams. It's not a scream of fright, or even frustration. No, he tips his head back and bellows toward the sky with what could only be years of bottled up, overflowing rage. I flinch back at the sound, hands flying to my mouth. The sheer pain behind his shout makes my eyes burn, and sends a flock of birds hiding in the leaves skyward. I don't dare risk moving, not wanting to let him know of my presence, to interrupt whatever this moment is. I can only watch, completely still, as his yells fade to nothing and he collapses onto the stone beneath him, exhausted.

The boy's face falls into the heels of his palm, sun glistening off his wet cheeks as he bends his neck to wipe the skin along the fabric on his shoulder. I squint, adjusting my glasses, and he lifts his head again, revealing his vulnerable, tear streaked face to me.

I know him, I realize, and the small town of it all will never stop freaking me out, how I see the same people *everywhere*. Even without the uniform, he stands out as the only other worker from Suzie's I've met, the graduated boy smoking a cigarette by the window. I deflate a little bit, because he hadn't been much help beyond pointing me to the Ledge. He didn't know the victims. And that meant I was stuck here invading a moment for this boy who had nothing to do with me.

I need to find the friends of the victims, the family, people who *knew* the inner parts of their lives. I need to differentiate the tragedy of these murders from the tragedy of everyday life.

Scanning the terrain beneath my feet, I gingerly wiggle my toes, deciphering whether I can move without freaking the boy out further. But even the smallest movement feels like it shakes the entire forest, and I freeze again. Only then do I realize that I hadn't been the one causing the noise. More footsteps echo off to my right, down the same path the boy had run down moments prior. They're calmer, more controlled, but heavy, and a second boy stops as soon as he steps into the sun.

I nearly lose my footing because I recognize him, too. I saw him only two days ago with Reyna in our kitchen. All of Anthony's conviction from that day at the soccer field has been drained from him, and he wavers almost as morosely as the boy on the ground.

He speaks. "You've gotta stop coming out here, man."

Too wrapped up in his emotion, the boy on the ground hadn't noticed the entrance of his... friend? Acquaintance? They must know each other, if the stiffening of his muscles is any indication. He frantically wipes his face, blinking rapidly as he stands. "Pretty sure a lot of people come out to the quarry at the uneventful time of five thirty to be alone. You shouldn't be here, either. Probably even more than me."

I press my back hard against the tree behind me, bark biting through my thin shirt and into my shoulder blades. They're too engrossed in each other, though, and I squint through the foliage as the new boy approaches. "Why not? I haven't done anything."

I don't like the pointed, malicious way those words come out, or the glint in his eye.

"Sure you haven't, Anthony," the other boy says flatly. "I don't think any of us can keep track of who did what anymore."

Anthony tilts his head, licking his front teeth. "Oh, I don't know about that. I know exactly what *you* did."

The Suzie's worker takes a step forward, almost like he might lunge at Anthony, but stops himself. "How?" he spits. "Pretty sure I'm the only one left who could tell the tale, and I haven't told you jack shit."

Anthony just laughs darkly. "I don't need your words. It's written all over you."

The only expression I see on the other's face is pure fury. "I could say the same about you. You know, I wasn't with you when it happened, but it wasn't all that hard to put it together."

Anthony stiffens, tucking his fingers into the pocket of his shorts. "Don't come out here again. Between Carlos and the others, I'm just waiting for them to knock my door down, and I don't want the assholes around here asking questions."

"No? Then keep your mouth shut."

"I'll keep my mouth shut," Anthony hisses, taking a step forward, "if you do the same."

They just stare at each other for a few moments, some sort of secret communication passing between the two, until the boy from Suzie's gives a curt nod, weighed down with something like shame.

And then, almost too low for me to hear, Anthony murmurs, "Tell Xavier I said hi."

My muscles tighten, even as shock courses through my veins at the name of one of the victims, and I ready myself for when the fists start flying, unsure what I would even do. But an unreadable expression just filters across the boy's face, and then Anthony disappears into the trees.

The other boy stares after him, finally saying, "You'll get what's coming for you," to his disappearing silhouette, before turning back to the quarry and staring into the water for a long, long while.

Chapter Ten

I AVOID LUNA FOR a few days, mostly because I feel guilty about the flicker of doubt I felt after seeing her at the hospital, and also because I spend some time actually trying to do my job. Sitting at home, I play that conversation in my head over and over again, scribbling down as much as I can remember, attempting to decipher their cryptic words.

Tell Xavier I said hi.

Keep your mouth shut.

The boy from Suzie's had said very clearly that he barely knew any of the victims, and he didn't seem all that affected by their loss. So why, then, had I caught him screaming at the world and discussing Xavier?

And why had I realized that the unreadable expression on his face when Anthony said that was guilt?

Worse, I haven't been able to look Reyna in the eye. Anthony hasn't come back to the apartment, but how do you tell your roommate that her brother has some sort of dark secret, certainly involving Xavier at the very least?

By avoiding Luna, I also avoid going to Suzie's, even though I'm itching to run into the boy again. But I know she goes there, and I don't have the energy quite yet. But after nearly five days, I'm running out of food, and I have the choice of either going to the grocery store or going to the local diner where I might actually be able to do my job. Elise would kill me if I didn't choose the second.

The walk to Suzie's is a drag, the thought of talking to people even more unappealing than usual. I can't even pinpoint where the desolate feeling is coming from, just that I want to curl up in bed and have nothing to do with this case.

Nevertheless, the smell of maple syrup calls to me, and I slide through the door. Thankful that I come in the middle of the afternoon on a Thursday, and that the only person visible is Jo, I walk a little faster towards the counter.

Jo looks up at the sound of footsteps, blonde hair tied back in a french braid. Her mouth spreads into a smile at the sight of me. "There she is! Have a seat, it's been a little bit, hasn't it?"

Five days, really, but I suppose longer for her since she wasn't working when I came on Saturday morning. "I guess I couldn't stay away."

"That's good to hear. For a minute there, I thought we scared you off."

I think back to what she said, about how new people are always leaving. The guilt spreads anew, and I sort of wish I'd just gone grocery shopping.

"Where have you been?" she asks, handing me a menu, and there's no suspicion in her tone. It makes me feel worse.

"Working," I lie, opening the menu and actually reading it. I should probably get a salad or something, something healthy. It might make me feel better. "It's a nice job, but sometimes the schedules can get a little bit wacky."

"Ah," Jo nods in understanding. "Work at night, sleep during the day, that kind of thing?"

I go along with it. "Yeah. That kind of thing."

"Well," she says slowly, knocking her knuckles against the marble counter, as though building up to saying something. I lean forward a little bit, curious, because I think this is the first time I've seen Jo hesitate. Or look at all unsteady.

I cock my head in question, but don't say anything.

Jo lifts her eyes to mine, and it's not uneasiness I find there, but something more mischievous. A knowing smirk. "Luna's been in here every day, though."

Though something catches in my throat, I speak as casually as I can. "Oh, yeah?"

It's clearly not very convincing, because Jo only smiles wider. "Yeah. She was asking about you, you know. Wanting to know if you came in."

I run a finger down the side of the menu, bounded in leather. "I don't have her number," I admit, thankful that I can say something honest. "And I didn't remember to tell her about my weird schedule when I last saw her."

"Mmhmmm," Jo hums, even though I'm telling the truth. "Well, she was in here earlier, mentioned that she had the afternoon off."

Trying not to look too interested, I curse myself. Five days spent avoiding her, and it all washes away. "Yeah?" I pause before asking the question, telling myself I should just go home. But Elise told me I was right, that I should keep these relationships. And I will. "And… and where does she usually go, on her days off?"

Biting her lip to hide her smile, Jo says, "You'll probably find her painting in her yard. There's a picnic table outside; she likes to paint in nature, like her mom."

"Even though she paints people?"

"Nature can inspire anything, Alex."

"I suppose so," I muse, unable to say or do anything else because I don't even know where she lives. I know she needs to pass my apartment to get home, but beyond that…

As if reading my mind, Jo scribbles something on the notepad she uses to take orders, then rips it off and slides it across the table to me. "You don't think she'll mind, do you?"

My eyes scan the words, reading a street name that I don't recognize, but it can't possibly be far. "No, probably not. Thanks."

"The picnic table's around the side of the house," she adds. "Just so you know."

I nod, avoiding the glint in her eye, and duck my head back down towards my menu.

I PACE BACK AND forth at the edge of her street for longer than I care to admit.

The street is parallel to the main road, a few blocks down from where my street intersects with it. The neighborhood became more spread out the further I walked from Suzie's, trees dotting nearly every yard, swings creaking on the porches of empty houses. By the time I arrive, I've already debated turning around no less than a dozen times, just going home, but the address Jo wrote feels like a weight in my pocket, along with the knowledge that she asked about me. I already feel guilty enough, I'm pretty sure ignoring her further isn't going to help my cause.

Steeling myself, I march the remaining blocks to her house. It's a small, one story cube, like most around here, painted in a deep, faded blue. A hooded porch hugs the front side of the house, with an empty swinging chair creaking in the wind. I glance back and forth between the two sides of the houses, trying to figure out where the picnic table is, since the whole house is shrouded by trees. Eventually, I decide on the left, because there's more room there.

As I tiptoe through the grass, I'm sort of afraid I might scare her. Does this make me a stalker, even though a mutual friend literally gave me the address and told me to go? Because it feels a little stalkerish.

Luna comes into sight through a cluster of trees. She sits hunched over, expert hands moving in slow, deliberate strokes. She's using paints now, I can tell from the colors dotting her skin, her face, from where she might have brushed a strand of hair away. Late afternoon light pierces down through the canopy, throwing dots of light over her nose, like reverse freckles-

I shake myself, realizing I'm staring. We're entering stalker-area, and that's something I'm trying to avoid. I make myself known before I can chicken out and run away. Clearing my throat, I say, as lame as possible, "A little birdie told me you might be here."

She's surprisingly unperturbed by the sound of my voice. Is that a thing, when you know everyone in your town? They just turn up out of nowhere all the time? It seems exhausting.

She lifts her head, the braid that her hair is tucked into falling over her shoulder, and her mouth falls only slightly open in shock before it's replaced by a smile. "Alex?"

I tuck my hands into my pockets and round the last tree between me and the picnic table. "Only a few days, and you're already hesitating on my name again?"

Luna bites down on a laugh, swinging her legs up onto the bench so she can extend them across the wood. "Was it Jo who sent you here? I feel like it was Jo, she's the meddling type."

I hold up a finger, unsure of whether I should sit down. I pick the safe route, leaning against the nearest tree. "She did not *send* me here. She gave me some information, and I utilized it." I slip the piece of paper Jo gave me from my pocket, waving it in front of Luna's nose. "The information just happened to be your address."

She swats the paper away, and I fold it back up with a laugh, if just to give myself something to do with my hands. She seems to be doing the same thing, twirling a paintbrush around her fingers. "You've been busy?"

I nod to her artwork. "My job isn't as glamorous as yours, and my boss is an asshole who likes to give me nights."

Luna tugs her knees to her chest, looking sympathetic. "You look tired, you probably haven't slept well."

Technically true, although for different reasons. Trying not to feel too guilty at the look of pity on her face, I motion to myself. "Is it that obvious?"

"Very," she confirms, ruthless. "Do you have a couple days off?"

Making up a schedule in my head, I nod. "Till Monday."

She shuffles back and forth in the same way a nervous high schooler might at the school dance, when they're just about to invite the pretty girl out to the dance floor. In spite of myself, I blush at the comparison.

She looks down once more, tapping the paintbrush she hasn't set down against her knee. "My mom was asking about you, too. Wanted to know if you wanted more *sculpture* lessons." She used her finger to make air quotation marks around the last two words, which makes me laugh.

"Don't look so bitter about it," I tease.

"I could give you painting lessons instead. It's much more fun."

I shake my head, tempting as it might be. "My grandma tried to teach me to paint, and it never ended well for anyone involved. I never had the patience."

"And you have the patience to painstakingly shape *marble?*"

"It's easier to take away than add, you know?" I admit. "Besides, I wouldn't call watching your mom sculpt, and playing with the chisels, *lessons*."

"Don't say that in front of my mom," Luna warns. "She's very excited about lesson number two."

I snort. "Then, tell her I'm in."

Luna lets out a squeak of protest. "She sucked you in. If you decide you like my mom better than me, I'm officially giving up on people."

I think to myself, *Sometimes, it seems like you have.* I don't say that, though, because then she might *actually* send me away.

Instead, I stalk closer to the picnic table, swinging one leg over the bench to sit down. I peer at the canvas Luna had been working on when I interrupted, three quarters of the way finished and glistening with fresh paint. It looks like a painting pulled from an old Greek vase, of two women intertwined in the grass, faces curved into each other. "Jeez, this is incredible. Like, art-museum-level incredible."

Heat rises in Luna's cheeks, and she ducks her head, swirling a paint brush through a glass of muddy water. "It's a work in progress."

I squint. "Well, I'd buy it as is."

"That's relieving, because I've spent the past hour battling with the thing, and I'm pretty sure the painting's winning."

I move closer, shifting so both legs are completely under the table, and I can carefully lean over the painting. "How so?"

Using the back of her paintbrush, she taps lightly against the cheek of one of the women, where a path of silver drips down the page. "I find tears... especially difficult."

I lift my eyes to see her still scrutinizing the canvas, thumb softly dabbing at the canvas to fix a smudge. I shift my gaze to the glimmering tracks traveling down the woman's cheeks, clear and shining with highlight. "Well, I wouldn't be able to tell. Just looking at the emotion on her face makes me sad."

"That's the goal," Luna sighs but sits back, looking slightly more content. I can tell in the way she pushes her palette away, wiping her hands on a paint splattered rag.

I pause, eyes caught on a streak of dark paint stretching down her cheek, shining like a cut. Clearing my throat and tearing my eyes away, I say, "What made you draw this?"

"The women?" she asks.

"No," I say. "Something so... sad." I think perhaps they're mourning in the painting; whether someone outside of the picture or themselves, I can't tell.

Lune rubs a hand across her face, catching on that thick streak of gray. Noticing, she picks at it with her nails, sending flakes drifting back down to the grass. "Hell if I know, I just... paint what comes to me. This is what came today." She pauses, a muscle feathering in her jaw, before continuing. "I haven't been feeling great."

"Yeah, well, that makes two of us."

She tilts her head, the hollow of her neck absorbed in the shadow of her chin. "Yeah?"

I shift. "Yeah. But, I mean, they say you need to go backward."

"Backward?"

"You know, the metaphor? Like, pulling back an arrow to shoot you forward?"

She snorts, leaning forward. "That's cheesy."

A ray of sun flashes across her face, illuminating the back of her hair with a golden halo. Hairs stand up on my forearm, even in the warmth of summer, and I tuck my arms closer to my chest. "I prefer the word *encouraging*."

All at once, the humor ebbs away, leaving her form with only tired muscles and a tired soul. She mumbles, "I'm starting to feel like maybe the rest of my life is just going to be backward. Further and further down the rabbit hole, until there's nowhere else to go."

"Rabbit holes aren't always bad, you know. Ever read Alice in Wonderland?"

Luna fires back, "Has *anyone* actually *read* Alice in Wonderland? Because I certainly didn't, and I'm fairly sure no one I've ever met has read it either."

I sit back, allowing my arms to fall from the table, unsure if the question is rhetorical. Even so, I admit, "I'm not sure that I have."

She snaps her fingers. "*Exactly*. I'm half convinced that it's a whole conspiracy, that some wizard thought up this idea and willed it into existence."

I play along, not entirely sure how we got here. "If this so-called *magician* willed it into existence, wouldn't he have just brought... the book itself? Which is sold in stores everywhere, even though, as you so kindly pointed out, no one ever buys it anyway?"

"Magicians tend to be over-exuberant. I'm sure the author- I mean, can we even consider him an author if he didn't *actually* write it? Anyway, I think the guy not only willed the book into *physical* existence, but also *mental* existence. Everyone just *knows* it."

"I think your mother just read it to you when you were, like, three, it stuck, and now you're seriously overthinking it."

"One might even say I'm going down a rabbit hole."

"Again."

Luna sighs, running a finger down her paper. "Again." *Again and again and again and again-*

"I wish I could will things into existence," I say softly, thinking of solutions and parents and relationships and family, of all the things I left behind that I never really had. Of all the things I'm searching for now that I can't seem to pluck up the courage to find. "But I'd choose something more valuable than a children's book."

Luna returns her gaze to her painting, left abandoned at her fingertips. Even so, her eyes are glazed over, and I can tell she's not really looking at it, or referring to her art when she mumbles, "Me too."

There it is, the voice in my head whispers, the journalist voice, the one that always needs answers when maybe the rest of myself might not want them. *An opening.*

"Luna," I say delicately into the silence. She remains in her soft trance, head bowed and shoulders slumped, but she jerks ever so slightly, so I can tell she's listening. "Can I ask you something?"

Luna's voice is tight and gravelly when she answers. "Depends on what it is, although I guess that means you'll ask it no matter what."

Not exactly a reassuring response, but I shove ahead anyway. "You know when we went out the other night?"

"You mean my most recent hangover? Yeah, Alex, it's seared into my brain."

The way she laughs as she speaks makes me want to backtrack, to make the choice to laugh with her instead of saying something that might make her stop. *Solutions and answers first, friends later*, the voice reminds me. The voice that never shuts up, the one thing I sort of wish could have stayed behind in my old, empty apartment. "Who was that woman talking about?"

Luna at last lifts her eyes to me, brows creased. "Who?"

I speak hesitantly, even though I remember exactly who she was. "I think her name was... Ruth?"

The confusion dissipates, replaced by an expression that's one part harsh, but mostly exhausted. Her fingers curl against the wood of the picnic table, nails scraping at the edge of her painting. "It was nothing."

Feeling worse and worse, I hedge, "Well, not nothing, considering you have the same expression right now as you did when she asked."

The same expression the boy by the quarry had, now that I think of it.

Luna speaks through gritted teeth, avoiding my gaze. "Well, if you knew this was how I would react, then why would you ask?"

"I just thought," I start, but I trail off, because I don't really know what I thought. "I don't know, it could have been about *her*, not her question."

"It was both."

Every muscle in my body stiffens, as if prepping to make a fast escape. "Well, I, um…" I stutter, cowering at the way Luna's hands tremble.

Before I can get another word out, she lets out a broken, "*I don't want to talk about this.*" It's not mean, or harsh, or loud, but rather pleading.

I nod quickly, swallowing hard. "Yeah, of course." The tightness ebbs from Luna's body, but her hands are still shaking. I tear my eyes from them, choosing instead to look over her shoulder. "I'm sorry. Sometimes it can help to talk about tragedy, but sometimes it makes it worse."

She lets out a quivering sigh. "I don't know if it would help. I just know that right now, the pain *way* outweighs any good it would do."

I nod knowingly, and before I can stop myself, I reach out, laying a soft hand over hers. The vibrations of her fingers slow to a stop, and I brush my thumb over her calloused palm. She looks up, and I hold her gaze. "I get it. And if you ever do, you know, want to talk, you should know that I'm not going anywhere."

She swallows roughly, wet eyes shining. "Thank you." A moment of silence passes, and she pulls her hand back, drumming against the picnic table as she tries for a smile. "Except you're gonna go somewhere right now, because I have to finish this painting before nightfall. And in order to finish it, I need to stare at this painting instead of you, so…"

Her voice wavers, and I realize she just needs to be alone right now, probably to finally let those tears fall. I don't acknowledge it, though, as I stand. I take out the note with Luna's address on it, snagging one of Luna's pencils and scribbling on the back. I slip it under a paintbrush, so it won't be blown away by the wind. "I'm gonna need you to send me a picture when you're done. I'm not convinced it can get any better than you've already made it."

This time when she smiles, it feels a little more real. "Deal."

I back away with a small wave before disappearing around the house, leaving Luna to paint whatever's inside of her instead of feeling it.

Chapter Eleven

WHEN MY RINGTONE WAKES me up in the morning, the sun has barely begun to rise, most of my room is still cloaked in shadows and darkness. Panicking at who might be calling me this early, I feel around my nightstand until I find my phone, dropping it twice before managing to bring it to my ear. "What?"

"Alex?"

I groan at the sound of Elise's perfectly fine and normal voice, even as the bubble of tension in my gut dissipates. "Why are you calling me at six a.m.?" I croak out.

"I wanted to make sure you were still alive."

I shove my face into my pillow, grunting even louder as I wipe the bleariness from the corners of my eyes. "And it couldn't have waited, say, three more hours? Maybe four if you were feeling generous?"

"You're alone in a foreign town investigating a combination of murders and disappearances," Elise says, a tinge of sarcasm coating her tone. "And I haven't heard from you in nearly a week. Sue me if I'm worried."

I settle deeper into my mattress, not willing to get out of bed right now. "Well, I'm not being held hostage by anyone except you, and you always have an ulterior motive, regardless of how much you might care about me. So what do you want?"

The line cracks with silence for a few seconds before Elise plucks up the courage to speak. "Your girlfriend's in the other room."

This makes me sit bolt upright in bed, my other arm getting tangled in the covers. "*Excuse me?*"

"Don't be mad," Elise begs quickly, words tumbling from her mouth before I have a chance to get my own in order.

Anger filters through my veins, images flashing through my brain of the last couple of times I'd seen Rachel; none good experiences. "I might ask what she's doing there at six in the morning, but I'd rather ask what she's doing there at *all*."

Elise sighs, sounding even more exhausted than me. "She just showed up, okay? She was, like, sobbing on my front porch, I think she was out all night, I couldn't just turn her away. She crashed on the couch."

I flop back onto my bed. "What did she say?"

"She wanted me to convince you to talk to her," she says. "I told her, 'fat chance.'"

"That's why you're the one I like."

She manages a laugh. "Too bad I'm taken. I think she was just really drunk, but, like... what do I do?"

"Kick her out once she has the strength and sobriety to stand on her own," I spit, but Elise knows the venom isn't directed at her. "You're not her babysitter, you don't owe her shit. And neither do I."

"I love the self-confidence," Elise says, and I can hear the hesitance in her voice. "Go you. But-"

"You know when you add a but after the sentence, it just completely erases everything else you said, right?"

"You need to talk to her. She needs some sort of closure."

"She doesn't deserve closure. According to her, the relationship was over before we even broke up!"

"But *you* deserve closure," Elise says delicately. "Running off to Vermont isn't going to give you what you need. Even finding your-" She cuts herself off, amending, "Even finding another sort of family won't heal you."

I pull at a loose thread on my blanket, watching the tiny stitches unravel one by one before I force myself to wrench the string free. "It works in the movies. They always go to Vermont."

Elise laughs, and I listen as the sound tinkles away into a sigh. "And you'll remember that in every movie, they eventually have to face the toxic ex in one form or another."

Except in the movies, the villainous ex is always one dimensional. They're just… bad. Bad people who never deserved the cool main character. The thing is, Rachel was never bad, never anything but good to me. Maybe there were signs I missed, red flags, but they say hindsight is 20/20, and I can't remember *anything* before our last couple of months.

I loved her, and she loved me. And then my dad died, and we both stopped acting like we loved each other. It all happened so fast, I still barely know how it all went down.

As Elise would say, probably because I never answer the damn phone.

I sigh, running a hand through my hair, grunting at the number of knots twisting around my fingers.

There's rustling in the back of the phone call, and the muffled sound of Rachel's voice makes its way to my ears. It doesn't matter how distorted and far away it is, I'd recognize her anywhere. The sounds haunt me, running over my skin like ice, and I have to pull the phone from my ear just to steady myself. Whether it's anger, regret, or pain I'm feeling, I can't be sure.

"You're right," I finally say, wanting to physically backpedal away from the phone despite the fact that we're not even in the same room. "And I will. But not right now, okay? Just… get rid of her."

"I can do that," Elise says, sounding like there's nothing she'd rather be doing, before giving me the greatest gift and hanging up.

I WONDER IF ANYONE else ever goes to the sculpture center more than once a year. I should probably find out before I start getting weird looks. Three times isn't outrageous, right?

I spent the better part of my morning pacing my bedroom, digging trenches into the carpet where my feet traveled, waiting for a text from Elise. One finally came an hour later, a small note reading, *She's gone, I dropped her at home on the way to work. She's a wreck.*

Not really feeling a lot of sympathy, I write back, *Sorry about her. Not sorry that she's a wreck. I was a wreck, too.*

She replies, *Don't I know it.*

She does. After I found out, I spent a week at Elise's place, and I cried the whole time.

Have a good day at work, I text back, before silencing my phone, not really wanting to talk about it anymore. In fact, there's only one person that I want to talk to right now. Considering I have exactly two and a half friends right now, it's not hard to narrow my options down. The half friend is Reyna, who I still haven't talked to since I added at least seventeen question marks next to her brother's name in my notebook. And between the other two, only one of them I know for a *fact* won't mention my ex-girlfriend.

So after wandering aimlessly around town, not hungry enough to go to Suzie's but too rattled to go home, I take the road towards the sculpture center and Luna. Given it's before lunchtime, the place isn't very busy, and Lucia ambushes me before I can even look for Luna.

"Alex!" she exclaims, coming out from the ticket booth. "Can I make the assumption that you're here for Luna, not the sculptures?"

Laughing, I say, "Why can't it be both?"

"Well, unfortunately, Luna doesn't work until this afternoon," she says apologetically. "So, I suppose you're stuck with me and the sculptures."

Even as disappointment clouds my stomach, I can't let it infiltrate my face. "That's not a bad deal, I don't think. Got any more tricks you can show me?"

"Are you hooked?" she asks excitedly. "It's an easy artform to get hooked on, I feel like I've hooked you."

The Morgan family as a whole seems to be pretty good at hooking me.

"Totally," I say seriously, motioning for her to lead the way to the studio.

Lucia's face splits into a wide grin, the corners of her mouth and forehead wrinkling at the action. As I've gotten older, and watched others get older, I've started to wish that people would stop being so terrified of wrinkles, particularly the ones like I'm looking at now. They're evidence that you've lived, that you've felt. That you've smiled. And sure, they hold evidence of frowns, and anger, but that's part of feeling, too. And from the lines marking Lucia's beautiful face, the one she passed on to her daughter, I can tell Lucia's felt a whole lot in her lifetime.

LUCIA LETS ME GO as soon as the clock strikes one. She claims she needs time to focus on a different project, but there's a knowing look in her eye that leads me to believe one o'clock is when Luna's shift starts.

I'm right. When I surface through the trees, I catch sight of her immediately, wearing loose jeans and an even baggier T-shirt.

A bandana threads through her hair, keeping her face clear, thin strands tucked behind her ears.

I drift toward her unconsciously, instinctually, like my body won't stop until I reach her. She stands on her tiptoes, peering directly into the face of a statue, using a rag to wipe away streaks of dirt. The statue itself is beautiful, crying out to me from even several yards away, stiff fingers reaching out toward something it cannot find. Water drips down from the washcloth, slow and deliberate, digging tracks into the grime accumulated across the woman's cheeks. Eyes big and hollow, made entirely of stone and yet somehow alive, tears fall steadily where Luna cleans, making an already sad statue all the more heartbreaking.

"One of your mother's?" I finally convince myself to ask, even though I know it's not, because Lucia doesn't sculpt people. I just can't think of anything else to say.

Wrenching her hand back and fumbling the rag in the process, Luna's heels drop harshly to the ground. She turns to face me, hair tumbling and swinging against her neck as she does so.

"You should stop being surprised to see me," I say before she can even open her mouth. I plunge my hands into my pockets. "I'm shockingly persistent."

Luna breathes out a small, "Clearly."

I shrug. "It's a gift."

"That's not the word I would use."

Flicking my brows up, I take a few more steps toward her, though several yards still remain between us. "Oh, yeah? And what word *would* you use? And don't say 'annoying,' because that's just not original at all."

She cracks a smile, though she still rolls her eyes. "I can't even think of a word. Indescribable, actually."

"Thanks. I talked to your mother this morning."

Luna's face morphs back into neutrality, not giving anything away. "Oh, yeah?"

"Yeah," I confirm. "We had another sculpting lesson."

"You actually went through with that?" Luna asks in disbelief.

Shrugging, I say, "Why not? I don't know if you've noticed, but I'm trying to make friends around here."

"If I end up having to compete with my mom for your attention, I'll never forgive you."

"I'm sure you'd win, anyway. You're pretty persistent, too."

Smiling again, Luna twirls back to the statue, resuming the job I'd interrupted. "The answer is no, by the way."

"What?"

She taps the forehead of the statue. "You asked if this is one of my mom's pieces. It's not."

"Oh," I breathe. "It's lovely, though."

She steps back until she's level with me, tilting her head. "It is. It's one of my favorites."

I peer closer, and even though that makes perfect sense, I ask, "Why?"

Giving me a brief look before returning her eyes to the statue, she asks, "Do you know who it is?"

"How would I *possibly* know who it is?"

Laughing, Luna concedes, "If you're not a mythology geek, I suppose you wouldn't."

Turning to her in surprise, I ask, "You're a mythology geek?"

"Sort of. I like the stories. They're some of my favorite things to paint. It's just… an infinite amount of source material that can be interpreted in a million different ways."

I think back to the very few of Luna's paintings that I've seen, and I suppose they did all fit that Greek aesthetic. Or maybe I just think that now that she's said it; I'm really not one to critique art in *any* way. "And this is someone from a story? Who is it, Aphrodite?"

Exasperated, Luna rolls her head toward me. "Is that the only Greek woman you know?"

Jokingly, I think about it. "I know Artemis as well." I pause, before snorting out a laugh. "Appropriate, isn't it?"

"Are you making a joke about my name?"

"Would she technically be considered the goddess of *you*?"

"Shut up," Luna laughs. "Although, you're surprisingly close."

"So it *is* Artemis?"

"No," she says, humor gone and replaced with contemplation, a sort of dreamy look painting her features. "It's her lover, actually."

I whip my head to her, eyes flickering between her and the still statue. I reach out, dragging my fingers along hers, the ones that, perhaps, are trying to find Artemis. "Didn't Artemis take a vow of chastity or something? Wasn't that her whole thing?"

Almost accusatory, Luna says, "You know more than you let on."

My hand drops back to my side, fingers still cold from where the warmth had seeped into the statue. "I did go to school, Luna. Yeah, I've got a handle on the basics."

She holds her hands up. "Okay, okay, well what you *don't* know is that back in the day, they didn't really count sex as sex unless it was between a man and a woman, if you catch my drift."

Leaning back on my heels, my mouth falls open with an, "Ah. Are you trying to tell me that Artemis was a Sapphic icon?"

"Don't let the homophobic historians hear you say that, but yeah, that's exactly what I'm saying."

"So Artemis would hook up with her hunters?"

Luna grins. "Well, she would hook up with *one*. Although, it's believed that all the other hunters had sex with *each other*."

"Hmm," I muse. "Nice loophole. Gently homophobic, of course, but very convenient for them. So, who's the lucky lady that got to have the literal *goddess*?"

Luna returns her eyes to the statue, gazing up at the waiting woman, who suddenly seems even bigger and more ethereal than she had moments before. "Callisto."

I press my lips together. "The Greeks really had some *weird* names."

Pressing her elbow into my ribs, she says, "It's a lovely name. It literally means *most beautiful*. I'm not kidding."

"How do you even *know* that?"

"Some paintings require more research than others," she muses. "And I've done… ample research on this particular story."

I stride forward, walking a slow circle around the statue. The woman is draped in a thin cloth, and it will never stop baffling me how sculptors manage to make stone look so convincingly like fabric. This one must have been here for quite some time, because vines and flowers have sprouted up from beneath the pedestal, weaving around Callisto's legs, up through her fingers and into her hair. "Tell it to me. The story, as long as it has a happy ending."

"It doesn't," Luna says bluntly. "Myths and fairytales rarely do, when they're observed in their rawest forms."

I consider this, but looking into the eyes of the statue once more, heart panging at the longing on her face, I say, "Tell me anyway."

Luna drops to the ground at the base of another statue, tucking her feet beneath her and tugging at the hem of her shorts. "So Artemis is a huntress, of course, and she had a group of women who hunted with her. And after a time, she fell in love with Callisto. Only problem was-"

"Besides the fact that they were both supposed to stay virgins?"

Luna ignored me. "The only problem was that Zeus, Artemis's father, happened to have a bit of a crush on Callisto."

"It feels weird to call a god's feelings a *crush*," I say slowly. "It doesn't really fit."

Luna leans into the statue she sits against, which seems risky to me, but she looks unbothered. "Would you rather I say he was *taken with her*, or *entranced* by her, like they do in bullshit history books?"

I wrinkle my nose. "No, that's worse. So he had a crush on his daughter's girlfriend? That's messed up."

Can't they just come to me?

"Hey, you're Reyna's roommate, right?"

Ask and you shall receive, I guess. Small goddamn towns. Anthony, Reyna's brother, slows to a stop as he approaches me, pausing what looks like a long jog if his heavy breathing is any indication. Pulling headphones from his ears and letting them hang around his neck, he uses the collar of his tee to wipe the sweat pouring down his face.

I just nod, because even though I'd been looking for him for hours, I have no idea what I should say. How do I start this conversation? *Hey, a couple days ago I overheard this super weird conversation between you and some other guy where you both definitely threatened each other and also mocked one of the dead guys who disappeared?* Yeah, I figure that wouldn't go over super well.

He smirks, that annoying one that he'd hidden around his sister. "Don't tell me you're lost."

Even though I'm not, I'm far enough away from the apartment that I definitely could be. Sheepishly, I admit, "How pathetic would it be if I was?"

"Pretty pathetic, I'm not even gonna lie to you."

I glance around. "Are you taking pity on me yet?"

He sighs, wrapping up his headphones and shoving them in his pocket. "I gotta talk to Reyna, anyway. Come on, this way."

We walk in silence for a few minutes as I sort out my thoughts. Only when we're relatively close to our destination do I force myself to speak.

"Hey, can I ask you something?"

He grunts, looking quizzically at me. "Depends, is it about Reyna?"

Chapter Twelve

LUNA SENDS ME AWAY during her shift, claiming she actually has to do work and she can't just tell me myths all day, but she says to come back to the picnic table around eight, once she's off work and the sun has set. That gives me some time, and I set off on a mission. I have two boys I need to find, but I'll settle for whoever I stumble across first.

I check Suzie's first, for the boy whose name I still don't know, but I only find Jo. I manage to duck out before she sees me. The high school is nearby, so I peek at the empty fields before turning around. I try my apartment next, but Reyna's door is open and her room deserted. I circle around all the quarries I know about, and come up with nothing.

Exhausted from hurrying around in the heat, I collapse down on a curb off a side street, wiping sweat from my brow and wishing I'd brought a water bottle with me. Checking my watch, I see there's only an hour until Luna would be expecting me, and I'd successfully wasted an entire afternoon.

interpret that as well, so I just look away. "I guess it's a beautiful story, in theory. I mean, it could have been."

"That's the kicker," Luna murmurs. "*It could have been.* I suppose it's not beautiful at all, then, is it?"

"I don't know," I say, deliberately not looking back at the sculpture. "I'd like to think it still is."

"They don't get enough credit," Luna says, indignant. "Their story gets overshadowed, like most sapphic stories are. The world is too busy being obsessed with Achilles and Patroclus, or Apollo and Hyacinthus, to care."

"If it makes you feel better," I offer, "I have no idea who Patroclus is."

Lips twitching, she says, "It does, sort of, and it surprises me. They have books and songs written about them and everything, while Artemis gets erased to a woman who hates men rather than a lesbian, and Callisto gets forgotten."

I stay quiet for a moment, weighing my words carefully. I gaze at Luna, her shoulder slumped so heavily I fear her spine might snap. "Not forgotten. You remembered her. And I promise I'll remember her." I turn away, breathing out with the cool breeze whistling past my ears. "Besides. There's nothing wrong with a quiet love story. It's still beautiful."

"Maybe," Luna whispers. "Make it too quiet, though, and it's like it never existed at all."

Eyes widening, Luna agrees, "You have no idea. Zeus, being the screwed up dude he was, transformed himself into Artemis to seduce Callisto, and got her *pregnant*."

Staring at her, I drag a hand down my face. "Why are myths always so weird?"

"So, she gets pregnant, and naturally Artemis is like, *What? You had sex? You betrayed me as both a virgin goddess and your girlfriend?* Even though Callisto routinely had sex with her, but I digress."

"Did they break up?" I ask, even though it feels ridiculous to ask such a mundane question of a goddess.

"You could say that. Callisto got kicked out of the group, and Hera, who's Zeus's actual wife, got so angry that Zeus cheated on her *again* that she turned Callisto into a bear."

Running the sentence through my brain again, I decide to ask about, perhaps, the *least* messed up part. "Why a bear?"

Luna merely shrugs. "I don't know, it's the story of the constellation, the bear one. I don't know the name. Artemis didn't know Callisto was turned into a bear and ended up accidentally killing her on a hunt."

I jerk up in horror, nearly face planting into the dirt. "*What?*"

Luna smiles grimly. "Like I said, no happy endings. But after her death, she was cast into the stars, so I guess she's got that going for her."

Leaving the statue behind, I cross my legs in front of me before lowering myself beside Luna. I glance briefly up towards the statue she still leans against, but it's something abstract, made of random shapes, and I don't have the mental headspace to

"No, if it were about Reyna, I'd ask her." I hesitate. "It's... those guys who went missing. They were a year above you, right?"

Anthony stiffens, his steps faltering, but if I hadn't been paying so close attention I wouldn't have noticed. His features smooth over, and he nods. "Yeah. Terrible, I know."

"Did you know them?"

He sniffs, clearing his throat. "Sort of. They were good guys."

Bingo.

If my track record and human nature is anything to go by, people are far more likely to shit talk about people they barely know. Those girls the other day heard nasty rumors about the victims in passing, but Anthony? Only two categories of people can see past an asshole's antics: long time friends, or family. And I know for a fact that neither he nor Reyna are related to any of them.

I hum, as nonchalant as I can. "It's crazy. You must be freaked out."

He doesn't respond.

I try again. "Any idea what the hell is going on? If... it'll stop?"

"Yeah," he says roughly. "I've got a theory."

We arrive at the apartment, and I let us in, taking my time with the key. "And what would that be?"

He clicks his tongue as the door swings open. "Nothing you'd understand, new girl. And nothing I feel like explaining."

Reyna came home at some point, her door now firmly shut, and I smile tightly in farewell, heading toward my own room. But his voice stops me.

"No," he says softly, making me turn back.

"Hmm?"

"You asked if I think it'll stop," he says, voice strangely blank and dull. "No."

He disappears into Reyna's room.

BY THE TIME I get into my room, I'm scrambling to shower and get over to Luna's in time. She said something about night painting, which sounded ridiculous to me, because seeing seems pretty important to something like art.

But when I find her seated in the same spot I found her last time, she is, in fact, painting in the dark, illuminated only by a lamp perched in the center of the table.

"This feels wrong," I say upon greeting. "This whole atmosphere that you've created."

Luna peers up at me and grins as I sit down across from her. I lean over to see what she's working on, but it's barely developed yet. She must have only started this piece when she got home today. "Night painting is surprisingly common, and surprisingly beautiful. That's what the lamp's for."

"I thought you don't paint from life?" I ask.

"I don't," she says, "And I'm not. *But*, I am painting a piece set during the *night time*, and sometimes painting at night can help with the colors and general mood. Painting a night scene in the sunlight... never turns out how you want it to."

"Probably because it's our instinct to make things brighter than they actually are."

"Maybe," she hums, swirling a pool of green-black paint. Or, at least, that's what it looks like from here. "Our senses can be misleading."

"But this works?" I ask. "Do you hold up your paintbrush to the backdrop or something to color match?"

She giggles, lifting her brush, the bristles weighed down by a heavy glob of dark paint. "Sometimes. Just look, you can see the way it blends into the trees."

"The silhouettes just look black to me," I say, peering over my shoulder.

Luna plops her brush unceremoniously to her paper, smearing the paint around the background. "Black trees aren't interesting."

Before I can respond, a buzzing travels up my leg, piercing the night with a rhythmic pulse. Groaning, I pull the phone from my pocket, praying it's Elise, but no such luck.

"Jesus," I mutter, rubbing at an eye as I gaze at the familiar number, the one I've tried to scrub from my brain. My other finger hovers over the answer button, trembling, fighting the instinct to press it.

Luna quirks an eyebrow. "You're running out of time, you know. Six rings are all you get."

It's true, because after another moment, the sound is cut off, and the world falls silent once more. And yet I continue to stare at it, at the missed call icon that seems to have become engraved into my notification center.

Luna nods to my now dark phone, and I drop it roughly onto the table. "Who was that?"

I contemplate whether or not to be a dick about it, whether I might respond in the same way she does when I ask about… whatever it is she's hiding. But I'm too tired for secrets.

"Satan," I say honestly, the phone with the missed call icon burning a hole into my thigh.

Luna nods knowingly, eyes flashing with understanding. "So, ex-girlfriend, then."

I snort humorlessly, drumming my fingers against the table, trying to get rid of the relentless restless energy. "Yeah. I'm glad some terms are universal."

"It seems raw," she observes, fiddling with her paintbrush. "The breakup."

I shrug, looking away. "It's not, really. I just hate her."

"Because she broke up with you?"

My eyes snap to her. "I broke up with her."

Luna's mouth opens slightly. "I'm sorry, I guess it's usually the person that gets broken up with that's the most upset."

I wave a hand at my phone. "She *is* upset."

"Well, if you're both upset, why did you break up?"

"If she was in love with me, why did she cheat on me?" I fire back. "The universe is full of stupid questions."

I glance up in time to see Luna's eyes soften. "It is."

I gnaw on the inside of my cheek, tracing the pattern of the wood beneath my fingertips. "You know, I wouldn't have been quite so torn up about it if it weren't for the timing."

"Timing?"

"Yeah," I say bitterly. "You know, if it hadn't been over two years into the relationship and three days after my father's funeral."

Luna winces. Like, actually flinches away at my words, and the simple recognition of the messed up scenario makes me feel a tad better. "People are terrible," she whispers.

I look down. "I know, right?"

Gently, Luna sets down her paintbrush against her pallet, making sure the paint isn't dripping. "I'm sorry," she says.

I wave her off, straightening my back. "It was almost four months ago, I'm more than over her. I just wish I hadn't wasted so much time, you know?"

"Yeah," she says softly. "Relationships should come with a warning label." She holds her hands up, as though showing a banner. "*Warning: Will end catastrophically.*"

I chuckle, the sour taste in my throat dripping away.

"I'm sorry about your dad, too," she adds.

"He was sick," I sigh. "I knew it was coming for a long time."

"It's still terrible to lose someone," she says, throat bobbing, and I wonder who she's lost. "The circle of life holds a personal vendetta against all living creatures."

I blink rapidly. "I like to think it's necessary, otherwise I just get angry about it. Death, I mean."

She picks her paintbrush back up. "I get angry about it anyway." Shoulders hunched, she starts painting again, hands moving with so much fluidity compared to the rigid bones of the rest of her body. She purses her lips, hesitating before finally asking, "Is that why you're here? Your… dad, your girlfriend… is that why you moved away from your old life?"

"Sort of," I say immediately, because it's the truth, and I feel compelled to give her something true. To feed her a morsel of myself that isn't a lie. And maybe I just need to voice this aloud to someone other than Elise. "I... you were right when you said most people wouldn't move to West Rutland without an ulterior motive."

Head tilting, her eyes flicker. "Don't tell me you're an undercover spy ready to reveal a secret drug ring in our town." She clicks her tongue humorously. "I knew it was all a conspiracy."

Chuckling uncomfortably at how close to the mark she comes, I scramble to say, "No drug ring, no town secrets. Just... some secrets of my own."

Luna just stares at me, humor dropping from her face, and she doesn't ask me to elaborate. She knows what it's like to have a secret, something you guard so close to your chest that it almost burrows into your bones.

But I can't stop now. I wouldn't lie about this, and if I wanted her to tell me something... I needed to tell her something in return. Maybe that's why it didn't work with Rachel. Because... I didn't give her anything when I expected so much. "I have this theory that you can never know someone completely until their life comes to an end."

Luna sets down her paintbrush completely, as if she can sense the serious tinge to my voice, the way I've chosen a shingle on her roof to stare at so I don't chicken out. "I hate that theory."

I don't argue. "Me too. But... people hide things." I keep staring at that shingle, not letting myself give her a meaningful glance because she wouldn't deserve it. "Can I tell you something?" I ask instead, hesitating. "Like, I know you don't want to tell me things, and that's fine, but can I tell you things?"

I didn't mean it in a bad way, and I can tell Luna understands, because her mouth quirks up. "Considering I don't have any friends anymore, I should probably listen to you."

I nod, but I can't laugh, because I'm too wrapped up in my thoughts. "It's in the nature of humans to hide, to project something to the world totally different from what we are." I can tell Luna wants to say something, perhaps ask in what ways I project myself on the world, but she stays silent. "This society we've built... we could have made anything, and we made something ugly. Something manipulative and painful."

"Not always," Luna argues, without much effort.

"Not always," I concede. "But each person is made up of their relationships with others, and even though we're wired to think *our* relationships are the most important, because we're all self centered, there is so much going on in every person's life." This time, I do look at her. "And we're not omniscient beings, we can only know what we're told."

Luna follows along, even though I know I'm babbling without much sense, but I need to walk the words around until I can come to a conclusion that I can handle. That I can bear. "I know the feeling. The people we love, we can't protect them from everything. We can't... always be there."

I shake my head, but I take mental note of the emotion in her words, filing them away for later. "That's not what I mean. I mean, yes, but, it's more that *they* can't protect *us* from everything. When someone is alive, they can hold their secrets close, like we all do, but after, they lose that control. They pass that weight of knowledge onto someone else. And it starts to feel like I never knew him at all."

She shifts forward slightly, as if she wants to pass right through the table and join me on my bench, but she settles for simply extending her arms forward, the movement almost miniscule. A fraction of a gesture, but I feel it in my bones all the same. "Are you- are you talking about your dad?"

I huff out a laugh, because if I don't laugh I might cry, and Luna and I *definitely* aren't at that point yet. "Rachel... My ex-girlfriend, I probably deserved what she did to me."

"No one deserves to be cheated on," Luna says immediately, with steely resolve and a hint of surprise.

I purse my lips. "My mom probably did. I learned from the best."

Luna sucks in a sharp breath, eyes softening. "Your dad..."

I duck my head. "I don't know. What she did wouldn't have *hurt* so bad if I hadn't just found out my dad had an affair when I was five."

Luna jerked back. "Why would you find out about that *now*?"

"It became pretty obvious," I say bitterly, "when I got the will, and I got most of his possessions, but there was a small amount reserved for-" I cut myself off, unable to say his name out loud. "For a son. A half brother I never knew I had."

Speaking it aloud makes the ball of tension, the guilt of lying, unravel in my chest.

Eyes nearly bugging out of her head, Luna seems to say the first words that come to mind, which are, "That's heavy."

Sputtering out a laugh, I lean forward so my chin can rest on my propped up fist, my head suddenly too heavy to hold up. "Yeah, I guess it is. Very full circle, right?"

Chuckling at herself, Luna rubs her eyes. "Not the parallel cheating, although that's pretty wild. I mean… a brother?"

I nod, and then I say it. "Yeah. And he's here."

Lips parting, Luna just stares for a second, almost like she doesn't immediately make the connection. I can hardly blame her, the whole situation is so bizarre, but her jaw finally snaps open, lunging forward and slapping her hands on the picnic table. "*What?*"

Jerking back in shock with a startled laugh at her enthusiasm, I just sigh and hang my head. "Yeah."

"Like, in West Rutland?"

"Somewhere," I breathe out. "It didn't take long. I found the woman pretty quickly; there was contact information. I guess she was from here, and when she found out my dad was married, she took off with the kid to get help from her parents."

Wheels turn behind Luna's eyes, as she searches back through her memory, but she just shrugs. "Honestly, I can think of *several* women with that kind of story. Showing up with a baby and nowhere else to go. How old is he?"

"Nineteen," I say softly. One of the few things I know about him. He's only five years younger than me, and my heart aches in memory of all the days I'd sat alone in that city apartment, my parents at events or out with friends, when I could have had a brother to be miserable with.

Luna's eyes soften, all the pieces clicking into place. "That's why you moved here. You came for him?"

I huff. "Sort of. I mean, I'm being a coward about it, but that's the plan."

"Moving to an entirely different state where you don't know anyone hardly sounds cowardly."

Curling my legs up beneath me, I try to remember why I'd decided to tell her this in the first place, but I can't stop now. And she doesn't seem to want me to stop. "I got his name from the will, but… that's it. I know I can look him up at any time, thank you modern technology, to find out what he looks like, but I just haven't been able to."

Genuinely confused, but not in a judgemental way, Luna asks, "Why?"

I lick my lips, searching for the right words. "My parents didn't have any siblings, and other than the affair I was an only child. They're both dead, which means there's *no one else*. And then the whole thing with Rachel, I just… I never really comprehended that a person could wake up one day and be totally and utterly alone. And this was almost like a chance to not be alone anymore, but the thought of looking at him, of not seeing a resemblance, or an inkling of my father and me… I don't know, it freaks me out. Like I will have come here for nothing."

"Looks aren't everything," Luna points out.

"Yeah, but if he were a full sibling it'd be one thing, but half, I just don't know."

Luna swallows thickly, eyes glazing over as her mind briefly goes somewhere else. "Blood isn't everything, either."

I want to ask. God, I want to ask her questions. It's been so long since I've met a new person, stuck in my routine of work, Rachel, and home for the past two years. I'd forgotten how many people this world has, and how many of them are good. But I don't dare open my mouth, not wanting to scare her off like last time.

Realizing I'm waiting for her to speak, she flushes, and says, "I'm sorry."

"For what?"

She licks her lips, and I can tell my theory had been right. She wouldn't say a damn thing about anything until I did. "I don't want you to be gun shy around me, like I'm a rocket about to go off at any moment."

Smirking, I question, "Well, aren't you?"

Laughing, she buries her face in her hands. "*No*. It's just been…" She trails off, unable to find the words. "You had your version of a hellish six months. Let's just say I've had mine."

"I get it," I say gently. "I was definitely a total bitch to all my friends before I came here, I just got it out of my system." And making friends here is sort of part of my job. Although sitting here, befriending Luna doesn't feel at all like an obligation.

"Are you calling me a total bitch?"

"Not directly."

Another laugh bursts from her throat, and she slaps a hand over her lips, like she's not used to making such a light sound anymore. "I'm working on it. The world deserves my darkness sometimes, but you don't."

I shrug, that guilt coming back, the lies sitting on my tongue, wanting to be thrown out the window like all the others I'd burned to the ground tonight. But I swallow them back down. "I can take it."

"You should look him up."

My eyes flutter closed. "I'm planning on it."

"No. Do it tonight."

My eyes fly open again, and I stare at her, suddenly panicking. "I don't know-"

"Do it," she repeats, almost eagerly. "I can help you once you do. I know every damn person in this town, and it usually sucks, but *please* let it be helpful for once."

She looks so excited that I can hardly say no. I wonder if she, too, is curious about the murders plaguing her town, if she ever looks into it with all of her connections because she can. "I don't even know what I'd do once I know who it is."

"I'm pretty sure you have to actually know what he looks like before we cross *that* bridge."

"God, I'm gonna fall *off* the bridge."

"Nothing good and interesting happens in this town," she says, pounding her fist on the wood to drill in the point, and it makes me laugh. She's very animated with her hands, and I like to watch the emotions seep out through her body when she won't show them on her face. I also notice that she says *good and interesting* and not just *interesting*, all too aware that a murder mystery steadily unfolds beneath her nose. "And I am always bored."

"I'm pretty sure you chose to live here."

"You would be wrong," she says immediately, and I cling to the information that she gives up. "I mean, it was a choice, but… it definitely wasn't."

I tilt my head, but she just flings her hands up. "Nevermind. We can talk about me later. But this is *way* better. Let me help you find your long lost brother."

I shake my head, glancing up at her to see her eyes shining, some powerful emotion hiding there that I can't describe. More than just excitement for a mystery. Maybe it's that she just promised to tell me more. At some point. "I hope revealing all my pathetic relationship failings doesn't make you like me less."

She lifts her eyes to the sky, but they're full of mirth. "I think I like you more now, actually."

I DON'T STOP RUNNING the entire way home, afraid that if I take too long to get to my computer I'll lose my nerve. Relief floods through me when the rest of the house is deserted, Reyna nowhere to be found, because I have no idea how I'd react if she asked me why I'm freaking out. I'd probably run right back out the door and never come back.

Safely closing myself in my room, I don't let myself hesitate. Despite shaking hands and a pounding chest, I pull open my laptop and start typing, sighing when the machine immediately connects to the internet and doesn't lag. If I'm waiting for a sign that I shouldn't do this right now, the universe doesn't give me one.

I enter one letter at a time, using only my index fingers, because that's the only way I know how to type, but also because I can't afford a typo right now.

Parker Jefferson.

I add *West Rutland, Vermont* at the end for good measure.

My fingertip hovers over the enter key, so close to the backspace, and it would be so easy to choose one over the other, but suddenly the page refreshes, and social media profiles and articles for West Rutland's High School Newspaper pop up.

My spine stiffens, because I can see a small thumbnail preview, showing off dark copper hair like mine, but the rest of the details are fuzzy.

He's here. This is confirmation that the will didn't lie to me, that I hadn't come here for nothing.

He's here.

I click on that same picture, blowing it up in size, gnawing on my fingernails as it loads. And all at once, my computer screen is overtaken by the only living family member I have left.

I sit back, eyes flying open wide. Because that's when I realize I recognize him. I've only met a grand total of eight people in this town, and even that might be generous, but...

I recognize him.

Chapter Thirteen

LUNA HAS MORE SELF restraint than I do, and like we agreed, she doesn't message me asking who he is. She leaves me alone with nothing but my thoughts and an inability to process what the hell is happening. We have a plan to meet at Suzie's tomorrow morning, so I have at least until then to freak out about the fact that I'd met my brother *weeks ago* without even knowing he's my brother.

I saw him days ago, screaming at the quarry as I hid behind a tree.

And both times I'd seen him, he was wearing that hat, covering the damning red hair that might have made me connect the dots.

I'd expected to smile when I saw him, to spend hours finding everything we have in common, scouring his social media for shared interests. Instead, I search through his pictures, his followers, barely even paying attention to him as four names of dead boys cycle through my head.

If I hadn't seen him the other day, if I hadn't heard him cry, his words at the diner would have remained true in my eyes. He doesn't follow any of the victims, and none of them follow him. They aren't in any of his limited number of posts, most being him and his parents, a few of him playing soccer. I notice, however, that even though he follows Anthony, Anthony doesn't follow him.

I spend my night panicking, returning to the conversation I'd heard by the quarry, to what Anthony had said.

Not many people find out the identity of their brother just to immediately question why they were lying about knowing a murder victim.

A shiver runs down my spine at thinking it so bluntly, so... I don't know. Like it's an actual possibility.

I push the thought from my head. I have a plan to meet with Luna. Luna does an excellent job of distracting me.

Oh.

Wait.

We have a plan to meet at Suzie's.

What are the odds of him working tomorrow when I go to meet Luna for a stack of maple pancakes? Really, he's only been there once out of all the times I've visited the diner, so what would be the odds? But I have no way to know what I'm walking into. It results in a night of horrifically fitful sleep.

That first morning I saw him, I'd been so fixated on the murders I hadn't paid much attention to anything else. I'd been so tired, so excited to talk to a new person, and someone closer to the age of the victims, no less.

But I can see it. His nose, mouth, and general face shape are different, but his eyes were the same rare green as both my dad's, and mine. The shiny auburn hair mirrors mine as well, falling just past his ears in the picture I found, but he's cut it shorter since then. His has more of a frizzy curl to it than mine, presumably from his mom, and I toss my phone aside before I can scrutinize it any further, leaving myself with only thoughts.

By the time the next morning comes around, I've managed barely three hours of sleep, and I'd been staring at the ceiling for far too long. I try to make myself look as presentable as possible, but I do a marginal job at best, heading off to the diner before I can call Elise and tell her that I want to abort mission.

Because he didn't ask for me to come here. He has a life, clearly. A family, a job. Does he know about me? Does he know who his father was? What if he does, and he hates him, and therefore hates me? What if he doesn't, and he doesn't believe me?

How do you tell someone you're their sister nineteen years too late?

I can't tell if I tense or relax when I find only Jo behind the bar, and I collapse into an empty booth, flipping through my journal where I'd written everything I could find on Parker last night. I realize that this is the first time I haven't sat at the bar, probably because this is the first time I haven't come alone. It feels weird, sitting at an actual table. More permanent.

"What is it that you're always writing in there? Plotting my murder?"

I slam the notebook closed, in a way that is definitely more suspicious than it needed to be. Luna peers down into my booth with a smirk, hand on her hip.

Throwing my notebook into my bag, I say, "You caught me. You'll never see it coming."

She doesn't have any art supplies this time, just a coffee she grabbed from the counter and a wide grin. "I knew it. You've been a serial killer this whole time. There's no half brother. The whole 'I just moved here' was just an elaborate cover and you've been living under the covered bridge like an evil troll. No wonder I've never seen your apartment."

"Honestly, the covered bridge would probably have better living conditions. There's been a leak in our roof since I moved in."

"Maybe you should get that fixed," she says, settling across from me. "If you plan on staying for a while."

"Why bother? It's dripping right into the kitchen sink."

She laughs. "So did you do it, or what? Because you look awful."

I lean forward, rubbing my hands down my face, as if I can pull the exhaustion out of my skin. "You go ahead and see what your new brother looks like for the first time and see how well you sleep."

"Who says I haven't?"

"Ha-ha," I deadpan as Jo comes over to take our order.

"Morning, ladies," she says brightly, not bothering to give us menus. How have I already managed to become a regular? "Alex, what happened to you?"

I throw my hands in the air, and Luna bursts out laughing. "She's going through a quarter life crisis. Didn't you know? That's why she moved here in the first place."

Jo's smile falls a little bit, and it twists in a weird way, like her mind travels a million miles away. "I've been there." I wonder if she'd once wanted to get out of West Rutland, if there had been a time when she had no interest in running the family business. If she ever longed for something else. "Will coffee help?"

"And maple pancakes," I say.

Luna taps her fingers on the table. "Same."

Jo winks and disappears, as I point a finger at Luna. "Let me be clear. You *also* seem to be going through a quarter life crisis, so you can't make fun of me."

Her lips curve up. "I wasn't making fun of you. I was making a statement. In fact, I probably have you beat. I think my quarter life crisis will extend into a mid life crisis at this point."

I gnaw on the inside of my cheek. "You can't blame me for being curious when you say cryptic shit like that."

She just gives me a small grin before sipping on her coffee. "Let's at least give your crisis a happy ending. You promised me you'd look him up when you left. *Who is he?*"

"It's been killing you, hasn't it?" I'd refused to give her the name last night, not wanting to hear anything before I had the time to do my own research. She sulked about it, claiming she'd go to the school yearbook and narrow it down purely by appearance, until I agreed to tell her this morning.

"Well, I didn't lose as much sleep as *you* over it," she teases me, and oh, I like this Luna, light and excited and not trapped in her own head. "But I did lose some."

Suppressing a laugh, I take my phone out. I hesitate for only a second, because what if Luna confirms my suspicions? What if she hates him, what if he's awful? What if she talks about him like those two girls talked about the missing boys? Before I can change my mind, I bite the bullet and slide the screenshotted photo across the table to her, not wanting to say his name aloud in the crowded diner.

But she recognizes him immediately and destroys all my efforts, blurting out, *"Parker?"*

I lunge forward, slapping a hand over her mouth, eyes wide as I look around, but everyone remains immersed in their food and their own conversations. Luna's eyes crinkle, smiling behind my fingers, and I shyly draw my arms back, flushing. "Sorry."

Unfazed, she just leans forward, palms face down on the table. "Parker Jefferson? Are you sure?"

I stare at her, sarcastically saying, "I don't know, I can check with my dad's attorney-"

She waves me off. "No, I just- There's a lot of single mothers here, like a lot, and last night I was running through all the possibilities of who it could be, but Parker wasn't one of them."

"Why?"

She looks around, aware of the volume of her voice, and murmurs, "Because as far as anyone knows, his *dad* is his biological dad. His parents have been married for, like, thirty years."

Lips parting, I sit back in the booth abruptly, wishing I could go to sleep right now and wake up six months in the past. "But that doesn't make sense. You have to be wrong."

"West Rutland folks are excellent at airing out each other's dirty laundry. I'm not wrong."

My mind runs through the timeline. So they were both married at the time of the affair, and the woman already lived in

West Rutland. Did they briefly separate? Was it just a business trip that went south? Maybe it hadn't been my dad who sent his son away. Maybe it was the mother who took him.

But this made things a whole lot worse. When I imagined dealing out the news, I imagined another soul, like me, coming from a broken family. I imagined that he'd been raised by a single mother, maybe a single child like me, and he'd be looking for blood, too. But he has a whole family already. He didn't need more.

Could I break up a family to save my own?

"Alex?" Luna asks delicately, but Jo brings out our food before I can respond. Probably seeing something on my face, she doesn't stop to chat, just shooting Luna a look before rushing off to help another customer.

"I shouldn't have come here," I whisper, appetite entirely gone as I push maple syrup around my plate with my coffee stirrer. "He... I'm the last thing he needs. He already has what I'm looking for."

"And what are you looking for?" Luna asks, also ignoring her food. Maybe we shouldn't have met here, but the public atmosphere keeps me from bursting into tears, so that's a plus.

I don't say the word *family* out loud. She seems to know.

"You can never have too much family," she says, and the words hit me like a knife in the chest. Because she's not talking about me, she knows I have no one left. She's talking about him. And maybe she's talking about herself a little bit, too. "And the truth is better than lies. There are a lot of things I wish I knew."

I swallow roughly, unable to speak.

Pressing her lips together, she looks up at me through lowered lashes and says, "I know what it's like to barely start loving someone like family before it's too late."

Our eyes meet for barely a second, and something watery reflects over her irises before she looks down. "I'm just saying, it's still your decision, but you can't make your decision based on the fact that Sadie Jefferson had an affair and never told her husband. Make it based on you, and make it based on him."

I poke at my pancakes. "It makes me hate him a little less," I choke out, voice barely a whisper. "Dad. Knowing that everyone else has secrets, too. Even me."

The corners of Luna's mouth curve up, and it immediately makes my heart lift, too, and I don't have the nerve to say anything else. To ask more. "Oh, yeah?" Luna teases. "What secrets might those be?"

I finally cut into my food, stomach grumbling, and she does the same. "I'll show you mine if you show me yours."

"Not a chance. What was that you said about secrets being integral to humankind?"

THE LINE BETWEEN *STALKER* and *investigator* gets greyer with every passing hour.

After leaving Suzie's, watching Luna disappear down Marble Road toward the sculpture center, I pull out my notebook and flip to the back page, where I scribble everything I know about Parker.

It holds only four facts: his name, his age, his mother's name, and where they live. I don't recognize the street name from any of my many walks around town, so I tap it into my phone and let the small arrow on the screen direct me to the south side of town, shrouded in thick woods and full of long, winding roads. As I walk, I gather all the information about the boy from the diner, integrating him and my brother into the same person, and what that might mean. His words haven't stopped echoing around my skull. *You'll get what's coming for you.*

Keep your mouth shut.

I've started locking my bedroom door at night, because Anthony had said those words, too. He'd said... a lot of things.

I hike up a hill, the small houses getting further apart as I go, until the dot on the screen that represents where I stand meets my destination.

Taking a deep breath, I lift my head to gaze across the street, toward the single story, green house with black shutters dotting the windows. A garden decorates the front yard, hedged in with that stereotypical white picket fence, flowers and greenery overflowing. The scene is so peaceful, a calm, rural life in central Vermont, far from the life he could have had with me in New York. Which life would have been better? I have no idea, even as I gaze longingly at the comfortable house, trying to imagine someone curled up on the couch within, reading a book, or cooking, or doing nothing.

A dog barks, someone walking their pet toward me, and I hurry further down the street, not wanting to get caught staring.

But I come back. I walk down the street, back and forth, past the house on the opposite street, no less than a dozen times, trying to work up the courage to knock on the door. On my thirteenth pass, the door finally creaks open, and I nearly have a heart attack, lowering myself to the ground to pretend to tie my shoe.

It's not Parker, but rather his mother. The similarities between the mother and son are far more obvious, her curly hair tied up with a scarf at the nape of her neck, freckles dotting her fair skin. She wears loose gym shorts and a ratty white shirt, sinking to her knees beside the flower bed, pulling a collection of gardening tools toward her.

I watch transfixed, shoelace beneath me abandoned. She's beautiful, but she looks nothing like my mother. My mom would never have taken the time to sit in a garden, pulling weeds and delicately watering the bulbs. A small smile paints her face, content and calm, and I wish I could join her, even though I know nothing about plants.

Maybe that's what it was, for my dad. Sadie made the world slow down for him, in a moment he needed it.

Maybe I need that, too.

But what Parker doesn't need is me. A whirlwind blowing into his calm life, tearing through the garden he's made. But then, I like to think that I deserve a garden, too.

Slowly, I stand, shaking out my foot that had fallen asleep from kneeling for so long. With one last look, I turn and jog back down the hill, unsure what I'm chasing but knowing what I'm running away from.

Chapter Fourteen

"YOU STILL HAVEN'T SPOKEN to him, have you?"

I hold a finger up, hopping into my usual spot at Luna's picnic table, peering at what she's painting today. I smile, seeing the same picture as two days ago, but nearly finished. "Let's be clear. I'd spoken to him before I even saw his picture, so I've already won."

She clicks her tongue, not looking up from the highlight she adds to the nose of a statue in a garden. "Let me amend my statement. Have you spoken to him as your brother and not as some random server at Suzie's?"

I grumble out, "*Shut up*," and she chuckles. It's sort of become routine for me to visit Luna either here or at the sculpture center. I find that she doesn't do well when she doesn't have something to do, and she much prefers using her hands at all times. I have to be careful, though, crafting up a fake work schedule that I stick to so that she doesn't see me around town too often and get suspicious. Another pang of guilt rings through me, but I barely notice it because it's pretty consistently there at this point.

The sun begins to set, and Luna flicks on the fluorescent lamp that seems to always stay out here. "You know, I defended you about the whole cowardly thing when you first said it, but you're starting to be true to your word."

I press a hand to my chest, feigning offense. "I'm going to pretend you didn't say that. Instead, I'll tell you that I'm working up to it and am no longer avoiding Suzie's. I actually sucked it up and went for some pancakes this morning. Jo is doing well, by the way."

"Wow, what a milestone."

"I know, right?" I say, momentarily content with just watching her add details to yet another masterpiece. Her fingers had clearly once been thin and nimble, but callouses built up over time, her forearms strong from her time in the sculpture garden. The muscles there flex as she dabs at her palette, mixing a soft pink that could have been plucked directly from a sunset. Only when she puts down her paintbrush to lean back and observe her work do I swallow and finally ask what I've been trying to do for days, even as I fear the answer. "Do you know him well, then?"

Seemingly waiting for this question, she responds, "I know him in the way I know every single person in this town, but we never went to school together. He was in, I think… eighth grade, when I was a senior in high school, and even though the middle and high schools are stuck in the same building, we were kept pretty separate. But my-" she cuts herself off, swallowing, and rephrases. "But I knew him through someone else, yeah. They went to some of the same soccer camps over in Rutland City, the ones they have in the summer. He was captain of the soccer team his senior year."

I exhale, because I needed to hear something good. He has to be *good*. I also smile because I have an incredible lack of athletic ability. My mom tried to put me in softball once in third grade, but I'd gotten a concussion a week in and never went back. "Is he… is he nice?" He seemed nice enough when I talked to him, if a little sleep deprived, but it was his job to be nice to me at the time. And that day at the quarry, with Anthony… neither of them seemed nice at all.

Luna smiles, like I'd said something she hadn't expected, and nods. "Yeah, yeah, he actually is. He was always nice to the younger kids at the camps, even though most of the other varsity players were elitist assholes. He stuck around to save up for college, working at Suzie's and an auto shop just outside of town, because his parents couldn't afford to send him."

My brows knit together, hopeful that the money sent by my dad could help, even though it wasn't an overwhelming amount. Although, how did his mom tell him about the small inheritance if he didn't know about the affair, anyway? He must know at this point. He's over eighteen, the attorney would have gone directly to him-

Pushing the logistics from my mind, I ask, "Did you ever speak with him? Or… or anything?"

A small shake of her head. "I mean, maybe in passing, but Carlos wanted me to stay out of his business."

I lean forward, and something about that name is familiar, like I've heard it before. "Carlos?"

Starting, Luna swallows thickly and looks away. "Yeah, Carlos. The one who went to the soccer camps with him." The devastation on her face is so distinct that I don't dare pry. "Parker was sort of his idol, he wanted to be just like him. I mean, all the younger kids did, but Carlos loved soccer."

I can't help but notice the past tense. Who, exactly, has Luna lost?

"Anyway," she plunges forward, picking up her paintbrush again, hand shaking slightly this time. She doesn't go back to painting yet, like she just needs something to hold. "I don't know him well enough to know how he'd react to something like this, but he's a good guy. I promise." She shifts, swirling her brush through a mug of dirty water. "What's your plan?"

"No plan," I admit. "Well, I think I might talk to his mother first. It seems wrong to just, like, accost him somewhere and drop a bomb on him."

"Wrong, maybe. Easier? Yes."

"I have a habit of choosing the least easy option of hundreds."

"Yeah, I got that impression," Luna says. "Instead of, you know, picking up a phone, you *moved to an entirely different state.*"

Rolling my eyes, I bite on my tongue, resisting the urge to defend myself that it's temporary, that I'd wanted it to be a vacation. "Go big or go home."

"And where is that? Home, I mean," Luna asks, glancing up at me.

I tilt my head. "To be determined."

We fall into comfortable silence, and I gaze at her across the two feet separating us, the nearly completed painted sheet of paper between us. I press my lips together, wishing she would look up at me, too, but she's started painting again. I watch in fascination as she does so. I would have thought the piece was done a while ago, but she keeps adding more and more, and every time she's right to add it.

"Do you think it's possible for people to say *I love you* too much?" I don't know what makes me say it.

"God, no," Luna says without missing a beat, much faster than I expected. "I sort of think we can never tell people enough."

I turn away. "Maybe. Unless they don't deserve it. I wish I could take all my words back from... her, to give to someone else." To give to him. To give to you. "The word feels small now."

"I think it is a small word. It's just so... obvious. Doesn't mean people don't love to hear it. Or feel it."

I hum, entwining my hands together. "I just wish there was a bigger word, and we could still use love all the time, but save this other thing for the real thing. Although, I suppose, we'd just start overusing the new word, too, because that's what humans do. Take until it's gone."

"Lucky for humans, you can't run out of love. It's not a finite resource."

"Oh, stop, you sound like my rabbi."

Laughing, Luna throws down her paintbrush once more, leaning against the table on her elbows. At first, I think she's staring at me, but then I realize her eyes are actually trained on the lamp. "Is the fluorescent lamp not harshing your mellow? Because it's harshing mine. Harshly."

"It totally is," I agree, squinting when I turn to look. "You know, I'd sort of rather live by candlelight."

Luna jerks toward me, eyebrows raising. She glances at the lamp illuminating the space, sharp and fluorescent, casting a circle of white light around it. "Are you telling me you want to live in the eighteen hundreds?"

"No," I snort, before pausing. "Well, maybe, if we got rid of the rampant racism and homophobia and misogyny."

"We can barely do that now."

"Yeah, well, maybe the people of that time weren't all that beautiful in the personality and basic human decency department, but my god, do I want to run off with my secret lover into a candlelit garden, escaping from the heteronormative ball where every suitor begged me to dance."

Luna mixes up what looks to be a soft green on her palette, but will possibly morph into something different come daylight. Everything does. "Admittedly, that does sound a little enticing."

I nod to the lamp, squinting at the brightness. "Everything in modern days is just so harsh, you know? So bold, relentless, so bright and dim at the same time. Sometimes I don't want a light, I just want a glow. If that makes… any sense at all."

Luna's movement pauses, before she holds up her finger. "Give me a second." With that, she switches the lamp off, plunging us into darkness. The only light comes from a small window on the side of the house, illuminating enough of the yard that I can watch Luna disappear towards her garage. My ears sharpen as she rustles around, something metallic clanging through the night. I shift uncomfortably on the bench, staring at the spot where she disappeared, waiting for her to materialize again.

People don't always do that. Come back.

Before my mind can run any further, the sounds of feet on dried grass grow closer, and I see Luna once again illuminated not only by the window, but by a small candle cupped in her palms. The glow paints a deep orange highlight across her cheeks and jawline, firelight dancing in her dark eyes, turning brown to molten gold even in the absence of the sun.

She joins me at the table once more, sliding the candle toward me. The orange circle brightens up the wood of the table, and I reach out my hand, allowing the reflection of the flames to dance across my skin.

"See?" I whisper. "Beautiful."

"It is," Luna agrees, scooting forward. "It makes everything feel like *more*."

You make everything feel like more, I think before I can stop myself. Or maybe it's just the candlelight.

"Does it mess with the painting?" I ask. "To have orange light instead of white?"

"No. I mean, yes, technically, but not in a bad way. I think the painting could use a little more, too."

I could use more. We could all use more. We deserve it, too.

I smile slowly, nudging the candle. The flame ripples inside the glass, making the glow masking Luna's flow over her skin. It reminds me of the reflection of water, the way the waves sparkle along the walls of an indoor pool. It makes her shine. "Doesn't it make you want to live by candlelight?"

She gazes at me, and her eyes are so wide and full of color. "It certainly makes me want to see by candlelight."

"Same thing."

"Tell me," she says, lips perfectly pink. "Why *do* you want to live by candlelight?"

Refusing to pull my eyes from her, wondering if I have that same ethereal glow radiating from her, if she's admiring me too, I toss the words around on my tongue. I try to find a way to describe it, to articulate how a world with the intensity turned down makes me feel. "Because," I say slowly. "It makes people look like you do right now."

She holds up her hand, admiring the pattern on her knuckles. "What, orange?" she asks jokingly, but there's a catch in her throat.

"Lovely," I whisper, because it's true. "Soft."

She swallows. "I don't think even a candle is enough to make you soft. You've got that tough look about you." She pauses. "You've got the lovely part, though."

"Maybe we need another one," I say with a smile, trying to ignore the swelling in my chest. I feel like the fire in front of me has transferred into my veins. "Would that be enough? Or two?"

She shakes her head. "No, because it makes you look like something else." She swallows again, licking her lips, like her throat is suddenly dry.

I observe the effect on my own skin, before lifting my gaze back to her. "Something good?"

"I haven't decided yet," she says. But she's smiling.

"YOU LOOK LIKE YOU'RE on cloud nine."

The voice nearly gives me a heart attack when I shut my front door behind me. It really shouldn't have, given that I don't live alone, but I wasn't really expecting her to be awake, let alone in the living room, when I got home from Luna's at nearly one in the morning.

"You need to stop sitting in the dark," I say with a laugh, allowing my heartrate to get back down to normal. "One of these days it's not going to be you, but a murderer, and I'll have let my guard down."

Chuckling, Reyna stretches, her shoulders and back popping. She probably hasn't moved for hours. "Well, for now, it's just me, dying to ask how your date went."

I flick my brows up, trying to erase the blush and smile from my face. "Not a date, although it's nice that you think I could get one here."

She shrugs. "It's not as hard as you might think, even though there's like three options."

"You're not being convincing."

She waves me off. "All I'm saying is, you look like a giddy fourteen year old when her crush just kissed her on the cheek."

I grit my teeth, because in actuality, I got less action than that. Even so, that warm feeling left behind by the candle lingers in my chest. Maybe it's because I feel like I did before Rachel broke my heart (I cringe inwardly at the phrase. I've always hated it, but in this particular scenario, it's fairly accurate).

Changing the subject, I ask, "How did *you* spend your night? Any good movie recommendations for me?"

She groans. "Your assumptions make me sound so lame, you know that right?"

"I just know a night in when I see one. I'm sure I'll regret not having one in the morning."

Sighing, she flips her laptop closed, leaning over to turn on the lamp instead. "Yeah, well, I had plans with Anthony, because I like to be a good sister, but he flaked on me at the last minute. Movies and pizza make for a good backup plan."

"It's because high schoolers are assholes. Common knowledge, and you can't even get mad at them for it."

She snorts. "Well, you're definitely right about that. *Emergency party*, which is odd, because I don't remember doing anything spontaneous in high school. Everything was so meticulously planned."

"Probably because nothing ever changes at that age," I suggest. "Although they think it does."

"He's certainly more spontaneous than me," she says, motioning around the room.

I consider her words, before throwing caution to the wind. "If that's the case, then we should do something sometime. You know, if what you said about there only being three people our age around here is true."

Her face splits into a grin. "Next time my brother bails on me, I'll let you know. Assuming you're not with... whoever you were with."

She knows I was with Luna, and I still don't really understand why she doesn't just say it. Maybe because she doesn't want to broach the subject. With that thought, I wonder whether or not I've made a mistake. I probably don't want my only allies in this town to hate each other.

If Reyna saw a change in my face, she doesn't let on, because she only says, "But for now, I'm going to bed, and from the bags under your eyes, you totally should too."

I lift my fingers to my cheeks. "Are they bad?"

"You look like you haven't slept since you moved here."

Even though I have, it sort of feels like I haven't. The days move too fast, even as nothing happens.

Well, not nothing.

"I'll take the hint," I say with a wave, heading toward my bedroom. "Goodnight." I pause. "Tell your brother I say hello, and to appreciate you more."

"I'll definitely do that."

I close the door behind me with a soft click, and moments later, I hear her do the same.

Chapter Fifteen

THE NEWS REACHES ELISE before it reaches me, mostly because I stayed out at Luna's last night, and I'd decided I earned the right to sleep the day away. But once again, I'm awoken by my phone ringing. I can't even be mad given the fact that it's nearly eleven. Moreover, any lingering anger dissipates when she starts speaking.

"Did you hear?"

I clear my throat, willing away the embarrassment of being woken up by my friend slash coworker so late on a weekday. Fear drips into my stomach as a million and one scenarios race through my head. Did Rachel come back? Did something happen to her? Did something happen to *Elise*, to the company? "All I'm hearing right now is you, what happened?"

"Alex, it's happened again. There's another one."

I know what she's talking about immediately, and stumble from my bed. Tripping over my feet, I peer out the window, only to see a deserted street. Not a single person in sight, the whole town holed up alone in their houses even though another boy is probably dead.

I can only think of one name. *Parker, Parker, Parker, Parker.*

Because he's involved, somehow. He's involved in... something.

"Alex? Alex, are you there?"

"Who?" I choke out. "Did they say who it was?"

"No name's been released yet, barely *anything*'s been released, it all just happened."

"Damnit," I mumble into the phone, lifting my fingertips to my mouth. For some reason, I find my throat constricted, my eyes burning, even though I have no way of knowing who it is. There's no indication that I've met him.

But I might have. Or I might know someone who knows him. I know this town now. I'm a part of it.

"*Damnit*," I repeat, this time kicking at the wall. "What the hell?"

"I know." Elise's voice is quiet and mournful, and I wonder exactly how she heard. Knowing her, she probably has a tab constantly open on West Rutland news. "It's... I know. But Alex, this... It's different this time. They found a body."

I nearly drop my phone, but my fingers have turned to stone. "*They what?*"

"They found the boy's body," she repeats. "He was only found this morning, but they said it was at one of the quarries. They're saying..." She trails off, swallowing hard. "They're saying it's likely that's where the other bodies were also disposed of, just... not visible."

I furrow my brow, asking questions even as my heart aches. "So he wasn't in the water, the boy? They found him on land?"

"No," she says. "He was in the water, but he was floating."

My stomach roils at the thought of a crime scene on the other side of town, of people having to pull a high schooler from the water because some psycho decided to go on a killing spree. The thought sends a chill down my spine, and I have half a mind to leave town right now. The past couple weeks, I'd somehow managed to convince myself that maybe, just maybe, there was nothing here. That these boys just up and ran away from their lives, instead of having their lives taken.

I wish I'd ignored her call.

"God," I mumble, rubbing my tender forehead, trying to will away the nausea. "What should I do? I can't just show up at the crime scene, they don't know I'm a journalist."

"Sure you can," Elise says, sounding just as disgusted at the prospect as I am. "Give it a few hours, though, let the news spread. I guarantee there'll be a crowd gathering."

The headache worsens. The nausea grows, and I want to leave.

But I can't. Not only because of my job, but I can't leave these people who are going to be hurting. Did Luna know him? Did *Parker* know him? I know he said he barely knew any of the other victims, but what if it was his friend, what if-

What if the victim *is* Parker?

"Okay," I finally say, voice weak and unsteady. "I'm... yeah. I'll be out and about all day, so forward me any articles that come out with new information, yeah? Any names, any theories, any suspects."

"Of course," she says. "I'm constantly refreshing the page, you'll know as soon as I know."

We hang up with a melancholy air hanging between us, filling the miles that separate us, the weight of it holding me here in this murder mystery town. Light filters through the small crack in the curtains, the sun making its way steadily across the sky. It pierces my eyes, too bright. Part of me longs to get back in bed, to shut out this dark and depressing world that my job has become.

But the sun has risen, stretching toward midday, and another boy is gone. So I rise, too.

I do as she says, though, waiting until early afternoon to head out. Reyna's nowhere to be found when I pass through the living room, and even though we don't talk much, I sort of hoped for the distraction. Something to hold me up at the door, to keep me here a little longer.

This is the job you signed up for, my mind reminds me. *Do your job.*

I walk slowly through the town, where lots of people mill about, talking in hushed and anguished tones. Some are just headed home, or to a loved one's, but I follow a steady stream of people towards the quarry. I pass Suzie's as I go, squinting to read a harsh *closed* sign plastered across the front door. With every other store I look at, I find the same thing.

It becomes plain that we're not headed to either of the quarries I'm familiar with, passing both paths as we trudge down Marble Road. I don't know why I feel so relieved.

Sound grows as we approach through the woods, a mass of people shouting coming into view. I catch snippets, most begging for information, others crying over the boy lost. I still don't hear a name, though. I don't even see anyone here that I recognize. I search for Parker, wishing he'd just materialize in front of me alive, but he's nowhere to be found.

The place is completely barred off with crime scene tape, not allowing the crowd to get a good look of anything beyond the tree line. I stand on my tip-toes, trying to get a good look at *anything*, but there's too many people. I'm not going to be able to find anything here, not now at least.

A name, though. If I listen long enough, I might hear a name.

"You heard?"

I jerk up, not expecting anyone to talk to me, but I look up to see Lucia peering down at me, eyes red and raw.

I swallow hard at the sight of grief, feeling suddenly out of place here. "I followed the crowd," I tell her softly. "It's just… horrible."

"I don't understand it," she mumbles. "This… this type of thing doesn't happen. Not here, not *anywhere*."

I almost say that serial killers are much less common than crime shows lead people to believe, but that feels insensitive. Instead, I simply say, "I know."

She shakes her head, wiping her nose. "They need to get this evil son of a bitch, they need to do *something*."

I don't know what to say. All I can do is nod, unable to supply any sort of comfort. Instead, I ask, "Do they know who he was?"

She nods, wiping her cheek with a knuckle. "Anthony Michaels, good kid. *Great* kid."

Lucia goes on, says something more about the boy, but all sound shuts off, replaced by a dull ringing in my skull. Because somehow, even though I know very few people here, almost none of them boys... I know that name. He'd been in my apartment only a few days ago.

He'd been at the Ledge telling my brother to keep his mouth shut.

And my brother had told him to keep *his* mouth shut in return.

Oh, god...

Reyna wasn't home. She wasn't in the living room, like she always is, and she's not here.

I scan the crowd, searching for Reyna, but I can't distinguish her through the mass of people, or the tears pooling around my eyes.

I don't know what I say to get out of the conversation. A stomachache, maybe, that being at a crime scene isn't sitting well. And really, it isn't. The thought that Reyna's brother had been found in that water mere hours ago was enough to make me keel over and throw up halfway through the woods.

Should I not go home? What if she's there? She probably won't be, she's probably with her family.

The family she has left.

Nowhere else is open, and I don't know where Luna is, so I leave Lucia behind at the scene. Home (or the only place close enough to home in a twenty-mile radius) is the only place to go.

THE FORTY-EIGHT HOURS that pass before I head out toward the crime scene again are excruciating. Two days, and I haven't seen Reyna. She's probably at her parent's place, and I've texted her half a dozen times to tell her how sorry I am, to ask if she needs anything, but she's been radio silent.

I think about how he canceled their plans, how Reyna went to bed thinking she'd see him the next day. I think about saying how nothing ever changes when you're in high school, but today... everything changes.

While I waited for the police to clear the scene, I did a deep dive to find out everything I could about the most recent murder. Because that's what they were now. Not disappearances, but murders. I make my round to the newspaper, the detective's office, every article published since it happened, but it doesn't give me much. I need to actually go to where it happened.

The path through the woods that leads to where the body was found lies used and trampled at my feet, wider than I last saw it. The walk takes less time than it did last time with the crowd holding me back, and when I arrive, the place is deserted.

Emerging from the trees, I step over the dozens of footprints left over the past couple of days. All that's left behind is what looks to be a memorial. I approach it slowly, kneeling in front of the pile of flowers and wreaths and extinguished candles. It all surrounds a single, framed picture of the boy I'd only met three times.

I wonder if Reyna brought it.

Over the past couple of days, I found that Anthony fit in with the other boys in the same way they fit in with each other. More than acquaintances, less than best friends, although he seemed particularly close with just one of the other victims. Xavier.

It feels a little bit more wrong, now, to tear into the lives of these people just for a job. It makes me stumble back from the memorial, unable to look at the picture any longer.

I wonder if I'll ever see Reyna again, if I'll finish the job before she comes home. If she'll come home at all.

I scope out the edge of the quarry for anything that looks out of the ordinary. They've released almost nothing about the report: just his name, and that the cause of death was drowning. They found no DNA on him, maybe because he drowned accidentally, but more likely because it all got washed away in the dark, gloomy quarry water.

It doesn't really make sense, though, why they found him here and not at the Ledge. According to Luna, the high schoolers are consistent in holding their parties there, but maybe they changed their location last night. Or maybe he just got drunk and wandered off. Scenarios run through my head, and it's times like this where it pains me that I may never know.

Being here is making me sick, so I do what Luna seems to do whenever she feels at the edge of the world. I go to the other quarry, the one that doesn't have death written all over it. Hoping it would give me signs of his life, where he'd been breathing and happy and partying with his friends at the Ledge.

It's a short walk and a straight shot. It would have been perfectly easy for Anthony to end up here the other night, to get from point A to point B. I try not to think about that as I follow what might have been the same path he took.

This quarry is as deserted as the other one and feels just as eerie. Only the absence of a memorial makes it feel a little more normal, a little brighter. A place of celebration, of parties.

It won't be for a long time, I bet. Maybe this way, people will stop disappearing.

I inwardly curse myself, because they're not just disappearing anymore. They're winding up dead.

Kicking the dirt up as I do so, I approach the edge of the quarry, peering over the railing and into the mysterious waters below. The one thought that keeps bugging me, over and over, is... how does someone drown in this thing? Anthony knew how to swim, according to gossip around town, and they found no evidence of blunt force trauma to the head, or anywhere else on his body. No marks, no signs of strangulation, no indication that Anthony was anything but completely awake when he was submerged. Nothing weighed him down, and the only remaining possibility is that his murderer got in with him and held him beneath the surface with their bare hands.

My stomach flips over at the thought, because who the hell could do that?

My toes play with a stone beneath my feet, and I run my fingers along the railing. It's in my way, standing five feet or so away from the edge. Too far. I need to look from above, not from a distance.

Delicately, I crouch below the railing, shimmying my way over to the other side. I hold the metal bar firmly as I do so, knuckles turning white. But once my footing is steady, I loosen the grip, allowing myself to walk along the edge

It's just a big bowl of water. And as far as I can tell, it goes straight down.

Down, down, down.

I let go of the railing completely, shuffling a few steps over. The edge doesn't slope toward the water, but rather shoots down like a cliff, the rock cut harshly back whenever the miners still worked here. The water ends about six inches below the edge, and I wonder how filled up it might be right after it rains.

I pull my glasses from my face, squinting to get a better look, but it seems to me there's nothing to look at. I'm not sure why I thought a body of water would hold all the answers, but I figure there must be a reason I'm drawn here over and over again.

Another reason flits into my mind, but I push it away, because now's not the time to-

I don't get the chance to finish my thought, because the ground isn't as smooth as it looks, and I feel my feet stumblebeneath me. Both my arms flail out to my sides: one hand searching for the railing, and the other hand holding my glasses, grasping hopelessly at the air. I lean to my left, trying to find something sturdy, but I'm too far. In my haste, my other hand opens up, trying to find a landmark sturdier than my glasses, and they slip from my grip.

"No!"

On instinct, and before I can stop myself, I plunge my body over the edge after them. A crippling mix of regret and fear wash over me before the water does, and the fall happens in slow motion, my hands grasping at the side of the rock, nails cracking as I try desperately to stop the descent.

The world goes cold. My feet make contact with the still, dark water, sending ripples across the entire basin while the rest of my body follows. In a moment, I'm submerged, the waiting water pulling me deep into its clutches. Panic climbs up my throat, and when I open my mouth to scream, nothing but bubbles come out. My limbs thrash around, trying to swim even though I seem to have lost all motor function. My heart thunders in my chest, growing too big for my body, making me sink deeper, deeper, deeper.

I remember what I'd thought when I found Luna out here the first time, how water like this isn't really water at all. It has a presence to it, a mind of its own, and it might just choose to keep me.

Rise, I remind myself. You need to go up.

Except there is no up. I move to swim, and find myself going nowhere at all. After a moment I convince myself to open my eyes-

Only to be surrounded by nothing but darkness.

A scream rips from my throat once more, except you need air to scream, and my lungs shrivel up, as empty as they've ever been. I blindly reach out, and I connect with what feels like stone, and it's blocking my way out, caging me in. I pound my fists against whatever barrier is above me (or is it beneath me? Beside me? It's all dark), but the water is slowing me down, making whatever strength I have futile, and I can't get out, I can't get out, *I can't get out-*

I realize all at once that this is it. This is exactly how someone drowns in a quarry.

The vague feeling of something else touching me, fingers wrapping around my wrist, stops me from gasping in even more water. I'm so distracted by that and the fuzziness in my brain, that I barely even notice myself being dragged, pulled away from wherever this water had taken me.

Light starts to snake through the water, piercing my burning eyes, until my head at last breaks through the surface. I gasp for breath, and regret it at once, half inhaling the water still in my throat. I cough and sputter, hacking up half a lung as I try to stay above the surface. A blurry film of water still blocks my vision, now joined by bursts of stars as I try not to pass out. My mouth bobs slightly below the surface again, but I'm wrenched up by someone, who manages to push me up against the edge of the quarry. The person punches fist after fist into my chest as I cough, trying to get the water from my lungs. A sharp piece of rock digs into my back, pulling at my spine, but I don't have the will to speak. All I can do is grip the person back, fingers digging into their shoulders, even as my feet can't find any bearing.

"Are you insane?"

I blink water from my eyes, recognizing Luna even through the many, many things obscuring my vision. In my drugged state, I realize I'd recognize her anywhere.

"Luna," I rasp out, coughing more at the attempt at speaking. Droplets of water fly from my lips, leaving my throat raw and destroyed.

She doesn't respond, only shakes me rougher against the rocks, grip around my arms now painfully tight. I hang limply in her grasp, trying to move my hands toward land, only to find more water. My fingers strain for something, *anything* steady, something that I can't drown in, but Luna is all there is.

"Luna," I say again, weakly, returning my hands to her shoulders. She wears a tank top, drenched and hanging heavily around her form.

"What the hell, Alex," she says through a voice crack, looking away, breaths scattered. I can feel them in the way she holds me. "Why did you- Why would you-"

"My glasses," I say weakly, turning to gaze at the water still twisting around us, rocking against the jagged cliff, trying to get a grip on me once more. I try to scurry away, even though there's nowhere to go.

"Your *glasses?*" she shrieks, letting go of me to pull at her hair. When the grip on my shoulders releases, I begin to slip under the surface again, but she catches me, settling me into the rocks again. I sob in relief, holding her tighter.

Through my tears, I nod, dumb and foggy, my brain still blurry from the water that made its way into my system. I don't try to speak, don't try to do anything else for fear that I might pass out. Then I'd *really* drown.

"Damnit," Luna croaks out, leaning forward to rest her forehead against mine. The sensation calms me down a bit, the feeling of something solid pressing against me, holding me steady. Her eyes are closed, but I keep mine open, peering at her face to the best of my ability through blurry vision. Her face is soaking wet from the water, but I can tell she's crying, too. Eyes lined with silver, red and raw, her lips tremble as we stay completely still, completely alive.

"I can see how dead bodies might end up here," I say weakly, recalling one of our first conversations. Those cave systems... all you have to do is get caught under one of those ledges, and it's nearly impossible to find your way out.

She doesn't laugh, only leans against me and rests her forehead against my shoulder, somehow still managing to keep me afloat. Her legs kick beneath her, knees and toes brushing against mine.

My fingers cling to her tighter, unsure whether it's to hold myself up or to hold her against me. But the crippling fear and suffocation around my lungs overrules the want to keep her close.

"Can we get out of the water now?" I beg, kicking my legs, heart seizing at the thought of fully submerging again. "Please?"

At the sound of my voice, Luna wrenches back, staring at me. "Yeah, yeah, we need to get out. Hold on, there's a pathway over to the left. Can you swim?"

Yes. No. Not right now. "Technically."

Luna nods, seeming to understand, and doesn't let go of me as we make our way along the side of the quarry. As we move over, the cliff behind us gets lower and lower, until it dips into land, a small trail waiting.

"Why is there an entrance?" I find myself asking, straining to reach the land, to get the hell out. "Doesn't that sort of defeat the point of the railings?"

"The railings are to keep people from falling in," Luna says flatly. "They don't stop people from making their own ways to go in. It's not really an entrance, people just used the path so often it's… ingrained in the woods."

I don't respond, because we've reached the edge. Almost weeping in relief, I lean over the edge, hugging the earth as I try and fail to pull myself out. My arms shake beneath me, unable to hold my weight, and I can't tell if I'm trembling from the cold, fear, lack of oxygen, or all three.

It's probably the lack of oxygen, because Luna hoists herself out with no problem. A wave of water tumbles from her clothes and skin as she stands, spilling into the mud at her feet. The land is sloped, and I watch as each drop of water rolls down the hill, inch by inch, back into the quarry at my side. My head follows the track, as water returns to water, home returns to home, ready to sink deep into the pit to wait for its next victim. This is perhaps the most disturbed I've seen these usually still waters, and it's wrong. This is supposed to be untouched, left alone, only to look at and admire.

I don't really think I'll be admiring a quarry anytime soon (as if the past couple of days haven't been enough evidence for that sentiment). I just want to get out.

"Hey, are you still with me?" Luna's gripping my face, wrenching my gaze upward once more. Her brows are furrowed, concerned. Maybe she thinks I'm having a meltdown.

"Yeah," I croak. "Mostly. Help?"

Crouching, she grips my triceps and pulls with everything she has, just enough to get me out of the water and lying face down in the dirt. Breaths stutter through my ribcage, and I dig my fingers into the soft ground beneath me. I curl in on myself, trying to hide my face as I shake and cry.

Luna only lets me rest for a moment. "Come on," she says, helping me up. "Out of the mud, onto the warm stone, let's go. You'll thank me in ten minutes."

Luna wraps her arm around me, taking the brunt of my weight as she lifts me. On quivering legs, we move slow as molasses up the small hill. I keep my eyes trained downward, focused on my feet to make sure they don't get tangled in one another. The dirt and weeds transform into stone, and we come out from beneath the trees and into the sunlight. I sigh at the warmth tingling across my skin, sapping the water from my clothes and hair. Luna's skin is warm against mine, and I wonder how that could be, because isn't she as wet as I am?

Together, we collapse onto the gravel, my back smacking harshly against the hard ground. The sun is painfully bright compared to the darkness of the water, and I raise my hand to the sky, blinking the brilliance away. Feeling overwhelmingly heavy, dripping with water and soreness and a weight I can't quite describe, I close my eyes once more, focusing on my breathing. On the *air*.

"I still feel like I can't breathe," I gasp, splaying my fingers across my chest, brushing the skin just beneath my collarbone. It's still cool from the water, but warmth bleeds in from where I touch, absorbing the sun and comfort Luna gave me.

"That'll happen when you almost drown," Luna agrees, sounding just as breathless. I tilt my head to the left where she lies, only to find her already squinting at me.

Furrowing my brows, I ask, "How long were you under?"

Huffing, she presses her lips together. "Not as long as you, but… long enough."

"How did you know I was under there?"

"I saw you," she whispers. "You know that I… come here sometimes, I had just gotten here, but I saw you and didn't want to interrupt, you know, whatever you were doing. I don't know why I didn't just leave."

I want to tell her she must know why, and that I need her to tell me, but I can't get the words out.

She continues, eyes lowered. A shining water droplet falls from her lashes, tracking down the curve of her nose and landing on her cheek. "I didn't see you drop your glasses, though, I just thought you… jumped in. I was so baffled I couldn't move for a good ten seconds, which was too damn long…" She trails off, words catching in her throat. "By the time I got to the edge, I couldn't even see you, but I just had a feeling you were caught under the edge-"

Before my mind can catch up, I reach out, cupping her cheek to wipe away what might be a tear, but could just be the remnants of the quarry water. "Thank you," I murmur, not having to speak any louder across the small gap between us. "I- Thank you. You didn't need to come in after me, I know how… I mean, I don't know *why*, but I know how you feel about the water."

"I didn't even think about it," she croaks out, making my heart skip a beat. "I just… I wouldn't lose you to that, not like-"

She cuts herself off, turning away, and my hand drops to the rocks below.

"Luna," I whisper, willing her to look at me again. She doesn't. "Tell me."

She flicks a strand of wet hair aside, sending it smacking against her shoulders. The way she's lying on her back, I can see the rapid rise and fall of her chest, stuttering and unsteady. Wind whistles through the trees behind her, a soft, warm summer breeze rustling her limp clothes. She's biting her lip so hard I fear she might draw blood, and we stay stone still, as motionless as the statues in her sculpture yard.

"One of the worst quarrying accidents in history happened right here."

I'd almost given up hope that she'd respond by the time she speaks, and I jerk back to attention. She's still staring up at the sky, eyes following the clouds, looking anywhere but at me.

"In this quarry? Or just in West Rutland?"

"This one," Luna confirms. "In 1893. They dropped this huge stone that they were pulling out back into the pit. Killed seven people, injured a lot more."

Horrified, but a little confused as to why an accident in 1893 related to Luna, I say, "That's terrible."

"It was, but that's not my point. A tragedy like that, it sets off a sort of chain reaction. Have you noticed that the water in this one doesn't seem quite as dark, it's a little more transparent?"

Honestly, I admit, "No."

She lifts a shoulder. "I guess you wouldn't, you haven't spent nearly as much time here as I have. Particularly over the past year or so."

I wait, keeping my mouth shut, not wanting to interrupt whatever flow she's gotten herself into.

She swallows hard, and the knot in her throat goes up and down. "It's easier to see through because it's not nearly as deep as the others. You know how I said most quarries go hundreds of feet down? How this one is shallower than the rest? It only goes about fifty feet down. Still deep, still dangerous, but not nearly as intimidating as the others. I find it's more psychological than anything."

Something clicks as I think about how this is the quarry that the high schoolers choose to go to; the path behind the school leads directly here. This is where the parties are, where there's the most history. And most importantly, this is the only quarry I've found Luna at.

She speaks what I've realized before I can.

"That accident is why they stopped mining in this particular quarry ages ago. It's why everyone chooses this one to go swimming in, to hang out at, to hold parties."

My mind races a million miles a minute, flashes of moments before coming back to me, images of someone getting taken, probably similarly to how I almost just got taken.

"Something else happened here, too," she says, that bitterness in her voice becoming more and more pronounced. "Something more than that tragedy in 1893, and it wasn't just an accident this time."

Inching closer to her, trying to send over some sort of comfort as she begins to shake, I ask, "What is it?"

"I have a brother, you know."

I jerk up, because, no she doesn't. I know for a *fact* that she doesn't.

As if reading my mind, she purses her lips and says, "Well, technically I don't, but it's felt like that for a long time. That he was ours."

I hold my breath, waiting for her to go on. I'm afraid if I move even a muscle, whatever spell she's under might break, and she might run off.

She goes on. "My aunt and uncle died in a car crash four years ago. They had a son." She swallows hard. "Carlos."

Something rings in my memory, and I do my best not to show it on my face. *Carlos. Son. He.* The *he* Ruth mentioned, the *he* Luna nearly breaks down over every time he's mentioned. The Carlos who my brother had once known.

And if I had to hazard a guess, he's probably the person I saw her visiting at the hospital.

I don't say anything though as she chokes on the next words, wrestling them with her tongue. "He was, like, eight years younger than me, and most of the time siblings with that kind of age gap don't have much in the way of a relationship-" I think of Reyna and Anthony, and my heart twists, "-but we were always best friends. That's why he moved in with us instead of my other aunt."

I do the math in my head. He must be, what, only a freshman or sophomore in high school? Fourteen? Fifteen?

"We never formally adopted him," Luna whispers, so low that if I weren't so close, I wouldn't be able to make out the words, "because we thought it would be disrespectful to his parents, but we might as well have. After the adjustment period, he became... part of the family. Even though he kept his last name, he was a Morgan. In my heart, at least."

Different last name. That's why he never came up when I researched her. I push the thought away, because my job is the last thing I should be thinking about right now. It's the last thing I *want* to be thinking about.

She chokes through the next words, and because she's lying down, tears fall down the sides of her face, toward her ear. Reaching out with a shaking hand, I wipe them away before they fall into her hair. "I... I-"

I almost tell her to stop, that she doesn't need to go on, I don't need to hear it. And it's true, I don't. But there's something about the way she lies there, staring directly at the sun with a heaving chest that makes me believe she might need to say it.

I move closer to her, reaching towards the hand resting on her stomach. I run my thumb across the back of her palm, slipping my fingers into hers. She grips my hand deathly tight, and I squeeze back. "I can't help heal a wound I can't see," I whisper. "You have to show me."

She turns to look at me for only a moment, eyes wet with silver, before looking back to the sky. "He got invited to a party," she says, voice weak and gravelly from the grief shaking her body. "He was so excited, because freshmen never get invited. But he played soccer. He'd spent all summer at this camp over in Rutland that was supposed to only be for varsity, but the coach thought he was too good to be stuck in the younger camp. That's... that's where he got to know *your* brother. Parker would give him rides to and from Rutland."

I imagine it, Luna and I linked far before we'd ever met.

"He had so much fun that summer, and he was *so bummed* when it ended and school was about to start. Which is why he nearly lost his mind when some of the upperclassmen from the camp decided to bring him along. Initiation ritual, or something ridiculous. They thought he'd be the first freshman to make varsity in, like, ten years." Her lips tremble, tears falling steadily now, too fast for me to wipe clean. "I offered to go with him, because I was nervous, but he laughed and asked what I would do at a high school party." She laughs wetly, but there's no humor to it. "He was right, of course, I had no place there." She pauses, sucking in a great breath through a hiccup. "I still should have gone, though."

"What happened?" I whisper, and even though I can't imagine the specifics, my mind is steadily approaching a heartbreaking ending. One that leaves a boy in the hospital since the end of last summer, when soccer season was still in full swing.

She gasps, trying to regain control over her vocal cords, and there's nothing I can do but hold her tighter as she sobs, "He got stuck where you did when they threw him in. *Exactly* where you did. Except they didn't find him as quickly as I did. They didn't find him in time."

I suck in a harsh breath, the remaining water from the quarry weighing down on me even more.

"He was under for too long, unconscious. It did something to his brain, irreparable damage. A lot of it. He flitted in and out of consciousness for about a week, and we thought there was a chance he might recover, but then he went under, and... stayed there."

With the last of the words out, she turns toward me and buries her face into the crook of my neck. Instinct takes over, and I throw one arm over the top of her, slinking the other one beneath. I pull her to my chest, trying to calm the sobs wracking her body, to still the trembling of her shoulders.

Nine months, the boy has been in the hospital unresponsive. Not dead, but... dead in every way that counts.

"I'm so sorry," I whisper into her hair. "I'm... God."

Sniffling, she stays pressed into me as she says, "I never found out exactly who did it. He had no outside injuries, no signs of anyone else's DNA, it's the same problem they're facing now. Nobody saw, and nobody talked. There were so many people at that party, it was a beginning of school thing, *everyone* was there..."

"People are terrible," I mutter, quoting what she had said to me only a few weeks ago. It had been true when she told me, but this... "People can be evil," I amend. "So, so cold hearted."

"I visit him every week in the hospital," she murmurs. "At least. I don't even know why at this point. Nothing changes, and all it does is tear me apart, but... I need to see him."

"I'm sure he knows you're there," I say, even though I'm not. "Subconsciously or otherwise."

"I hope so."

I don't ask whether or not the doctors think he'll ever wake up. The answer is written all over her face. Instead of saying anything, I just squeeze tighter, shielding her from the blinding sun and everything else.

Chapter Sixteen

I DON'T KNOW HOW long it is before Luna rolls away from me, just slightly, her shoulder and hand still pressed to mine. All I know is my clothes and hair are completely dry, and the sun has traveled quite a bit across the sky. It shines through the trees behind her, peeking out from the hollow between her neck and shoulder. She shifts, nestling her cheek further into the stone and closer to me. Tangled hair spreads out behind her, tickling my fingers when I try to catch a strand in my hand. The glow of what seems to be the beginning of a sunset turns her entire being into a golden orange, casting an ethereal haze down her hair and neck. It reminds me of the candle, and I figure living entirely during that time just before dusk wouldn't be terrible, either. I dig my shoulder into the ground, keeping myself nailed down when I long to reach out and caress those warm spots of skin exposed to the sun, exposed to me. To hold her not simply because she's hurting, but just for the sake of holding her.

Even with her face cast into shadows, the slow spread of her lips and delicate curve of her lashes transfixes me. It soothes my heart to see her smile, as weak as it might be.

"You're staring," she scolds me.

"I am," I admit dumbly, shameless. I'm surprised she hasn't called me out on it earlier. "Do you want me to stop?"

"Only because I look like a gremlin who's been crying for a day and a half." Her voice is scratchy, raw from crying, and she clears her throat.

I turn my head, letting it swing in the other direction, where the still quarry waits. Always waiting. Just looking at it now makes my stomach flip, for more than one reason.

I return my gaze to her, eyes blazing in the sun. "Show me somewhere else?"

Her lips part. "What?"

I motion behind me, not wanting to look at it again. "Just looking at it makes me want to pass out right now."

"Welcome to the club."

I pause in my thoughts, eyes widening. "I can't believe you jumped in after me."

This time, it's her that reaches out, playing with a strand of hair plastered to my cheek. "I'll always jump in after you."

"No, you won't," I say seriously. "Not here, anyway, which is precisely why we should get out of here. To someplace that hasn't caused... an insurmountable amount of pain."

Luna's throat tightens, a muscle feathering in her jaw. "I used to love it here, like everyone else. I always begged my mom to let me go swimming in it when I was a kid, but she wouldn't let me. I get it now."

I hoist myself up onto an elbow, the strength I'd lost during my almost-drowning still returning. My shadow falls across her chest, and she stares up at me. "So, take me somewhere else. Somewhere happier. I know it's a small town and all, but there must be someplace better than here."

Luna blinks, considering, before her eyes flash with an idea. "Yeah, okay." She hoists herself up, and I rise with her, our hands falling away from each other for the first time in what feels like hours (it actually might have been). My legs wobble, and Luna reaches out to steady me. "Still woozy?"

"For more reasons than one," I say. "But it's not from the water, if that's what you mean."

"It's what I meant," she murmurs, although she now looks like she kind of wants to know what *I* meant. She doesn't address it, though, and instead nods toward the path leading away from the clearing. "Let's get out of here. Preferably as fast as possible."

"YOU BROUGHT ME TO *another* cliff?"

She had me pull over onto a small ridge on the edge of the road. A road which precariously drops down to a river about fifteen feet below.

"*One*," Luna says as we both climb out of my jeep, "it's not a cliff. Two, the quarry is also not a cliff considering you can only fall approximately six inches into the water. Three, we're not even there yet."

I wonder why we stopped driving if we're not there yet, but I decide not to question her and simply slam the door shut. The sun had completely set during the twenty or so minute drive, and we walk together up the dark, dirt road, the only illumination coming from the clear night sky, the moon and the stars.

"You should know that my expectations are exceedingly low," I say as we hike uphill, and I peer over the side of the road to see that the cliff is getting smaller and smaller. My eyes follow the edge, up and around the corner until the road leads to-

A covered bridge.

I glance at Luna, and from the way she's slowing down, I can tell this is our destination. "The spots in this town are so weird," I breathe.

Luna gazes at the tall bridge before us, giving me a tentative glance. "Technically we're not in West Rutland anymore, but covered bridges are about as Vermont as you can get, even more so than quarries."

We walk until we're standing just in front of the mouth. The bridge is in a fairly obscure spot, so I'm not surprised that there's not a car in sight. "I've never actually seen one of these in real life. Just pictures, or paintings. I always thought they were pretty. *Rustic.*"

"Rustic's definitely the word for pretty much everything around here."

I glance at her. "So, what is it about the bridge? Or did you just want to show me something pretty. I wouldn't be opposed, it's working."

Luna smiles, and she must have just licked her lips, because they're reflecting the moonlight. "It's not just pretty. This is a special one, I've got it rigged."

"You've got it *what?*"

Grabbing my arm, she pulls me into the entrance, where we're engulfed in darkness. Slivers of light flicker in through the windows on the side, and I hug the walls, running my finger along the ledge. "Here," Luna stops us when we reach just past the midway point, and to my surprise, she hops up on the ledge.

"Luna," I say carefully. "What-"

"It's safe," she says, reaching up and out the window, towards the roof. And to my never ending surprise, a rope ladder tumbles down in front of her. Swinging herself through the window, she gives the rope a tug, securing the bottom to a tiny hook at her feet.

"Are you kidding me?" I gape as she places a foot on the first rung. "Please tell me you weren't the one who put that there."

Her head pokes between two of the wooden rungs, and she rests her chin on one. "Technically it was me and my high school friends, but I'll happily take the credit."

Warily, I say, "That doesn't look secure."

"It's stable." She knocks her knuckles against it, the sound of bone against wood echoing around the hollow bridge. "It's never failed me in the past seven years. I'll even go first, if it makes you feel better."

"You do realize this might result in me falling into *another* body of water?" I say skeptically.

She grins and repeats the same words from earlier. "If you do, I'll jump in after you. But you won't." She snorts. "Besides, you didn't even fall last time, you *jumped.*"

Suddenly defensive, I say, "I sort of fell." I also sort of jumped.

Luna taps her toe on the ground, lifting herself further up the ladder. "You wanted me to take you somewhere. Now you have to keep your word."

The moon is behind her, so I can barely make out the silhouette of her face. But as I squint, even without my glasses, I can see how soft and vulnerable her face has become, fingers gripping the ladder like she was gripping me earlier.

I seam my lips together, before spreading my fingers over the window sill. "Make room, then."

Smiling as wide as ever, and making my heart soar, she begins climbing the ladder, allowing me to take her spot on the ledge. I have an iron grip on the nearest rung, which is actually fairly steady since she tied off the bottom. My legs tremble, but I watch as Luna pulls herself onto the roof with ease.

It's only five rungs or so. It's barely anything at all.

Luna peeks her head back over the edge, and she seems to be lying on her stomach. "Don't be afraid," she whispers.

"I'm not," I say, even though I am.

She holds out her hand, she fingertips just out of reach. It's enough for me to put my weight on the ladder, and begin to climb.

The roof is surprisingly flat. I don't know why I expected it to be slanted, but as soon as Luna hoists me over the edge, I feel like I'm on solid ground. I fall down beside Luna, gripping her waist as I laugh.

Luna looks up from where she's positioned over me, surveying our surroundings. "Feels good, doesn't it?"

The wind and height snatch all the breath from my lungs, and I place my hand over my beating heart in an effort to calm it. And even though I don't want to move out from under her, I sit up, because I want to see, too.

My eyes widen at the view. Mountains and trees and greenery tower around us, rising to put us in some sort of valley. The night is made up of blues and purples, black and greens, and I don't need to wonder whether Luna has taken painting inspiration from this view. Whether she consciously paints from life or not, I know she has. I can tell from the way her eyes shine as she takes it all in, the same way mine surely do. That same river flows beneath us, water glimmering with the white reflection of the moon. It looks nothing like the quarry water, which was dark, and gloomy, and all encompassing. This is… calm. Light, peaceful. Just a thin stream of water that will briefly pass through our lives, only to leave again.

That's what water should do.

"Thank you," I whisper. "This is exactly what I meant."

Luna turns to me, her smile more dazzling than the stars. "I know. You should have trusted me."

I huff. "I trusted you, I just didn't trust the ladder." I tip my head back towards the sky, at the galaxy winking back at me. "I can't see the stars in the city. I mean, I can, but… not like this."

Nothing is like this.

"The universe would be empty without stars," she says. "It would be… nothing. We would be nothing."

"It's a good thing there's too many to get rid of," I say, overwhelmed by the number of dots dancing above us. I never fully comprehended that the sky would look so different without all the light pollution. I thought the bad view was mostly due to distance, that I'd need to get a really good telescope in order to see what they show in pictures in real life.

Turns out I just needed to come here, where there isn't an unnatural light in sight.

"How would you even do that?" she asks. "Could you even get rid of a star?"

"I hope not. I know they explode sometimes, but that has nothing to do with us. It's nice that there's beauty out there that we can't touch."

She gives me a sideways glance. "Because they're too hot."

"I was thinking too far, but yeah, that too."

Luna laughs before reclining back onto the wood of the roof. To my relief, I don't hear a single creak, only the rustling of her skin against it as she settles in. Taking her cue, I lean back as well, only a tiny bit afraid of sliding off.

Reading my mind once more, she says, "It's flatter than you think, it's all in your head. Relax."

I huff out a breath, but do as I'm told, lying down so my shoulder presses into hers. She's wearing a tank top, and her skin is warm where it touches mine.

She hums beside me, before turning her head to look at me. She's so close, the warm puff of breath flutters across my cheek. "Do you ever think about how if we stayed out here long enough, still enough, we'd eventually see the stars move?"

I gaze up, stars flashing against my eyes, so that even when I close them, long remnants of light remain against the dark backdrop. "No. I guess I've never sat still long enough for that to be possible, or to even have time to consider it."

"I always forget," she says softly, voice smooth as silk. "That we're the ones moving, and the universe surrounding us stays the same, keeping us still."

"How long would it take?" I ask. I raise my hand, pointing towards the sky. "Like, if I stood and stared at the star just above that tree, how long until it disappears behind the branches?"

She shrugs. "Too long. That's what makes the illusion that the stars are constant."

"The stars *are* constant," I correct her. "We're the ones that aren't."

"I don't know," she says, turning to face me. "I feel pretty constant right now."

The only thing that feels overwhelmingly constant right now is where our hands brush together, making my stomach swoop low. "Is that good?" I ask, ignoring the way my voice catches. "Consistency?"

"Depends. Most of the time? No, I'd like some change. But right this moment?"

I feel her head loll to the side before I see it out of the corner of my eye. The tip of her chin brushes my shoulder, and even through the thin cloth of my T-shirt, it makes me shiver. I remain eerily still, trying to catch my breath, but my lungs quiver with the effort.

"I don't want to ever move," she whispers into my neck. "I'd stay up here for eternity."

The words sink into the pit of my gut, and I decide all at once that I won't make her move. I'll do it myself.

Rolling to the side, I shift so my upper body hovers over her, bracing a hand on her far side. The momentum makes me press into her, a small gasp fluttering from her parted lips. She settles further onto her back as she watches me, eyes wide and bright from all those stars, the ones I'd never noticed before.

"Me too," I whisper.

She comes to me. A flare of impatience mixed with a smile crosses her face as she lifts herself, reaching toward me. Her lips meet mine before I even have a chance to move, bridging the last of the gap between us that's been wearing thinner and thinner all evening. Perhaps the entire time I've known her. I don't have the time or strength to act surprised, allowing my body to ease into hers as her arms snake up around my hips, pulling me down into her, closer. Cold fingers trace patterns into my skin, trailing up and over my hip bone, across my back, beneath the hem of my shirt. Her touch slow and methodical, I imagine her with a paintbrush, inking us against a canvas and making us into something beautiful.

A vision of Artemis and Callisto, had they gotten the happy ending they deserved.

I'm so distracted by what her hands are doing I almost forget to pay attention to her lips. Cupping her face with the hand I'm not using to hold myself up, I fall deeper and deeper into the kiss, exploring the soft curves of her mouth. A bubbly feeling courses through my veins, and I can hardly contain my smile,

Her hands are still roaming around my hips, lingering near the hem of my jeans.

"I'm sort of afraid of falling off the roof," I murmur into her lips, and I can feel her smile. "I'm slowly losing control of my motor and mental controls."

I pull away just enough to get a good look at her face, and I actually *do* almost fall off the roof. Her pupils are blown wide, making dark eyes even darker. Blood rushed to her face and neck, peppering her dark golden skin with a rosy tint. She doesn't give me long to look, though, because she's looking at me, too.

Murmuring a soft, "Good," she fires back up toward me, twisting us until I feel the hard wood panels pressing into my shoulder blades. Pressure comes from both sides, and I kiss her back readily, basking in the fact that my hands are finally free.

Shivering, she pulls at my bottom lip with her teeth. "Better?" she asks, effectively pinning me down.

I nod mutely.

She leans back into me, softer this time, pressing a delicate kiss to the corner of my mouth. "I won't let you fall."

I won't let her fall either.

Chapter Seventeen

"PLEASE TELL ME YOU'RE not hooking up with the townspeople. I'm actually begging you."

I don't have the energy to be annoyed, eyes still stiff with sleep. My mattress threatens to lull me back to bed, and I have half a mind to just hang up on her if this is what she called about. "One, I am definitely not hooking up with multiple townspeople. Two, how do you even know I'm hooking up at all?"

Elise sounds like she's pacing around the office, because her speaker is muffled like she's moving. "Call it an instinct."

"Well, your instincts suck," I say, wrestling myself out of bed. Elise is making a bad habit of waking me up before nine a.m., and I'm not loving it.

"You've been there for over a month," Elise presses into the phone. "Am I going to have to drive to Vermont to drag you back home when this is all over and done with?"

I laugh, but there's no humor behind it, because a sour taste has dripped into my throat, a remnant of the night before.

"Seriously," Elise says, all hyperbole gone as I stumble toward my dresser. "I need you to remember that you have a life here. I know your last couple of months were shit stacked on shit, but you can't think about that. Your life, your *good* life, is waiting, okay?"

My stomach twists, and I rub at my temple, a headache already creeping in. Knowing that I might be giving myself away, I mumble, "I'm not talking about this."

"Alex!"

"I'm not *talking* about this," I stress, "because there's nothing to talk about. Stop being a pest."

"Fine," she grumbles, sounding unconvinced and pissed off. My head begins to pound even more. "Although if either of us is a pest, it's you."

"Just tell me why you called," I say, desperate to change the subject.

"Asking for an update. If you haven't been too… busy."

I ignore her. "There's not much, the body they found revealed pretty much nothing about who did it because they found him in the water. We're shit out of luck."

She pauses a moment, the only sound being a few papers ruffling. And then-

"Maybe we should call it quits?"

And there it is. My head completely explodes.

"What?" I ask, trying to keep the desperation from my voice. "What- what do you mean?"

"Change courses. Find your brother, and *come back home-*"

The thought is so ludicrous I almost hang up on principle. "Elise… I'm not just here for that anymore. There's *so much more here*."

"Are you even finding anything?" she asks. "I mean, is there anything to find at all?"

"Elise, five boys are dead."

"And no leads."

"They found a body less than a week ago!"

"With no evidence!"

I groan, kicking my bed frame, but before I can argue any further, my ears perk up. I whip my head towards my door, through which is the unmistakable sound of a key turning. And the only other person who has a key is-

"I have to go," I say, hanging up before Elise can get a word out. Tossing my phone on the bed, I practically sprint from my room, flinging the door open to find her just closing the front one.

It occurs to me too late that this might have been a mistake, that I should have given her space.

But then she turns around to see me, and I can't back away.

"You're back," I say, which is just about the lamest opener ever.

Dark bags circle her eyes, hanging low on her cheek bones because she probably hasn't slept in days. "Yeah, I- temporarily, I have to…" she trails off, voice shaky and frail.

"I'm so sorry," I whisper, barely loud enough for the words to travel across the room. "Your brother, I…" I trail off, too, because what do you even say?

She closes her eyes with a nod, walking further into the room. "Thank you."

I stand awkwardly in my doorway, and I have half a mind to just go back inside and leave her be. But she clearly has other ideas, because instead of entering her own room, she stalks toward me.

She braces herself, hugging her bag to her chest. "So. Have you found anything?"

My blood freezes. "What?"

"I know why you're here," she says, and to my relief she sounds not angry, but eager.

I, on the other hand, turn into a stuttering mess. "Wha… h-how, I don't-"

She jabs her thumb to the wall, where our two rooms wait. "Extraordinary thin walls. I've heard a couple phone calls. Noise travels."

Cursing myself, I run a hand through my hair. "Um."

"I wasn't even trying to listen," she says. "But you didn't think I was home, so you were talking rather loudly, and-"

"It's okay," I say quickly, even as panic swirls in my gut.

She lifts her hands, beginning to pace. "I mean, at first I thought you were an undercover cop, and then I started spiraling because I was like *what if she's with the FBI* or something ridiculous, but there's no way they would let you have a roommate-"

"Reyna," I try to calm her down.

"I'm not gonna rat you out or anything. I just…" Her hands drop, desperate. *"Have you found anything?"*

Oh, God, this is so much worse, because I have to look her in the eye, and painstakingly shake my head.

Her face falls, but she doesn't look overly surprised. "I... yeah, I sort of figured. Nobody..." She pinches the bridge of her nose, and for a moment, I fear she might cry. But she just inhales deeply, and asks, voice wavering, "You're staying, right? You're... you're staying to help, you're gonna do... whatever it is you do?"

Elise's voice echoes in my head, but it's quieter than before, and I can almost act like I can't hear it at all. "I'm staying. Until we know exactly who this monster is."

I IGNORE FOUR MORE calls from Elise before lunch, and it's starting to feel like I left not just one ex-girlfriend behind in New York, but two.

It's only when I finally leave the house to get something to eat, tiptoeing past Reyna's room, that I push everything from my mind, until only one person remains.

And remains and remains and remains.

When I reach Main Street, I linger in front of Suzie's for longer than I care to admit. What time is it, noon? The odds of her being on her lunch break are... high, to say the least, and Jo will be in there. If Elise could read me over the phone, I can't *imagine* the story my face is painting. I mean, this isn't *exactly* the walk of shame, but isn't it though? It sort of feels like it.

"You look stressed."

I spin around to see Luna approaching me with slow steps, eyebrows high on her forehead. She's dressed in simple jeans and a dark blue tank top, and she slips her fingers into her pockets.

Flustered, I stutter, "No, I... um-"

Lips pulling into something between a smirk and sheepish smile, Luna says, "You're well known in there at this point. You sort of look like you did when you first got here."

Anxious. On edge. Out of place.

The corner of my mouth quirks up. "Is that an insult? You didn't like me in the first week."

Slyly, she says, "Oh, I liked you. Don't convince yourself that I didn't."

Last night, I dropped her off at her place. It's always so much easier at night- the moments after- when we're both hiding in the shadows, content with silence. You can never be quiet during the daytime, or else people comment on it. I thought about inviting her over, because I have the courage to do that when the sun is down, but she shook her head. She had an early shift this morning, and she said if she came over to mine, she wouldn't sleep at all.

The memory makes me flush, and eases my nerves.

"Would it be weird if I kissed you?" I blurt out, cringing. God, I've been single for five months and I've already forgotten how to operate.

Her face splits into a teasing grin. "I think it'd be weird if you didn't."

We kiss in the daylight, and the ice breaks now that the sun has risen.

"Are you done with work for the day?" I ask when we pull apart, needing conversation, some sort of distraction to remind me that we're still standing in the middle of a public street.

"Yeah," she says, and the way her smile lingers makes my stomach twist. "Are you?"

No. Never. Not while I'm here.

"Been up since the crack of dawn," I lie. "I'm all yours."

Biting her lip, she takes my hand and drags me into the diner. "Good. The way to my heart is an omelet."

"I think I've got that covered," I say, sliding into a booth next to her.

"Ladies!" Jo's voice booms across the diner, and she slides out from behind the counter to join us. A smile paints her face, but her posture sags a little heavier than usual.

The whole *town* is a little heavier than usual. Maybe it's because when they're only disappearances, you can convince yourself the boys are still alive. It's a little harder to do that now. They might as well have found all five bodies last week.

"Fancy seeing you here," I say, trying to keep my voice upbeat, because the hint of melancholy behind her eyes is too much for me to take.

"Good one," she says drily. To my relief, she doesn't make a comment about Luna and me, or how close we're sitting, and simply asks what we're eating.

"She took it hard," Luna murmurs as Jo glides away, hunched over as she heads toward another couple a few booths away. "Anthony's death."

I turn to face her, tugging one of legs up beneath me. "Did she know him well?"

"She knows just about everyone, but yeah. He never worked here- too young- but a bunch of his friends do, he comes in all the time after practices and stuff."

The words *too young* echo around my skull, and they make me realize something. During my one, brief conversation with Reyna's brother, he told me he was going to be a senior in the fall. Not a fresh graduate, like the rest of the boys. He's a full year younger than every single other victim.

Why? Accident? Victim of opportunity, or did they just get the wrong guy?

I push the thoughts away, eyes returning to Jo as she disappears into the kitchen. "It's horrible. She's seen so many go." A memory surfaces, and I twist back toward her. "Hey, remember when you were first telling me about the quarries, and you mentioned how they had dead bodies?"

"Vaguely, but that's because people make that joke a lot." She pauses, tracing a finger along the table. "We probably won't be doing that anymore. At least for a while."

"Did you suspect, then, that the boys might have drowned?"

She shifts, blowing air out through her nose. "Not entirely. They've found more than one body there in the past, but I figured it could be a possibility. Especially since they searched every inch of the town and didn't find anything. The only places they missed were beneath the water."

I shiver at the thought of the search parties earlier in the summer, before I arrived. They went out week after week, disappearance after disappearance, and got nothing. Only increasingly desperate and hopeless.

Jo comes back to deliver the food, sliding the plates in front of us. Her eyes flicker between the two of us before saying, "I forgot to ask, checks together or separate?"

Before Luna can speak, I hold up a finger. "Just the one."

Jo smiles, and for the first time in a while, it's genuine. "I thought it might be. Enjoy the food, girls."

Luna leans back, giving me a sideways glance. "Is that your way of claiming this as a date?"

I shrug. "Hey, I'm plenty chivalrous."

Teasing, Luna traces a finger along my knee and mutters, "Pretty weak first date."

"Um, I'm pretty sure this is our *second* date." I lift my brows, even as I shiver at her touch. "What, was yesterday not satisfactory enough?"

She swats at my leg. "It's not a date if you don't go in with the intention of it being a date."

"Oh, I think you went in with plenty of intention. You cornered me on top of a bridge."

"*You* kissed *me!*"

Technically not true, although I'll concede that I initiated it.

I grin. "Oh, sure, yell it a little louder. I don't think the entire town heard you."

She slices into her omelet, and I pull my plate closer. "I actually think it'd be possible. Our entire population could fit into one of your city's snazzy apartment buildings."

"No, it couldn't," I insist, pulling up short. "Right? No. There's no way."

She swallows. "It's true. Our population is barely fifteen hundred on a good day, and there can be up to a thousand apartment spaces in a single city building. And sure, maybe some rooms are singles, but some of them will also house four or five. You do the math."

My jaw goes slack as I do just that, finding that she's right. "God, I hate perspective."

"Perspective is a bitch," Luna agrees. "Humans should be allowed to remain ignorant within reason."

"And the knowledge that this whole town could fit in one building is something I certainly never needed to acknowledge," I agree. "Is it weird that this place feels bigger the longer I'm here?"

"West Rutland?"

"Yeah, because you're right, when I first got here, I was like, a medium sized giant could step on this town with his one big toe, but now..." I shake my head, gazing out the window. "Maybe it's because it's started feeling like an actual place, and not just a cardboard cutout of a place."

It's true. When I arrived, all West Rutland was to me was five names on a page, and a whole lot of unknown. Now it's one name, and that name has nothing to do with the job I came here to do.

Luna's scrutinizing my face, and I only notice once I pull myself from my thoughts. "I could tell, you know," she says, taking a bite of hashbrowns. My pancakes didn't come with a side, so I reach over and scoop some into my spoon.

"Tell what?"

"That this was temporary," she says, a sliver of nerves entering her voice. "Even before you told me about Parker. I mean, you chose to move here, but you looked miserable," She smiles, poking at the corner of my mouth that seems permanently upturned in her presence. "You look less miserable now."

I huff out a laugh. "Oh, just less miserable? That's reassuring."

"Progress is progress. I'm just saying, you know when you uproot a tree?"

Surprised by the change, I slowly drawl, "Not in practice, but yes."

She rests her hand flat on the table. "Right, so when you take the tree away from its surroundings, it freaks out, and doesn't immediately adapt to its new habitat. And in that time period, its life starts to flounder, until it takes root. Then... it starts growing again."

"Are you trying to say I've finally taken root?"

She smiles, not quite shyly, because Luna doesn't seem to get shy, but about as close to shy as I've ever seen her. "Well, I'd like to think so."

My hand reaches out to hers, fingers entwined together, and I think that if Luna were to paint it, she'd show two roots coming together, finding solace in new, sturdy ground.

Chapter Eighteen

"WHAT DO YOU DO besides painting?"

Luna follows me from the diner, and I swing around to hold open the door. "Like… what?"

I shrug. "I don't know. The only two things I've seen you do are paint and work."

"Oh, well if that's how we're playing this, the only things I've ever seen you do are…" she trails off, glancing at me. "Nothing. I mean, not in a bad way, and it's probably because you always come to find me, never the other way around, but…"

"It's my lack of roots. Don't take it personally."

"I totally take it personally. Tell me what you do." She holds up her hand before I even have a chance to open my mouth. "And not what you do for work. What do you *do*?"

I think about telling her that I lied that night in the bar, when I was trying to turn the topic away from my real career. That I actually do spend more than a fair number of times with my nose in pages: my own writing, or otherwise.

And then I remember that she specifically told me *not* to mention my job.

And *then* it occurs to me that I... can't really think of anything else.

I slow to a stop on the edge of the road, running my hands down my face.

Luna smiles hesitantly, nudging me. "Is that a... hard question?"

I look at her tiredly, nearly twenty five years of exhaustion hitting me like a brick. "You have no idea."

"Tell me," she says, tugging at my hand to keep walking. She turns around to face me, walking backward, and she can do that because she knows this town like the back of her hand. "I don't care how you answer the question, just... answer it."

I think about whining about how I asked her first, but then just end up sighing. "I don't know. I don't know if I ever said, but my parents were extremely... work centered."

She slows her pace, returning to my side. "You didn't. You've never mentioned them, besides the fact that they..." Died. And that one of them had an affair. Yeah.

"We never got along," I say coolly. "I mean, I guess technically we did, in all the cordial, surface level ways. But we never really knew each other, if that makes sense. I never got the chance."

"Because they weren't home?"

"Yeah. And even when they were, they weren't actually *there*. Technology is a great thing, but it also eliminates boundaries and breaks. I suppose it doesn't matter, they never wanted a break anyway."

"Capitalism can be a crime sometimes, I swear."

I focus ahead, although I don't really know what I'm looking at. "And it's fine, whatever, they did what they had to do and so did I. But kids mimic their parents, don't they? Whether they admire their parents or not."

"It's a pride thing," Luna supplies. "It's a kid's natural instinct to want to make their parents proud. Particularly when the parents don't show their pride."

I glance at her, the words panging deep in my chest. "Makes sense. I guess that's what I was trying for, because I picked a career so freaking young, and proceeded to focus on… nothing else. No hobbies, no extracurriculars, just this… one thing, because that's what they did."

Luna squeezes my hand.

"And I grew up in a city," I add. "So there's that. Maybe exploring New York could be considered a hobby."

"That's totally a hobby," Luna assures me. "There are so many things to do in a city like that, you could waste away a lifetime. But maybe I only think that because," she motions around us. "I mean, come on."

I grin, because I'm thinking about the population again.

"There is one other thing," Luna says once we've reached my apartment. "That you do."

"Oh, yeah?"

"Yeah. You're officially a sculptor. My mother has decreed it."

I snort. "Two lessons make me a sculptor?"

She pokes me. "I know it's a foreign concept, but remember. Hobby, not career. Fun, not money."

I breathe deeply, before my smile breaks out wider. I had really enjoyed the lessons, and I decide on the spot to give Lucia a call as soon as possible.

"Besides," Luna adds. "Two lessons is impressive. Most people quit after the first one."

"I think that's just you."

I lead her up the stairs, fiddling with my key until the door creaks open. It's an old lock, and it took me a while to realize I had to pull the door towards me to get the lock to shift.

"Don't tease me for the shitty apartment," I warn her.

"I can't," she says, stepping over the threshold. "They're all shitty here. This isn't the fancy city."

I toss my keys on the table, kicking my shoes in the corner. "Oh, they're shitty there, too, unless you live in a rich neighborhood. I don't count them, though."

"What was your old apartment like?"

Old apartment. As if I didn't just pay July's rent.

I look around. "Actually, relatively similar to this. A bit bigger, maybe, with a much better couch. Only real perk is that I had the place to myself."

She glances between the two bedroom doors, just noticing them. "Oh, you have a roommate?"

As if on cue (maybe it is on cue, now that I know how little privacy the walls offer) that door swings open, revealing a haggard Reyna.

"Alex- oh," Reyna cuts herself off, registering the third person in the room, foot only halfway through her door. She hadn't been smiling, but her already dim expression grows somehow flatter, recoiling.

Luna, however, stays unfazed, face crinkling with sympathy. "Reyna... long time."

Reyna nods slowly, dripping through molasses. "I- yeah, I suppose it has been."

"I'm so sorry for what you're going through," Luna says, looking anguished as she gazes at her old classmate.

"Thank you," Reyna whispers, a flicker of pain plaguing her features.

Luna starts to take a step forward, but seems to think better of it when Reyna closes her body language. "Look, I know we aren't close or anything, but if you ever need anything..." She trails off with a shrug. "I know what you're going through."

Something shifts in Reyna, this time unreadable. "I suppose you do."

An awkward silence falls between us, and I feel even weirder at the thought that I'm somehow acting as the bridge between these two women who've known each other for their entire lives.

After a moment, Reyna clears her throat, hoisting a bag I hadn't even realized she was holding over her shoulder. "Well, I need to..." she points toward the door.

"Sure," I say quickly. "I'll see you...?"

Reyna shrugs, glancing at Luna. "You'll have the place to yourself for a while."

And then she's gone.

I stare at Luna, who stares at the spot where Reyna disappeared. For a moment, I think she's going to comment on Reyna's odd behavior (behavior that she hadn't exhibited this morning, alone with me), but she simply turns to me with watery eyes.

"Whoa," I say, pulling her over to the couch. "Are you okay?"

She shakes her head, leaning forward to press her fingers into her eyelids. "I'm just… so freaking tired. This town has faced a record breaking amount of devastation over the past year. It just keeps on coming and coming, and we don't deserve it. *She* doesn't deserve it."

I grip her hand tighter, her fingers enveloping mine. "You don't deserve it."

She looks up at me though her eyelashes, eyes reflecting the light streaming in through the thin living room curtains. "Neither do you."

I tilt my head in surprise, because all things considered, nothing's happened to me.

She sighs out a dull laugh. "You moved here at the worst possible time. I promise this isn't a horrible place."

"I never thought this was a horrible place."

Luna collapses back into the cushions, shoulders sagging. "Maybe because you don't know better. Or maybe you're just used to crime. Is crime really bad in the cities?"

"I guess. Definitely more common, there's just more people. The more people there are, the more bad apples in the bunch. Add in the night life, and you've got yourself a recipe for jail time."

Luna glances out the window, eyes dull. "One thousand, four hundred something. I don't know the exact number because people are moving away every day. But with that few people, the odds of a serial killer seems… small."

I gnaw on the inside of my cheek, the thought putting me on edge. "You know what else is weird? I think that's the first time I've heard someone call this guy a serial killer."

"Before last week, we didn't know for sure anyone was getting killed."

And now we do. Even I came into this thing hoping and praying that those boys would turn up, alive and well, having gone off on some wild summer adventure. A journalist longs for a good story, but... not one like this.

"It feels weird when it's something you're watching unfold," I hum, "not part of a TV series or something."

That's what it felt like, when I arrived. A show I decided to insert myself into, where I became a part of the story. Except I wasn't, for a while. I was still just watching from the sidelines. I never thought my heart would ache the way it does now.

"That's what people always say," Luna says dully. "About everything. How it won't happen to them, it can't. Bad things are myths, whispered stories in the night, until they're not. Everything's a myth until it's not."

I pause, considering, before turning my whole body to face her. "Tell me about another myth."

Her trembling hands still. "What?"

"Another myth, like the ones you paint, like the one with the bear constellation. Callisto. Are there others?"

"Of course," Luna says. "There are dozens of constellations, and every single one has a corresponding story. Some excuse as to how a person or animal ended up there. And even more myths about... everything else."

"So you must know another," I press. "One that's inspired you before, to paint, or to just exist. But I want a happy one this time."

Luna gazes at me sadly. "Myths are never happy, unfortunately. That's what makes them beautiful."

I shake my head, not wanting to hear any of that, because I need to see her smile. Happy, sad, she likes the stories. "No, what makes them beautiful is that they're fake. Fiction. Unreachable. But they're still beautiful to think about, to fantasize a world so poetic, so tell me anyway."

Luna rubs her fingers along my thigh as she thinks, and I don't think she even realizes she's doing it. Something about that makes it better. "There's so many. I took a mythology class in college, but they only covered the boring ones. The Iliad, the Odyssey, the Aeneid, all that. They're important figures, or whatever, but I would spend hours and hours reading the good stuff. Not about war, but about love." She glances at me. "I think it's bullshit when people say you can't have one without the other."

"People insist you need both to make stories interesting."

"Maybe that's true," Luna murmurs, before raising her eyes to me. "Do you want another constellation one? Those are my favorite."

Thinking about gazing at the stars on top of a bridge, I smile and lean my head against the couch, lining myself up with her. "Yes," I whisper. "Make me believe we'll one day be cast among the stars."

Chapter Nineteen

THEY HAD TO GET a court order to search the quarry waters for the other four bodies. Apparently, it takes quite a bit of money to scrape the bottom of a quarry, but finding one body finally gave them the leverage they needed to search the rest of that particular quarry. And if necessary, all the other ones.

"When is it happening?" Elise presses me.

She spent the better part of the past ten minutes reaming me out for hanging up on her, and ignoring her for the past few days, but Elise forgave me relatively quickly once I dropped the news that broke this morning.

"They're starting this afternoon," I say, trying and failing to build a sandwich with one hand. "The court order passed yesterday, and they spent all morning getting the necessary equipment."

"Okay. So how long is this thing gonna take?"

I shrug even though she can't see me. "There are four quarries in town, so probably a few days."

"I'm assuming they're starting with where they found the kid?"

I push aside my plate. This conversation is doing nothing for my appetite. "That's where they're set up. But between you and me, I don't think they'll find anything there."

Interest piqued, Elise asks, "What makes you say that?"

I shake my head, tucking my arms against the counter. "I don't know. It just doesn't make sense that they found him at the quarry they did. From what I've gathered, the kids in town have one hangout place, and one hangout place only, and it's a different quarry."

Elise hums. "Well, wouldn't that make more sense? From the sounds of it, the party quarry would be the first place they'd look. You don't want to dump a body in a place frequented by that amount of people."

I bite my lip. "I guess. But also, no, because as long as the body sinks, it doesn't matter, no one can see it. And besides, what would Anthony have been doing at the other one? Reyna said he was with friends that night, and I'd bet money I could guess where they were. So that means Anthony would have been dragged through the forest, a quarter mile from one quarry to the other at the very least, without leaving a trace? I'm sorry, I don't buy it."

Elise sighs into the phone. "You'd certainly know better than I do." She pauses, and the dull background noise of the office thrums behind her. "It's weird, you know, to hear you talking about these people like you know them. Like, saying his name or whatever."

I do know them.

I clear my throat. "I'd feel weirder just calling him the victim."

A few moments tick by where Elise stays silent, and I wish she would tell me what she was thinking, but she goes right back to business. "Tom's expecting a draft soon, so send me whatever you've got. All your notes."

I swallow, glancing at my notebook. "Yeah, you'll have them by tomorrow."

"So, what's your plan? Are you going to watch, see what happens first hand?"

The mere thought makes me sick. "Yeah, I'll stop by. I figure there'll be a bunch of people there so I can blend in, but if not, I won't be able to stay long."

"It won't matter," she says. "The only perk of a small town is news spreads like wildfire."

AND SPREAD, IT DOES. By five p.m., everyone in West Rutland knows that no other bodies were found in the first quarry. They examined it left to right, top to bottom, and Luna was right. All they found was a wrecked car, belonging to a Kevin McLaughlin who still lives off Marble Road. He'd claimed it was stolen to collect insurance money back in the nineties, but really, he and a bunch of other dumb teenagers just set fire to it and let it sink.

Sleep evades me, and I spend the night tossing and turning in bed. The weather somehow turned sweltering, and I throw the sheets away, padding to the bathroom to splash cool water on my skin. Trying not to think about what the households of the missing boys look like on a night like this, how no one in town is getting any rest tonight.

Dawn can't come quick enough, but I hold myself back, forcing my way through a sandwich as I type up my notes for Elise. By the time I finally check the clock, it's past noon, and I trudge out to the familiar trail, toward the quarry that nearly swallowed me, too. A bitter feeling has settled into the pit of my stomach, a strange echo of *knowing*.

If they're not found here, they won't be found at all.

The streets and path are mostly deserted, but it becomes apparent that this is only because I came so late. A crowd bigger than the one who came out to see Anthony's body waits for me when I arrive. A wall of eerie silence overtakes the mass of bodies, only communicating through whispers and vague head nods. I'm aware of every step I take, every twig I snap.

"I thought you might show up eventually."

Luna waits on the outskirts, leaning against a tree, eyes flashing ominously back and forth between me and what's waiting behind the wall of people. Over their heads, a crane stretches into the sky, plunging deep into the still waters.

I shuffle over to join her, and she shifts so I can use the tree for support, too. "It looks like the whole town did."

"It feels wrong," she says, still staring at nothing, arms folded tight around her chest. "Waiting and watching this like a show."

I gaze at the people, but they don't look like the crowds that gather in New York City. There are no eager looks, no chatter, no phones recording. Instead, they wait solemnly, like they owe it to their community, to the four boys they wait for. "I like to think it's not for entertainment, but just for answers. This question's been hanging in the air for quite some time."

"Too long," she says. "I don't know if this will make it better or worse, though."

She's right. It's closure, but... not really.

"How long has this been happening?" I murmur.

"An hour or so. It's slow going, but doing whatever they're doing takes less time than draining the water. And it's safer."

Good. Those death pits have caused quite enough destruction. "I'm glad they waited until after Anthony's funeral- if there's going to be more."

Softly, so I almost can't hear her, she whispers, "There will be."

I glance at Luna again, registering the tightness of her features, and she's sucking on her lips so hard they've almost disappeared. Her fingers curl into fists at her side, and I reach tentatively out, brushing my thumb against the back of her hand. The muscles around her shoulders and arms loosen, her grip easing, and I'm able to slip my hand into hers.

"Maybe you shouldn't be here," I murmur.

Swallowing hard, throat struggling, she chokes out, "This didn't happen with Carlos."

"What?"

"The crowd, the people. At least not immediately, and not here. They found him at night, washed up on the edge. They got him to the hospital before anyone even noticed something went wrong."

I crinkle my forehead. "I thought he got caught under the ledge? How was he on land?"

She nods bitterly. "I don't know, all I know is they found water in his lungs. Someone must have pulled him out once they realized he got stuck."

Aghast, I turn to her. "Wait, so whoever did it, they didn't mean to hurt him? And then they just... left him?"

"I don't know," she whispers. "Or maybe they're truly sadists, and they meant for him to only be halfway gone, because where he's at... it's somehow worse than death."

I don't argue with her, and I certainly think it's worse for her. The thought of her cousin, *brother*, lying alone in a hospital bed, and the thought of her watching it happen... A fissure slivers through my chest, and I lean closer to her.

"I need them to find the bodies," she says through gritted teeth. "This waiting, this... hopelessness that they're feeling, I feel it every day. I need it to stop for them."

My eyes burn, and I wonder if they're here. The families of the boys at the bottom of the water. I gaze over the crowd, peering through gaps between heads, jerking back when I see a familiar dark head of curls, staring intently ahead, like his life depends on it. His eyes, green like mine, burn through the air, and the fervid nature of his body posture makes my head tilt.

It's then that I follow the path down his right arm, where his fingers interlock with a girl's. No, not a girl's. A woman. An older woman, with graying hair and trembling shoulders, who seems strangely familiar.

I know what the gasp means as soon as it reaches my ears, wrenching my attention away from the pair. The sharp intake of breath, of horror, travels over the crowd, and suddenly they're pushing forward. Screams and shouts lift into the air, cries as people fall into each other's arms.

Two. They just found two of them.

My lips part as I listen to the sorrowful whispers, to the sobs of friends and families at the sight of two bodies. *It's them*, they're saying. *It's them.*

I lift a trembling hand to my mouth, clamping down on the bile rising in my throat. I'm glad the crowd obstructs my view, and I can't see anything of the boys who were lost to the quarry. Luna makes a strangled sound, and I turn to see her fighting off the sobs escaping her throat. Trembling, she holds her head in her free hand, as if she might be able to screw it on tighter, to make herself see something else.

"I'm sorry," I whisper, surprised to find that I'm crying, too.

If they found the first two… It says everything that needs to be said, really.

I look back over my shoulder, finding Parker in the crowd, surprised to see the look of muted anguish painting his face as he clings to that same familiar woman, fingers digging into the fabric of her shirt. Shouts and cries rise up to the sky, but I can hear that woman above them all, screaming, *"Xavier, no. Please, God, no."*

Like a mask, the sorrow vanishes, and Parker just stands with a blank expression, eyes glazed over, eerily still as he holds her back. Staring at a spot on the ground as he tries to remain upright. They shift, the woman pulling away with a shaking hand over her lips, and I get a good look at her face. Paired with the name coming from her sobbing lips, it clicks where I know her from. Yet another person I'd stumbled across in my research. Xavier's, one of the victims, mother.

One of the victims that was, apparently, just found.

A single tear tracks down Parker's cheek, and he holds her tighter, but it doesn't make sense. I think back to our one and only conversation, where he said he hadn't known them, he hadn't been in their grades, he wasn't affected by their death at all. But he clearly knows Xavier's mom.

And he's clearly mourning over something.

Tell Xavier I say hi.

Luna wipes her nose, trying to regain control over her breath. She speaks through hiccups, her body fighting against the words. "I- I've had enough of this. I can't-" She turns to me abruptly. "Will you take me somewhere?"

I don't even ask where. I just squeeze her hand tighter, kissing a tear away from the corner of her eye. I take one last look back, only to find that Parker has disappeared, before dragging her after me into the forest.

WE SIT IN SILENCE in my car until Luna stops shaking, and until I stop crying.

Luna's cheeks have dried by the time the A/C makes the car bearable in the insufferable heat, and I finally swing the door shut. For a second, I think it's good that the bodies were in the water, otherwise the heat would have decimated them, but then the burning in my throat reminds me that there was nothing even remotely good about anything that transpired today.

Luna's phone chimes, and she wrestles it from her back pocket, eyes flitting over the message. She squeezes her eyes shut. "They found the other two bodies. Different quarry."

I exhale, hitting the butt of my palm into the steering wheel. So, there it is. Five dead. "Like you said, though. At least the families know now."

"At least."

Except, is it even better? Everyone says it is, to know what happened, to get rid of all hope.

I shift in my seat, voice strong enough now to hold a conversation. "Did you have anywhere in particular you wanted to go? Or was it just... anywhere but there?" I wouldn't blame her if she chose the latter.

A hush falls between us, and I look up to see her lips pressed together, her throat bobbing again. I wish I could shove the words back into my mouth. "Today's the day I usually go to the hospital."

Sorrow overtakes my veins, stretching to my fingertips as I grip the steering wheel. "To visit Carlos."

She nods slightly, looking away out the window. I think about what she said earlier, about how there will be more funerals. There won't just be four more, for the bodies found today. At some point, she and I both know there will be a fifth.

My hand tingles, longing to reach out towards her. To take her hand, stroke her cheek, *something* to make her feel better. But she's not looking at me, and I'm frozen on my side of the car, so I just shift the car into gear. I look back to check in the rearview mirror, searching for any pedestrians, but I don't know why I bother. Everyone who might be walking past my driveway are all in the same place. Where we just left.

How long will they stay there, now that they were found, and there's nothing to wait for? Maybe they're already on their way back, but maybe they stayed, falling to the ground and clinging to each other. I wonder where Jo is. Whether she has someone to hold onto.

I wonder where Parker is, how he knew Xavier, and why he claimed that he hadn't.

The drive to the hospital is long and quiet, and I'm acutely aware of the way Luna fiddles with her phone, her bracelet, anything to keep herself from sitting still. The only words flitting through the silence are Luna's soft directions and I don't bother telling her I already know where the hospital is, because why would I?

When I pull into the parking lot, Luna murmurs, "You'll come in, right?"

I don't realize until she asks that I spent the entire drive wondering whether she'd want me to wait in the car. So now, I simply nod, and we both slip back into the summer heat.

More silence stretches between us as we walk through the sliding double doors, and I don't know why I've never felt further away from her. Inches apart, and I can't reach her. She stares straight ahead, following a path she must have walked dozens of times.

Toward a brother who will never wake up.

In the elevator, she presses the *three* button, and the doors shut with a quiet *ding*.

"Do your parents come with you?" I ask. "When you visit?"

Swallowing, she shakes her head. "Dad never does. Mom used to, but I think it started tearing her apart more than helping, so I told her she should start staying home."

"Does it help you?"

She bites her lip. "I don't know. But I don't really want to stop to find out."

"I'm sorry," I say as we reach the floor. "That you spent so long having to come alone."

"I would say I'm used to it..." She looks to me, gaze soft. "But can you ever really get used to something like this?"

Probably not. Definitely not. I can tell in the way her steps are heavy as she leads me down the hallway, how her fingers shake when reaching for the doorknob. She hesitates, bracing herself, before pushing inside.

You wouldn't know that a young boy has lived here for the past eight months, although he isn't doing anything close to living. Freezing in the doorway, I stare at his frail form, layered in blankets, lying completely still. Monitors beep on the other side of the bed, and tubes flow in and out of his body, but I don't know what any of it means.

Luna clearly does, though, because her face cracks after reading whatever it is the monitor is outputting. I can decipher her expression well enough: No change. Not good.

I think about asking her about it, but I'm too focused on his lack of movement. The slack, uncomprehending fall of his jaw. There's nothing there. His eyes are closed, but I can tell that nothing- no awareness, no consciousness, no life- lies behind them.

And that could have been me. Caught under a ledge, suffocating until all of my remaining air traveled in bubbles towards the surface, leaving me in the dark to die.

If Luna hadn't pulled me out, nobody else would have.

"Is it possible?" I croak from the doorway. "At this point, to ever find out who did this to him?"

I don't bother asking if he'll ever wake up. I know that answer already.

Solemn, she shakes her head, perching herself on the edge of the bed. She does it delicately, even though she knows it's impossible to disturb him. "After this amount of time, the case turns cold and dead. Has been for months. Unless someone actually comes forward and confesses, which I just know won't happen." She shakes her head with a shrug. "I guess you can't always know."

I guess not. I've been running into that problem for a while now.

I enter fully into the room. I don't know what to say, so I just pull up a chair beside her, so our knees press together. Luna's smoothing down the covers, straightening a sheet that seems to be tangled around his foot. I can't get over how young he is, how motionless. Those two things should never go together.

"We're gonna have to let him go at some point," she whispers, fisting the blanket between her fingers.

I lean forward, my knuckles brushing her knee. I don't ask what she means, because I know what she means.

A tear slips from the corner of her eye, but she's not sobbing like earlier. This isn't something coming from nowhere, sneaking up from behind. I can see it in her face, the way she knows. "He's been living on machines for months now, and they can't... they can't-" Her breaths stutter. "They can't let him go until we sign."

I close my eyes, because what a terrible position to be in. He's as good as dead right now, but they have to make a decision to make it final. "That's not fair, that you have to make that decision."

She sniffs, wiping her cheeks. "It's not me. If it were, I'd have done it months ago. I can't stand the idea that deep down he's suffering, or something, and just can't tell us." She shakes her head, looking up toward the ceiling. "It seems like the right thing to do, but my mom..."

I nod. "Makes sense. I don't know what I'd do, in her position."

"I guess I don't really, either," she says. "Maybe I'd change my mind if I were. I'm not the one who will sign his life away."

I scooch closer, until I can fold her hand between mine. "You can't think of it like that. There's... not a life to sign away."

She nods. "I know that. I mean, I've known that for a while. I don't even know why I keep coming."

"So why do you?"

She signs. "Irrationality, mostly. Because, like I said, there's a slim chance that he's suffering, which also means there's a slim chance he's aware. That he lies here alone, every day, waiting for me to visit. Could you imagine if he spends his week counting down the days, and I eventually don't show up?"

Her eyes are damp again, and she tumbles into my arms, resting her forehead in the crook of my shoulder, trying to catch her breath. I don't know what to say, how to comfort her.

Whether telling her that he's gone will ease the burden or just add weight.

I think about her mother, who has only ever seemed happy around me. When Luna told me what happened, Lucia didn't even cross my mind, that she'd lost both a nephew and a son.

"My mom almost didn't let him go that night," she murmurs. "She... I think that's why she stopped visiting, she felt so guilty. I do too, except that's why I *keep* coming here."

"You can't feel guilty. You weren't there, how could you?"

"Exactly," she says, pulling back. "I wasn't there."

I gaze at her sadly, because I'm now realizing that there's nothing I can say to lessen this burden, to shift it from her shoulders and discard it completely.

"I think forgiving yourself for a mistake is much harder than forgiving anyone else," Luna whispers, gazing at the boy laying stone still in the bed, where we both know he will stay.

"I think you're right." I lift my eyes to her. "And have you ever managed?"

Her lips form a thin line, and she leans forward to bring Carlos's hand to her lips. "Every day."

Chapter Twenty

A SOFT MELODY MELTS from the speakers as I drive. They're old, and it makes the sound come out slightly muffled, but I think it makes the music more real... Like someone could actually be playing it from the backseat.

We've been driving for over an hour now. I didn't want to go home in case Reyna went back, and Luna didn't want to go home to deal with her parents, so instead she directed me out of town, where trees and fields stretch for miles and miles. We chased the night, until the sun set around us, extinguishing the light until we could both breathe easier.

"I'm sick of sunsets," Luna says.

I smile. "How are you sick of sunsets? That was beautiful."

"I'm tired of people glorifying endings."

I sigh, rubbing the steering wheel between my thumb and index fingers. "Me too. But if no one makes them beautiful, how will we ever get through them?"

"I'm not sure we do," she says, and when I look over, I can only see a soft silhouette, the details of her features fading into a dark shadow pressed up against the backdrop of a starry sky. "I think we're stuck in them forever, and we have to just… live there. And maybe we'll get to the point where we can ignore that we're stuck, where we can forget, but… we never actually move."

"Do you feel stuck?" I ask.

She bites her lip. "Not yet. Do you?"

I disprove her theory with one sentence. "No. Not anymore."

She stays silent for a moment. "You were stuck before." It's not a question.

"I spent my whole life stuck," I admit. "Without realizing I was stuck, like you said."

Luna turns to me, and a passing street lamp illuminates her face, her wide eyes. "What made you realize?"

I can't help but laugh. "What do you think?"

Except Luna doesn't smile. "It can't be me. I'm pretty sure all I do is stay still, and make the people I love stay still with me."

I reach out, fumbling unceremoniously around in the dark until I find her hand. "Or maybe we want to stand still with you. Still doesn't mean broken."

Luna looks back at me, and this time her lips are turned upward. She squeezes my hand tighter, bringing it to her lips. "Maybe that's why you can enjoy a good sunset."

"Oh, I think you could, too, if you really looked at it."

Her smile splits open. "Looks like we'll have to do this again tomorrow, so I can give it another chance."

"I can make that sacrifice."

She pauses, hesitating, before asking, "Do I really make you feel that way? Unstuck?"

"You make me feel a lot of things. But yeah."

Even in the dim light her blush is clear, and she looks away to hide her smile.

My words are interrupted when the song melts away, replaced by the dull voice of whoever's running the radio show. "I know the hosts are necessary," I say, nodding to the stereo, "but if given the chance, I would not hesitate to fire every single radio host there is."

Luna laughs. "You and everybody else." He doesn't talk for long, though, because he quickly introduces another song, the peaceful strum of a guitar filling the car in his place. Luna sighs happily. "I love this song," she murmurs, leaning forward to turn the volume dial.

The music swells, and it's a song I don't recognize, but I feel like I do. Distant but familiar in the way the lyrics trinkle out softly like a lullaby, so soft I can barely hear what they're saying, but it doesn't matter. The song somehow makes me feel like I'm floating anyway, like my heart is soaring even though my body remains frustratingly grounded. I lean my head against the back of my seat, sneaking glances at Luna's profile and squeezing her fingers, and imagine that this song was made to be listened to exactly like this. At night, and with her.

"Do you ever get overwhelmed by the urge to create something beautiful?"

Wrenched from the melody, allowing the song to fade into the background, I turn to Luna. "Isn't that all you do? As an artist? Seems like you're an expert in beauty."

"I'm an expert in *creating*," she corrects me, and I only stare at her, not really seeing the difference. With a sigh, she rubs at her jaw with her free hand, still clinging to me like a lifeline. "I feel like a machine."

I want to tell her that we're all machines, just operating to get the job done until we can immediately be assigned another one, but I figure that's probably not what she wants to hear right now. "How so?"

Letting out an excruciating sigh, low and gravelly in a way that makes her always seem tired, she says, "It's just… never ending. Being an artist, you tend to feel rushed, like you have to create, create, create. Like you have to crank out something *now*, and it has to be new and inspired every single day, otherwise you're a failure."

"That doesn't seem like a super realistic mindset," I say honestly.

She huffs. "Probably not. But sometimes, I feel so pressured to just *finish* whatever it is I'm working on that… I never really like what I finish. It never says what I want it to say."

Trying for a joke, I ask, "Can a painting ever really say anything, anyway?"

She looks up at me through her lashes. "It's supposed to."

I think back to her work, at the flashes I've seen, and realize I've never seen something completed, only half-filled pages and canvases. I wish she would show me something whole, if just to hear exactly what she has to say.

Running a hand through her hair, fingers catching on a few tangles made by the wind, she nods toward the forgotten speaker. The music swells into my ears and consciousness once more, but it's a different song. Somehow less than.

"I watched your face, when you were listening to that song."

I shift uncomfortably, hoping my longing hadn't been written all over my expression. "Was it interesting?"

To my surprise, she says, "Very. You went somewhere else. It *took* you somewhere else. That's what I want to do, to make you feel like you felt."

Smiling, I say, "You do. It might not have anything to do with your art, but… you do."

Throat bobbing, she kisses my hand again, and lets me drive us back home.

LUNA AND I PART ways the next morning in front of Suzie's, while she goes to work and I go in for breakfast. The place is a ghost town, not a single person in sight besides Jo, slumped behind the counter.

"Business a little slow?" I ask, reclaiming my spot at the counter.

Jo straightens and offers me a weak smile that doesn't reach her eyes. "Just a little. I can't say I'm surprised, though. I expected it."

I pull the cup of coffee she pours toward me, warming my fingers. It's blazing hot outside, but cold prickled my hands at the sight of the sharp death behind her eyes. "Well, you'll always have a customer in me."

She smiles sadly. "That's because you don't know any better. You have nothing to grieve."

I nod slowly. Technically true, although with the amount of time I've spent with these boys, looking into their lives, trying to figure them out when they can't tell me anything, I feel like I have the right to grieve for them, too.

Jo reads my eyes, but reads it wrong as her eyes soften. "I'm assuming Luna told you what happened to Carlos, then."

I exhale through my nose, because since the visit to the hospital, I've been grieving him too. "She did."

Jo looks down, and I'm surprised to see she looks on the edge of tears, and I wonder just how well she knew the boy. He must have come in here often, probably with the soccer team, or with Luna and Lucia. "He's the one I'm stuck on. It's like this town's entered Groundhog Day since that night, and we can't get out."

"It sure seems that way," I say, thinking of the cycle of death plaguing the town. "None of these boys deserved what's going on, it's just…" I shake my head.

Jo shakes her head. "Carlos sure didn't. I've never met a kid sweeter than that boy, more genuine. When he first moved here, and once he started to come out of his shell a little bit, it's like he breathed fresh air into a dead town."

"He must have been amazing, to be loved so much by the town that took him in."

Jo chews on her lip. "Lucia, she introduced me to him, not long after he arrived, asked me to look after him on some days. He came during the summer, you know, so school hadn't started, but Lucia still needed to work." She motions around. "So, she brought him here. He had a permanent table, over there." She jabs a finger toward the booth across the way, where I first saw Luna sitting.

"This seems like a great place to hang out. I'm sure he loved it."

She snorts. "Yeah, well, he didn't at first. Wouldn't speak to anyone, not even me. He wouldn't order, wouldn't tell me what he wanted. He'd just... sit there and stare out the window. Until one day he came in, and said, *'My cousin gave me a few recommendations on what to order. I'd rather hear it from you.'* " She shakes her head with a laugh. "As if I hadn't tried to tell him a thousand times."

"He sounds like Luna," I say instinctively.

Jo nods with wide eyes. "So incredibly alike, those two, you'd think they actually *were* siblings."

I think about Luna's words, how it'd become her instinct to call Carlos her brother, how she had to correct herself. As far as I'm concerned, they *did* become siblings.

Jo sighs, still gazing past my shoulder at the empty booth, eyes filled with the ghost of memories and tears. "I knew what happened to him before he came, to his parents. Anything I could do to make him more comfortable, to feel more at home here, I was ready to do." She nods to the menu that I hadn't even realized I had beneath my fingertips. "His favorite was the same as you. Maple pancakes."

"I think it's an out of stater thing."

"Must be," she says softly.

"Lucia must have trusted you quite a lot," I murmur. "To leave him here."

Jo smiles sadly. "Lucia and I go way back, further back than most people know, I think. I met her much in the same way I met you. Here, and during her first week in town."

I grin. "Really?"

She nods. "God, I must have been only, what, eight? I hate to think of thirty nine as old, but it sort of is, isn't it?"

"I'm gonna plead the fifth on that one."

This makes Jo crack a smile. "Anyway, she came in with Roger, they'd just gotten engaged when they moved here. They came in and sat at that same booth, looking so lost on where to start. My grandma was still running the place at that point, but sometimes when I stopped by, she'd have me come on her rounds with her, helping her take orders and bring people their drinks. She never let me touch the food, but she said that the drinks were worth spilling to give me something to do."

"Did you spill orange juice on her or something?"

"Almost. I spilled *cranberry* juice on her, because I got distracted by the beautiful ring on her finger. It was simple, but bigger than any I'd ever seen before. Neither of them came from money, but she said it was a family ring that got passed down, an heirloom. I didn't even apologize, I just grabbed her hand and pulled it to my face, admiring how *sparkly* it was."

I laugh. "Was she wearing white?"

"No, thank God, and she wasn't even a little bit angry. She didn't pull her hand away, and used her other one to take some napkins to wipe away the juice. And then she turned to me and told me about the ring, every detail about where it came from, how her fiancé had given it to her. And then she asked if I wanted to eat lunch with them."

The thought makes me smile, of tiny Jo climbing into young Lucia's booth. The passage of time can be confusing as I try to imagine them as younger than they are now. It's difficult to consider people's lives before you know them. "Instant friends, then?"

"Something like that," she says. "I'd consider us friends now, but back then she became more like a big sister. She'd come in all the time, and once they opened the sculpture center, she'd take me there while she worked. Even though I've never tried- I was always too afraid of the tools, and cutting my finger off- I could probably sculpt something relatively successfully from the amount of time I spent watching her."

"You could probably do better than me, and she's actually given me a few lessons."

Jo looks down, the happy nostalgia being overtaken by the sorrow of the present day as she drops back into reality. "She looked after me, back then. Sometimes more than my own mother. She sort of took me under her wing, gave me something to do besides school and the diner. She encouraged me to be a kid, and she knew I would do the same thing for her and her kid."

"I'm sure you succeeded in that," I say softly. "And I'm sure she sees all that you did for him, and for her."

Her smile turns tight, a sort of fractured wall behind her eyes. I think back on every other time I've seen Jo, and whether that look has always been there, and I just haven't noticed. "I hope so."

"I wish we knew who did it to him," I say, gazing at that booth that used to belong to a young kid, but now has become as generic as all the rest. It's haunted, filled with ghosts. "So we could make them pay."

"Me, too," she says, voice bitterer than I've ever heard. "Me, too."

"IF I'D KNOWN DATING you would lead to manual labor, I might have reconsidered."

Unfazed, Luna shifts her grip on the marble. "Sunlight is good for you. The city light pollution makes you pale."

"I'm pale no matter what!"

"There's a difference between pale and dead."

Luna had texted me as I finished my food.

Luna: *Work is killing me. Might hurt less if you come distract me.*

It took me about zero seconds to agree, but now work is killing *me*.

"This is stressful as hell," I pant as we move a new statue across the garden. They got a shipment this morning, but the delivery people only took them so far. "What if it breaks?"

"Let's not will that into existence," Luna grits out, sighing as we release our hold of the statue, placing it on the pedestal we'd already moved. It snaps into place, and I practically jump away from it. "Although if it makes you feel better, it wouldn't be the first time."

I grin, wiping my forehead. "Are you trying to tell me you've destroyed a precious work of art?"

"I was young and weak. I felt terrible."

"Well," I say, knocking my knuckles against the sturdy statue. "We made it through. This was the last one, right?" I try not to sound too pleading.

It doesn't get past Luna, who exaggerates a heavy sigh. "Yeah, Alex, that was the last one. I release you."

"Whoa, whoa, whoa, I never said I wanted to be released."

Which is how I end up at the ticket booth as Luna polishes a sculpture across the clearing. I asked if they had to do that everyday, but she said only when it rains, and it poured last night.

I jerk up when there's a knock on the window, frantically sliding it open. This is why I'm not made for customer service.

The boy grins at me, and I freeze. "I didn't think it was possible to sneak up on someone whose entire job is literally to sit and wait for people."

I let out a breathy laugh, hoping Parker doesn't notice my awkwardness. I do a horrible job of casually saying, "Yeah, well, I have a special talent in- oh, hey, I've met you. You work at Suzie's, right?" As if that's the only way I know him.

"Right," he responds, jaw tightening. "You're the new one who came in with a bunch of questions."

"I still have a bunch of questions," I say lowly, glancing towards the trail that leads to the quarry. *Act normal.* What even is normal, anyway?

"You're not the only one. I'm pretty sure every high schooler's been questioned at least twice at this point."

Leaning on the counter is a failed attempt at nonchalance, I ask "Did they question you, too, then?"

He shakes his head, although I don't miss the way his throat bobs, and I narrow my eyes. "Didn't know the poor guys well enough, I guess, thank God for that."

Images flash behind my eyes, of the tear on his face, of Xavier's mother clinging to him like a lifeline. Like another son.

"Parker!" a woman calls out from the entrance. "Is there a problem with the tickets?"

My eyes snap to another familiar face, where Sadie Jefferson waves with a concerned face. He sighs before shouting back, "No, just give me a second, Mom!" He turns back to me. "It's her birthday, she loves this place. Three tickets?"

I charge him for them in the way Luna told me to, tucking the bills into the register. "Okay, um... enjoy."

He nods, no smile gracing his face, and then he's gone.

One sentence sticks out in my thoughts. *Your brother has done nothing but lie to you.*

I try not to overthink it, because what's the harm in lying to a supposed stranger? He doesn't know me, he's not required to tell me details about his life. But something about the way he goes a little bit rigid at the mention of the subject. Hadn't he said that the police didn't question him because he didn't know them well enough? Did he lie to them, too?

Why... Why would he do that?

Realizing I'd left the window open when he left, I slide it closed, burying my face in my hands.

Another sharp knock alerts me, and I jerk up to see Luna's nose pressed against the glass, concern dripping all over her features. I open the window, and I don't even get to say anything before she hisses, "You talked to him!"

I groan, chin still buried in my fingers. "Luna... I have a theory. And I'm scared it's a stupid theory, but I'm even more afraid that I'm right."

Her brows furrow, and she leans in closer.

I open my mouth, then close it, unable to find the words. How do I say I have a theory about the town murders without making it seem like I've been investigating? "I saw him that day at the quarry, when they found the bodies."

She doesn't seem surprised. Everyone was there. "So?"

I press my lips together, biting down on them. "Okay, so when I first met him, I was curious, right? About everything going on. I asked him about... the boys that went missing, and he said he barely knew them."

"Okay... I mean, yeah, that matches up. They weren't in the same year, from what I can remember he had a pretty tight knit group of friends that he was in band with, didn't necessarily hang out with the other soccer boys all that much."

Pausing, I wondered whether I would sound crazy. "He-

"Luna!"

Her father is waving her over, and she mouths *sorry* while holding up a finger, and hurries off to help him, leaving me with the same number of questions I woke up with. But I'm almost relieved at the same time. I didn't really want to voice something so awful out loud.

But then I see her, and those questions start to multiply.

I stand from my chair, leaning forward until my face passes outside the still open window, eyes tracking as Reyna storms in through the entrance without so much as a second glance to the ticket booth. Luna has disappeared down one of the trails, but Reyna heads toward a different one, the one I know leads to where I take my lessons with Lucia.

I bite my lip as I watch her push through the trees, eyes darting between her shadow and the empty entrance. I squint, trying to make out any figures, but it looks clear, even though my vision hasn't been all that reliable since I lost my glasses to the water. Taking a moment to debate, curiosity gets the better of me and I shove out of the booth, striding across the clearing until I, too, am surrounded by trees.

Making as little noise as possible, I follow the only path this trail takes, and therefore the only path Reyna could have taken. She wasn't exactly sneaking, so I figure she wouldn't have gone off the path. She's heading straight for something, and the only thing I can think of that has any merit is Luna's mom, who I know for a fact is in a sculpting session.

Luna and Reyna were a year apart, and in no way friends. What the hell could Reyna want with Lucia?

I stumble to a stop when I see the familiar statue, the one Lucia had once snuck up on me admiring, and it's not the only thing that tells me I'm close. Voices drift down the path from where it ends a few yards away. I shimmy myself between two trees, wedging myself out of sight behind the statue to listen. Guilt pangs in my chest at the thought of eavesdropping on two of my friends here, but Reyna doesn't anger quickly. And there's only one thing she's angry about right now.

"I'm not playing these games," Reyna is hissing, only partly trying to be quiet. "You think I don't know? Of *course,* I know. I've always known!"

Lucia's voice comes out brittle and dry, unlike anything I've heard come out of her mouth. "Known what?"

"You know damn well what, lady, don't play dumb with me."

What if she isn't playing dumb? What if Lucia genuinely has no idea what's going on? Worried that Reyna might be spiraling, I think about inserting myself into the conversation before it gets ugly, but Lucia speaks again, so I hold back.

"I'm not playing dumb, Reyna, I don't know what you're talking about. Are you alright?"

To my surprise, Reyna laughs, but there's no humor behind it. "I will be, but only once you're straight with me. I-" she cuts herself off, trying to calm herself. "I need you to be straight with me. All those families, they got their answers when their kids got pulled out of that quarry. Now I need mine."

Silence stretches between the two of them, and I don't know what I'm scared might happen, but dread pools in the pit of my stomach. It takes Lucia a long while before answering, "Reyna, this is not the time to have this discussion, nor the place. I cannot help you."

"*Bullshit!*"

I wince at the cry, as Reyna breaks down and yells, "That's *bullshit*, you need to… And I know why, he told me what he did, but at least *own* it-"

"He told you?" Lucia's voice is sharp now. Reyna doesn't respond, but I assume she nods, because Lucia clears her throat. My heart pounds as I wait for a response, for just one of them to say what the hell they're talking about. "Then it sounds to me like you have your own secrets. And I'm done discussing this right now."

"Fine," Reyna says. "Then you know where I'll be tonight."

And then Reyna's storming off once more, sniffling as she does, unaware of her roommate nestled into the trees off the path's edge.

Chapter Twenty-One

I WAIT SEVERAL MINUTES before stumbling out of the forest, thanking my lucky stars that Luna hasn't returned from wherever she went off to, and that there's nobody waiting at my abandoned post at the ticket booth. For a moment, I stand in the main clearing, looking back and forth, before running after where Reyna undoubtedly disappeared.

She hadn't made it far in the few minutes head start I gave her. I find her stooped over about a quarter mile down the road, dry heaving into a bush. Frantic, I approach to hold her hair back, but as soon as my fingers graze her back, she jerks up so fast that she almost takes me down.

I spread my arms out wide, incredulous. "What the hell was that about?"

"Sorry," she says, seemingly thinking I was referring to just now. "You scared me."

I shake my head, eyes wide. "No, I'm not talking about that. That's the least surprising thing to happen in the last ten minutes.

I'm talking about your *screaming* match that I just was subjected to."

Her face goes completely blank. "You heard that?"

"Well, you weren't exactly keeping it down, were you?"

Something like regret washes her features, but she mostly just looks tired and angry. "I thought we were alone."

"I followed you," I say honestly. "After watching you bowl through the field like a wrecking ball. You have to pay to get in there, of course I noticed you."

"I wasn't there to look at the statues," she says, as if that makes it any better.

I fold my arms across my chest. "Clearly. So why *were* you there?"

She sets her jaw, looking like she might explode any moment. "Didn't you hear?"

"Sort of," I say. "You were about as vague as possible."

"Yeah, well, so was she. That's sort of my problem."

I stare at her. "What exactly *is* your problem. What did she *do*?"

Reyna opens her mouth, before seeming to think better of it. "Nothing that you'll find interesting. Or believable."

"I'll believe almost anything. That's my job."

Reyna huffs, face flushing redder and redder by the moment, stretching down her neck and all the way to the tips of her ears. "Yeah, your bullshit job."

The anger is there that I hadn't seen the last time I saw her. The sadness, the grief, has at last been replaced with pure fury, and she has no space for kindness. Not for me, not for anyone that gets in her way.

"Yeah, my job. I'm on your side," I remind her. "I'm trying just as hard as you to find out what's going on here."

"Yeah, but you're only doing it for a paycheck!" she exclaims. "You can go off and write your little article and then split town, but I have to live with what happened to my brother *forever*."

"Article?"

I freeze at the voice coming from only a few feet behind me, losing control of my jaw as my mouth falls open in horror. Reyna's eyes flicker over my shoulder, widening ever so slightly at who she finds there. I know exactly who it is.

But I can't turn around. My whole body has turned to stone, no different than one of those statues I left behind. It doesn't matter, though, because the stone road crunches around me as Luna circles us, until she's between Reyna and me.

"You ran off," she says weakly, gaze dull. "I came to… to look for you."

I search for words, but nothing comes. A string pulls tight around my throat, and the only thing I can choke out is, "Luna."

She looks back and forth from Reyna to me, fire building behind her eyes. "What were you… your job?"

I can't say anything. I can't think of a single thing to say. My entire job is to think of words and write them down, but right now my vocabulary is being obliterated, and I can't seem to think of a single one, except, "Luna, *no*, I-"

"No, what?" she asks, crossing her arms across her chest to hold herself together. "No, what she was saying isn't true? Or no, stop talking?"

The second one. I can't say that, though, and I glance helplessly at my roommate.

For a moment, Reyna looks so shocked that I think she might backtrack, but instead she just glares at me before turning to Luna. "Oh, you didn't know? You're girlfriend's here on a job, and a job only. And not the bullshit tech support one she used as a cover."

Luna takes a step back, as though retreating might make her go back in time. "Wait, I don't understand-"

"Reyna," I say. "Stop."

"Oh, you don't want me to tell her?" she asks. "You want me to keep lying to her, like you've been doing this whole time?"

"I haven't been *lying*-"

"What would you call being an undercover journalist?" Reyna muses, feigning nonchalance even though I can feel the rage and resentment pummeling me. "Certainly not someone telling the truth."

"Alex," Luna says, voice cracking when she says my name, which makes something crack within me, too. "Alex, what she's saying... what *you* said..."

I still can't say anything. I can't catch my breath, and how have words suddenly stopped existing? This whole time, talking to Luna has felt easier than breathing, and now I can't seem to do either.

It doesn't seem to matter, because my panic says everything I can't articulate. A wave of emotion surges across her face, from confusion to shock to anger, until it finally ends on hurt. Her entire face and body crumples.

"So, you're telling me that this whole thing," she says, waving her hand around so it almost smacks Reyna in the face, "*all* of this... has just been a cover? So you could wring out a *story*?"

Her words wrestle me from my voicelessness, and I stumble toward her, but she holds her hands out as though in a protective shield. "*No*. No, of *course* not-"

Luna just shakes her head, and the way she looks at me is as though she doesn't even know me. "Yes, it is. Everything you've said here is built on a lie."

"Not everything," I choke out. "Not even close. I-"

"I told you *everything!*" she shouts, jabbing a finger into my chest. "I gave you *all* that I had left, didn't you realize that? How much I-" She violently cuts herself off, clamping her teeth down on whatever she almost spoke into existence. On the words I might never hear now.

My stomach twists painfully, and I nearly start dry heaving like Reyna was. But I swallow my bile, shaking my head until I don't know how to do anything else, until I'm dizzy with denial. The thought of her thinking that I don't... that I... "I never lied to you about us. I never... I wouldn't-"

"But you were gonna leave," she snaps, anguished. "I told you everything that I've lost, and you were gonna *leave-*"

"*No-*"

But I can barely get the word out, because then she's holding up her hand and looking away, throat bobbing painfully. "I... I... You..." Whatever had taken my voice takes hers too, and all she can do is look at me, eyes rimmed with red, disbelief painted over her sorrow. Then she shakes her head and runs away, back toward town. Away from me.

I want to chase after her, to make her listen, but my mind has gone empty. What could I even say, if I could think of a single thought? I watch her fade into the distance, until she's nothing but a smudge at the end of the road.

"What's wrong with you?" I whisper once she's gone, when Reyna and I are left alone.

"The same thing as you," she says, chest heaving. "I seem to destroy everyone around me."

"DID THEY FIND ANOTHER body?" Elise asks immediately upon hearing my panic, the sounds of my ugly sobs flowing through the speaker, all the way to New York City. "Oh, god, I thought them finding all the other ones would deter the murder a bit, are you serious-"

"Elise," I snap, desperate for her to shut up, unable to stop my circling around my room. Reyna hadn't followed me home, she just sat down in the grass and started sobbing. Any other day and I would have stayed, at least tried to put her back together, but I couldn't use my own pieces to assemble hers. We'd just end up getting jumbled together.

"Whoa," Elise says at my outburst, voice softening. I hear a door close, and I imagine her shutting herself in an empty room, settling down. "So it's something else."

I stop just short of screaming into the phone, but only because my voice box isn't cooperating. "It's all… This whole thing is falling apart."

"The job? What do you mean, aren't you actually getting somewhere now that-"

"Not the *freaking* job!" I yell. "None of this is about the goddamn job anymore."

She doesn't think that, she doesn't know that, and she'll never believe you. She'll think you were only using her for information, that you never-

Sounding alarmed, Elise's voice drifts through the fog around my brain. "Alex, take a breath. *What* is going on?"

I don't realize I'm crying until my voice comes out watery and raw. I drop to the ground, thinking sitting will help me breathe better, but it just makes my lungs cave in on themselves, so I lie down on my back. "She found out why I came here. About… everything."

"She? Oh…" Elise trails off, realizing. I never technically told her about Luna, but Elise knows me pretty damn well. "Is this your way of telling me you're hooking up with the townspeople?"

"I will *not hesitate* to hang up on you."

"Please, don't," Elise says, frantic, and something crashes in the background. "I'm sorry, just… don't. Stay on the line."

I close my eyes, the damp lashes sticking together. "I mean, that's the whole point of being undercover, right? I couldn't tell her, I couldn't tell *anyone*."

"You couldn't," she agrees. "You were doing your job."

"Yeah, well, I've started to hate my job these past couple weeks."

Elise sighs heavily. "I know."

Her response surprises me enough that I pause in my misery. "What?"

"I know," she repeats, voice soft and gentle as ever. "I may not have been able to see your lovely face, but I could hear it in your voice, the way you talked. You started calling less often-"

"I was busy," I say, defensive, the thought of Elise feeling neglected almost setting me over the edge. "It was never about *you*, I always want to talk to you."

"I know that," she says for the third time. "If you had let me finish, I would have said you started calling less often about the job. Half the time you just wanted to chat, you'd change the subject whenever I brought up the case..." Her voice falls away. "You were trying to tell me."

"I didn't try to tell you shit."

"Yeah, you did," she says sadly. "You wanted to, we came close a few times, but I..." She exhales heavily, and I look out the window, towards the direction where New York and Elise wait, expecting me back. "I didn't want to hear it. That you might have gotten sucked into that place."

"I didn't get sucked into Vermont," I say, the heaviness returning to my chest, and I don't think I could sit up if I wanted to. This weight might just keep me here forever. "I got sucked into her."

Elise's smile lights up her words as she says, "I know that, too."

"God, why do you keep saying that like we're breaking up?"

A beat passes before Elise is cackling so hard that even I crack a smile. "It does feel that way a little, doesn't it? I've always thought that a platonic falling out is the equivalent to a breakup. Sometimes worse."

My fingers still round my phone. "Wait, we're not actually breaking up, are we? Because, seriously, the *last* thing I need right now is a second one."

"Alex, we're never breaking up, and that's a promise. I like to think of it as... deciding we're about to go long distance."

The smile slips from my face. That might have made me grin like a maniac yesterday, but now... "I can't stay here. Not after today."

"Today was a hiccup," she says breezily. "You were just doing your job, and I stand by that. Does she need to hear from your manager that you were acting on our orders? Because I can totally make that happen."

"I'll keep it in mind," I say dryly.

"Anyway, you despise lying, nothing you did was malicious. I'm sure you spent the whole time aching to tell her."

I do hate lying. It tore me apart at the beginning, and then, just like anything else, I got used to it. That's sort of what makes it all worse.

Elise's words are reassuring, but I can't get the way she looked at me earlier out of my head. The scene flashes in front of my closed eyes, her eyes widening with realization when I couldn't bring myself to deny it. The pain, the regret, the setting of her jaw as she made that decision to walk away. "She hates me," I whisper.

"She doesn't," Elise says. "No one could ever hate you. Look at Rachel."

"That's not a good example. She's the one who fucked *me* over."

"True, but you were a total bitch afterward. Not that it wasn't warranted," she adds before I can chew her out, "but you were, and she still loved you."

I shake my head. "Rachel never loved me. I won't deny that I loved her, but… she never looked at me like… never *talked* to me like…"

"Your townsperson," Elise supplies.

My townsperson.

"Luna," I breathe. Just saying the name makes my taste buds turn sour, even as my fingers tingle, searching for the hands they got used to holding.

"Luna," Elise repeats, testing the name out. "That totally sounds like the name of a person you would fall in love with. The kind of person."

She is. She… really is.

"Her brother almost drowned in the quarry," I tell her. Not because of the job, but because I want to talk about her. And because if I talk about this instead of her outright, it might make this horrible feeling go away. "Last August, he's been in the hospital ever since, braindead."

"Jesus," Elise mutters. "They should really consider just filling those things in. If they're causing this much damage."

"They put up railings," I say. "People don't just fall in. They're either thrown in, or they jump."

I don't mention that of the two, I fall closer to the latter category. I probably won't tell anyone else about that, ever.

"Still," Elise says. "Drunk high schoolers are stupid, they should have knocked the threat out ahead of time. Especially since they're not being used anymore."

"It's the party quarry where it happens," I mumble, throwing my arm over my eyes to shield them from the light shining directly from my window. I think about shifting into the shadows, but my back is so tired that I don't bother. "*The Ledge* is apparently what it's called, if you can believe it."

"High Schoolers will do anything to make their lame activities sound cool. *The Ledge* sounds like they were partying at a rock concert, not getting drunk next to a body of water."

I shake my head aggressively, eyes widening. "No, no, no, you haven't seen these things. They're not just bodies of water, this isn't a pool. They're terrifying."

"I've seen them."

"In pictures," I say. "Trust me, it's not the same."

I saw it from within. I saw every little thing, and the thought that Carlos saw exactly what I saw makes my skin crawl. Pushing up on the solid stone, no idea which way is right or left, whether he was swimming toward the surface or further into the abyss.

God, he must have been so terrified. I could tear apart the people that did this to him, I could *destroy* them. If I just knew who they were-

My thoughts trail off, because suddenly my mind is sending me back to that day Luna pulled me from the water, where she told me about Carlos and everything done to him. The conversation flashes before my eyes, as she laid out the story of how Carlos came to end up in that quarry, and then the hospital bed.

I pull the words from the back of my memory, drawing them back into the sun we'd laid in that day. What had she said about who brought him? *Someone* brought him, because he was a freshman, and freshman don't get invited to the ledge-

Some of the upperclassmen from the team decided to bring him along. Initiation ritual, or something ridiculous.

Before the season started.

After that summer camp I keep hearing about, with the soccer-

"Oh, God," I whisper, fumbling my phone.

When I pick it up, Elise is yelling through the receiver. "Alex? Alex, what happened? Did she text you?"

"Oh, *God*," I say again, my thoughts running a million miles an hour, so fast my mind can't catch up. My hand covers my mouth as I consider, and... yeah. Yeah.

Springing to my feet, I practically run toward my computer, fingers flying over the keyboard and making about a thousand typos while my phone stays wedged between my cheek and shoulder.

"Alex, are you okay? Is it about Luna?"

"Technically," I say. "Let me call you back. I need to-"

"Alex, you sound like you saw a ghost-"

I did. Six, actually. With only one of their companions still alive.

I pause in my typing, moving to hold my phone. "I need you to trust me, okay? I'll call you back tomorrow."

"Okay," Elise says, not sounding entirely convinced. "I love you, you know that."

"I love you more. Thanks for not breaking up with me."

Pressing the end button and shoving my phone away, I frantically search up not West Rutland High, but Rutland City High School for the roster I'm looking for. I scroll back to last summer, to a catalog of names archived from their day camps, scanning it for seven in particular. It's not hard to find. Soccer's one of the few sports they offer during the summer. My eyes read them one by one, counting them steadily on my fingers.

One.

Two.

Three.

Four.

Five.

Six.

My finger shakes, brushing over Parker's name.

Seven.

Chapter Twenty-Two

I DON'T BELIEVE IN coincidences. Not when they're staring me in the face like this. Out of all the victims, Xavier was the only one who didn't play soccer, so it wasn't a solid connection before, but he went to that camp. Whether he wanted to start playing as a Senior, or if he just needed something to do with his friends, I'll probably never know, but it doesn't matter, because here they all are. Parker had just graduated, so he was listed as an assistant to the coach, and the rest were rising Juniors and Seniors.

This can't be a coincidence. I stumble toward my laptop, pulling up a million instagram and facebook tabs, the roster still on my phone. None of the five victims have anything posted from that night, or anything from the week or two after. I've looked at their profiles enough to be absolutely sure.

But I start peeling through the rest of the camp roster, digging into the lives of each boy who is still alive. Sam, Miles, another Jason. Adam, Wes. I pull up short on the profile of a boy named Jeremy. Like the victims, he also went radio silent for a while afterward, but he posted something that Saturday in August, when the party just started. Before it happened, before they even got to the quarry. Before that last day of camp came to an end.

The picture is of nine boys lined up on a field. One, two, three, four, five victims. And a sixth victim, who I now recognize from a hospital bed, and from a soft resemblance to Luna. And only three others who are still alive from that soccer camp, one of which is my brother.

Oh, God.

Falling from my desk chair, I barely have time to shove my phone into my pocket before bolting to the door. Tearing it open, I sprint from my room, from the apartment, and all the way down the road, maneuvering toward my destination. Over and over, I run what I found through my head, trying to find a flaw, a hole, where it doesn't make sense, but none appear. It's the *only* thing that makes sense.

I stumble as I pass Suzie's, colliding with a hard body and tumbling to the ground. Gravel digs into my knees, and I whip my head up to see an alarmed Parker standing over me, arms extended.

I never thought I'd feel scared looking at my little brother.

"I'm sorry!" he exclaims, reaching a hand out to help me up, and I'm so dumbfounded that I take it. "I didn't see you coming, although to be fair, you were sprinting *way* faster than a normal jogger should be."

Gasping for breath, I just stare at him, and I try to imagine him doing it. Parker didn't hang out with the soccer boys, but he took Carlos under his wing. He *cared* about Carlos. Could he have really... Could he have it in him, to get that kind of payback?

When I don't respond, he awkwardly adds. "I was just going to work. So..."

"You said you didn't know the victims. But you played soccer with three of them, right?" I don't hesitate to consider how crazy this must make me sound.

He stiffens, glancing left and right, before rigidly saying, "Sharing an extracurricular doesn't make you friends."

"And you were in band with Xavier. He signed up for a soccer camp with you."

His eyes widen, his breathing picking up in a panic, and he steps back. "Who are you?"

I stare at him, wanting to say more, but I can't think of the right question to ask, if it even exists. As a matter of fact, he *is* looking at me like I've lost my mind, and I curse myself for ruining everything. "I have to go," I say, taking off even though I don't quite want to leave him alone. But he's going to work, and that gives me time. Time to get to her. A stitch starts to tear at my side about halfway there, but I don't slow down, only one person on my mind.

A person who really doesn't want to see me.

I arrive anyway, first checking the picnic table, only to find it deserted. I should have known she wouldn't stay there where I could find her, where I would know to look for her. Resorting to the front door, I knock as loudly as I can, the wood of the door burning the side of my hand.

I feel like Rachel, calling a phone that will never answer.

"*Luna!*" I scream, tearing my throat hoarse. "*Luna, I need you to open the door.*"

There's no response, and I nearly start sobbing as the thoughts continue jumbling around my head. I know I'm right.

I have to be right.

"*I'm not fucking around, this is serious!*" I shout, wondering if she's even home. My arm's getting tired, so I switch to pounding with both fists.

"*Luna!*" I bellow, not caring if I wake up her neighbors, the street, the entire town for that matter. I'm relatively close to just breaking in when the door swings open, and I nearly tumble inside from my momentum.

She doesn't let me, though, because before I have a chance to regain my balance Luna's roughly shoving me back, hand pressed into my chest, until I land sprawled out in the grass.

She glares down at me, eyes puffy and red, and the sight makes the hairs on my neck stand up. "I told you I needed you to leave me alone. I *told you that*."

I hold up my hands, leaning back on my elbows as I gasp for breath. "I know. But I need you to listen to me more than you need space."

"I don't *need* to listen to you. You lied to me."

I stumble to my feet, keeping my distance so she doesn't run away again. "I know. I know that, and I'm... so unbelievably sorry. Like, I've almost thrown up twice today, sorry. And I want to talk about that, I want to tell you how none of the other stuff was fake, how you shouldn't doubt a *word* I ever said about us, but that's not why I'm here."

This seems to pique her interest a little. At least, she plants her feet, and doesn't look ready to storm back inside. She clearly still wants to tear my eyes out, though. "Oh, is there something more important? Another bullshit excuse?"

"It has nothing to do with us, and everything to do with you," I say, breathless, the run over here still making my lungs squeal. "It's about Carlos."

Her eyes flash. "Don't talk about him."

I rub at my temples, gripping my head between my hands to keep seeing straight. God, not having my glasses is really giving me a constant headache. "Luna, *listen-*"

"No!" she cries. "You don't get to come over here after *stomping all over me* and talk about my *dead brother.*"

I shout over her, because that's the only way to make her hear me. "I know who hurt him! I know what happened that night."

Luna's eyes darken. "Alex, don't you dare try to distract me with more lies."

"I'm not," I say desperately, heart pounding against my ribs. "That's why I'm here, isn't it? In West Rutland? To figure out why all these bad things have been happening to this town, to you? I'm not making this up."

Her gaze clears, lips parting. But I don't let her speak, not yet.

I hold up a finger, ready for the part I've been dreading. "First, I need to get this out of the way, and I seriously need you to be completely honest with me. And whatever you say, I'll believe you, because even though you don't trust me, I trust you." I pause as she waits, looking like she's on her past thread of patience. "Are you doing it?"

Anger gets replaced by genuine confusion, and she asks. "What?"

I wave my hands around crazily, because maybe I'm on my last thread, too. "The murders, the revenge for your brother, are you doing it?"

"Am I *murdering* people? Jesus, Alex, no- wait, revenge?" She looks so heartbrokenly shocked that I know she's telling the truth immediately. "What revenge?"

I run my hands through my hair as I pace in front of her, trying to get my thoughts in order in a way that she'll believe me. "You might not know who hurt Carlos, but someone does. And they're drowning them in the quarry."

"Alex, what the hell-"

"It's *payback,* don't you see?" I plead, turning to face her dead on. "Someone's killing your brother's killers in the exact same way that they hurt him."

"Alex-"

"I know it," I say, not giving her the chance to argue. "Your brother got hurt when he was at a party with a bunch of soccer players, right? That's what you said?"

She nods dumbly.

"Every single kid who's gotten killed went to that summer soccer camp that you were talking about, they were all at that same party with him." I pull something up on my phone, shoving it in her face. "And they were all in the last picture taken of Carlos alive. Alive and well, at least," I correct myself.

Luna snatches the phone from me, staring at the photo with so much intensity her eyes begin to water. "I've never seen this picture."

I breathe a little easier, because she won't run away now. She might not believe me yet, but she's on her way. I crouch down, resting my elbows on my knees. "Because before right this moment, these boys didn't matter to you, at least not together, or in regard to Carlos. But... Luna, these two incidents- what happened to your brother, and these murders going on now... they're not separate, Luna. They're the same freaking thing."

Luna sways from side to side, and I jump up to catch her just in time as my phone flies from her hands, smashing on the walkway. I barely spare it a second glance, instead focusing on Luna's blanched face and clammy hands. I lower her to the ground, until she's settled in the grass beside me, head pushing into her hands. It tears a sharp pain from my chest not to keep her in my lap, but I force myself to slide away, until we're not touching at all.

I watch Luna's labored breathing become steadier and steadier, her fingers clench tighter and tighter. "I never wanted to lie to you," I whisper. "I should have told you why I was here, but then it was too late, and ... I'm not lying now, I swear to you, I'm as sure as I've ever been."

"I know," she whispers, still not lifting her head. "I know, just..."

I wait, not so patiently, as her back rises and falls with the rhythm of her erratic breaths. She's wearing a baggy T-shirt that falls past her shorts, and she hugs that shirt around her, trying to keep her lungs in place.

I bite my lip. There's no point waiting. "There's something else."

"Oh, god," she moans, finally jerking back up. "What else could there possibly be?"

I press my lips together. "If this whole thing is revenge, which I think it is… that means the person doing it has to be extraordinarily close to Carlos. And by extension…" I hesitate, because her eyes are already widening. "Close to you."

Luna's breathing starts to pick back up, and I slide closer to her. I don't reach toward her, don't hug her. I just let our legs brush together, to let her know I'm still here. Before she loses her grip on reality, she needs to know that I'll always be here.

She opens her eyes, turning toward me. "Or maybe not. Maybe it was one of his friends, someone who saw what went down at the party."

I suck on my lip. "That's my other theory."

Luna thinks back to the picture, eyes somehow widening even more. "Parker."

My throat bobs. "He… That's what I was going to say earlier, he's been lying about knowing the victims, but I *know* he was close with Xavier, I saw him with his mom, and I heard him in this screaming match with Anthony-"

Shaking her head, Luna holds her hands up. "You can't seriously think-"

"I'm accusing your family right now," I say. "It's only fair that I accuse my own, too."

Maniacally, Luna asks, "But if it's not someone who saw it, how could anyone *possibly* know exactly who did it if Carlos wasn't *awake?*"

"Parker could have been at that party," I say solemnly, even though it rips my heartstrings to say out loud. "But you said Carlos' brain activity fluctuated for a few days. Was Carlos ever fully alert after they found him, even just for a minute or two? That can happen sometimes, a patient will wake up briefly, before..." I trail off. She knows what happens next.

She shakes her head. "I mean, he opened his eyes a few times, but I never heard him talk."

I seam my mouth into a line. "*You* never heard. Who went to visit Carlos those first few days?"

Luna shakes her head. "I don't know, but Alex, this is ridiculous. How could... how could someone-"

"Anger can make someone do a lot," I whisper.

Rubbing her face, she asks, "But why wait so long after Carlos? *Months passed*, Alex, *why now?*"

I sigh. "Anger can get worse once it's built up over time," I say in a hushed voice. "Keep it in too long, and it'll explode eventually, in one way or another."

Horrified, Luna says, "It shouldn't have exploded like this."

"No," I say. "But it did. *Who went to see him?*"

Swallowing, tugging on a strand of her hair, Luna thinks. "Me, my mom, my dad. My other aunt's family came up, but that was a few days later, and by then..."

By then he'd stopped opening his eyes.

"All the nurses and doctors, obviously," she adds, desperate to think of someone outside her immediate family. "And anyone could have visited, really, they didn't need our permission to go."

"But you were there the whole time, so you would have seen them."

She hesitates, lip wobbling. "I- I mean, not twenty four hours a day, but..." She trails off, voice faint. "Yeah. We barely left him alone."

I put my face in my hands.

When I look up again, Luna's shaking her head, standing up to walk around the yard. She walks circles around me, stomping so hard she tears tracks in the grass. She finally stops in front of me, jaw set. "Neither of my parents did this. And neither did your brother."

I gaze up at her, because what if she's wrong? "Then who did?"

Chapter Twenty-Three

IT TAKES ME ANOTHER twenty minutes to work up the courage to tell her about Lucia's fight with Reyna, and the sun is well on its way to setting.

"That's why I ran off," I explain after painstakingly recalling every word I overheard. "To go after Reyna and ask what the hell that was about."

We've moved around the house to the picnic table, and while I've sat down on the table, feet propped up on the bench, Luna continues pacing around the yard. "Back up. What made you follow her in the first place?"

I shrug. "Call it a gut feeling?"

Her eyes narrow. "Is that something all reporters have?"

My stomach flips. "First off, I'm not a reporter. I'm a journalist. Second, yes, I'm sure they do. It was just the way she was acting, the look on her face. She was so furious, she had to be going *somewhere*."

"And she was angrily going to see my mother," Luna repeats numbly.

I nod, resting my elbows against my knees to steady myself, because all Luna's pacing is making me dizzy. "Like I said, I missed the beginning, but there was definitely some yelling going on. She wanted Lucia to *tell* her something."

"And Reyna didn't tell you anything when you went after her."

I shake my head bitterly. "I might have burned her down eventually, but you walked in on her yelling at me about… much of the same things you yelled at me about."

"Glad me and her have something in common," she mutters. "But now I'm sort of wishing I hadn't noticed you left for a few more minutes."

I shrug. "Maybe I would have gotten it out of her, maybe not."

Luna takes a deep breath, turning to face me as the panic starts to overtake her features again. "Just because Reyna thinks she's guilty of something, doesn't mean she *is*."

"I totally agree," I say honestly. "And it doesn't mean she's guilty of… what I'm thinking."

"But someone is…" Luna trails off.

"Yeah. I'm sure of it. But going off my 'reporter gut feeling,'" I quote her. "Your mom knows something. *I'm not talking about this right now.*' That's what she said. Who says that if there isn't something to talk about?"

"Someone trying to get rid of a lunatic?" Luna suggests with wide eyes.

My eyes flash. "Reyna's not a lunatic. She's an angry girl with a dead brother, trying to figure out who killed him and why."

"My mother didn't *kill* anyone!" Luna bursts out incredulously, breathing scattered, chest struggling to draw in air. "She's not *capable* of that."

"I never said she was-"

"You're *implying* it," she snaps. "You're implying... all over the place right now."

"Luna, something's going on here-"

She points toward the road. "Then go find me evidence. Go search for the evidence that none of the cops have been able to find. *Go.*"

I can hear it in her voice. She's done hearing me out, done humoring me.

I hop off the table. "Like I said, I don't know anything for certain except that these two things are connected."

Something gutters in her eyes. "Maybe they are, maybe they aren't. But if they are, then I *know* who hurt my brother. I don't want to know anything else." I exhale, but she's still pointing toward the exit, unmoving. "If you'd never come here, *none* of this ridiculous bullshit would even be on my radar. I don't *want* it." The last words tear from her throat in a sob, like she's trying to convince herself far more than me.

All I say is, "You should," before backing away, desperately trying to think of a plan B.

I'VE ALWAYS GENERALLY HAD good morals when it comes to my investigating, but Luna somehow makes all logic go out the window. I would normally hesitate about tearing a family apart, like I have been all summer, but when I finally knock on the front door of Sadie Jefferson's house, I don't hesitate at all.

Parker's at work, and I'm happy his step dad is somewhere else, because only Sadie is home when she answers the door.

She doesn't seem to recognize me, which makes this a whole lot harder, and means it's going to take a whole lot longer. "Hi. Can I help you?"

I skip over the formalities. "My name is Alex Brown."

She recognizes me, then. She knows that last name, because she breathes it out. "Brown... You're Henry Brown's daughter."

I swallow. "I am. And you're Parker's mother. My... my..." I can't bring myself to say *brother*, or even *half brother*, not right now. Not under the circumstances.

Her expression breaks, and she steps back, motioning inside. "You'd better come in, then."

She makes us both hot cups of tea, and I perch on the couch next to her, trying to find the right thing to say in order to get the answers I need. And even though I want to meet him, I want to have a relationship... Those aren't the answers I need right now. I've been building up to knocking on that door this entire summer, and I came for the opposite Jefferson.

"I'm sorry you had to find out about Parker this way," Sadie says gently. "And I'm sorry about your father."

Emotion catches in my throat, but I don't have time for that now. "Thank you. I've been trying to figure out what to do about him ever since, but every idea I got seemed like a bad one, until I just... couldn't wait anymore."

Sadie sighs. "Well, he's at work right now." As if I don't know that. "Which is probably for the best. He... didn't take the news of his real father well."

Curiosity getting the better of me, I ask, "He only found out when the inheritance came in, then."

She nods, eyes welling up. "I never... I never imagined that Henry would leave him anything, we were together for such a brief time, and we agreed it would be better to part as if it had never happened, despite the baby. We both had families." She smiles wetly, eyes crinkling. "He had *you*."

I open my mouth, searching for what to say. "I want... I wanted to.." I trail off. "He hates his father, doesn't he? Hates us?"

Her shoulders slump. "I tried to explain the situation, that we were both at fault, but you know how personal biases can work. He didn't want the inheritance, he didn't want... anything. I tucked it away in a bank account, because I think he'll come around someday, but for now..." She shakes her head. "I'm afraid you've come all this way for a brother who isn't ready for any more life changing news."

My throat bobs. "And does he know about me, then?"

Does he know he has a sister? Does he know that when his father abandoned him, I didn't get a chance not to?

Her eyes softened. "Yes."

My heart cleaves in two. "And he- he doesn't want to meet me?"

Her face tightens. "You have to understand. He's already lost so much."

"How could gaining a sister possibly be a loss?" I'm crying now, unable to keep the emotions that have built within me for months now from spilling out.

"Finding out what you could have had, but didn't, can be just as painful. When he thinks of you, he thinks of a girl who got raised by both of her biological parents. Who wasn't lied to all her life."

"I *was-*"

"I know," Sadie murmurs, effectively shutting up my defense. "But not in the same way." She pauses with a sigh, shaking her head. "You've seen what this town has been going through."

There it is. An opening, and even as I mourn something I never even had, tears dripping down my cheeks, I take it. "I have. Did he know those boys well, then?"

She seems to hesitate, but her face crumples, and she whispers. "Just one of them. He knew them all, of course, but… yes, one of them was very special to him."

Was she speaking of Carlos? Or Xavier? Or one of the others, perhaps, because I couldn't trust anything anyone told me.

"I should go," I say, standing abruptly and wiping down my lap even though there's absolutely nothing there. "Do you mind if I use your bathroom first? I just…" I scrub at my face. "I need a moment."

Sympathy plagues the lines of her face, and she says, "Of course. Just down the hall." She leans forward, grabbing both of our mugs, mine still untouched, and heads off to the kitchen.

It hadn't been a full lie. I had truly been crying, I'm not talented enough to conjure up fake tears. But I'm also good at my job, and I know a good opportunity when I see it.

There are only three doors down the hallway, all wide open. It's nice to see. Something about open doors implies trust, and it's nice to see proof that he has a good home life. The first is clearly Sadie and her husband's room, and the second is the bathroom, where I'm supposed to stop.

Instead, I go all the way to the room at the end of the hall, painted a muted blue color, dull from years of wear. I don't have time to hesitate, slipping in until I'm out of sight of the doorway. I don't even know what I'm looking for. What sort of evidence does a serial killer leave in his room with an open door? That alone is almost enough evidence for me that he couldn't have done this, but I dive ahead anyway, observing the space.

It's a mess. Not in a usual teenager way, with clothes strewn about and a few plates left behind. No, this bedroom looks like it hasn't been cleaned for weeks, and that it might have actually been intentionally trashed. A stack of papers has been strewn across the floor, like someone threw it, and there are several dents in the wall at foot level. But what catches my eye is a pile of torn up pictures shoved into the corner of the room, jagged edges poking this way and that.

I approach, knowing this is a *huge* invasion of privacy, but I don't have *time*. I need to know. I need him to give me something.

The pictures are polaroids, consisting of only two familiar faces. One of them is, of course, Parker, smiling brightly in a way that I've never seen. Whatever smile I might have seen him wear at Suzie's, it wasn't his real one, and I feel a drop of shame that I can't tell the difference. Here, he's glowing with the other boy, whether curled into his side, nestling into his neck, or kissing him.

I remember that day at the quarry, hugging Xavier's mom with a mixture of grief and what I now know to be disbelief. Because I now know why he was lying.

He and Xavier had been together.

My finger floats across the one photo that remains intact, buried at the bottom of the pile. He must have missed it, or maybe he'd reached it last during his tirade, unable to destroy that last piece of evidence that he had loved a boy and a boy had loved him back. They don't smile at the camera in the picture, but rather each other, like they forgot Parker was even taking a picture. Xavier had his fingers over his mouth, suppressing a laugh, and Parker gazed down at him with such love that my entire body shakes with the weight of it.

One of them was very special to him, his mom had said. Special, indeed.

"Alex?"

I jump, the picture fluttering from my fingers as I hurtle around with wide eyes, hands up to signify innocence even though I most certainly am *not*.

"I'm sorry," I say, tears coming back immediately, because I mean it. "I'm so sorry, I just, I was just curious, and I needed-"

Sadie isn't angry. In fact, she does the last thing I expect, and envelops me in a bear hug. The kind of hug parents give their children, the kind that I don't think I've ever had in my entire life.

This woman didn't raise a killer.

"It's okay," she murmurs into my hair as I sob. "It's okay. I know. It's okay."

She pulls back, hands on my cheeks, wiping away my tears. She's about to say something else comforting when her eyes catch on the picture I'd dropped, panic replacing any other emotion. "Oh." I look over my shoulder, heart fluttering in happiness at the picture of what he'd had and sinking at the sadness of what he'd lost, but Sadie just seems horrified. "You can't tell anyone."

Confused, I turn back. "Wha- oh." My brain catches up, because this isn't New York City. This is a small town where kids who aren't the norm still live in fear, and hide in the shadows. Hide in the confines of torn polaroid pictures taken in private. "I would never." I pause, realizing I need to give her another nudge. "Even though I never had to stay in the closet, I never would have wanted to be outed without permission."

She sucks in a breath. "You-"

"We're more alike than just in looks, I guess."

Her shoulders relax, and she blinks away her own tears. "This town. I love it for everything it's given me, but I hate it for how behind it still is. They pretended like they weren't even friends, too afraid someone would figure it out." She shook her head, letting out a small laugh. "Parker even signed up for band to spend more time with him, even though he hated the trumpet. Xavier went to some soccer camp with Parker after his graduation to make it up to him." She blinks rapidly. "They would have done anything for each other."

And there it was. His lying, the secrets… it all made sense, and my soul found a semblance of peace. "I understand. I'm sorry that he's had to go through that. I'm even more sorry that he lost him."

"Me too." She looks back up at me, almost desperately. "So you understand even more, now. Why he can't handle, well, *you* right now. It might just end him. I can't believe he's still standing as it is."

And even as it pains me, I need to move on, because I have other questions that need answers right now. "I understand."

Chapter Twenty-Four

SUZIE'S HAS THEIR SIGN flipped to *CLOSED*, which is weird, because they don't usually close until nine. I wouldn't have even stopped my stride if I hadn't noticed it, but now it's an instinct to look through the diner windows, to see if they're busy, if Jo is working. If Parker is working.

He isn't, but she is. Well, not working, but inside, along with another silhouette that I immediately decipher as Lucia. Deja vu barrels toward me, and I'm thrown back to my first time going inside the diner, when I joined them at the counter. The same counter they lean over now, speaking in hushed, fiery whispers.

I almost go to the door and knock, to ask why they closed early. But Lucia's speaking with the same intensity I heard in her conversation with Reyna, so I hold back. I quicken my pace, watching their animated faces and positive they don't see me as I round the side of the building. There's a dumpster pressed against the brick wall, and I squeeze myself behind it. I'm not sure what I'm waiting for, but I stay and wait anyway.

Several minutes tick by, the stench of the disposed trash curling towards my nostrils with every passing second. I breathe through my mouth and snake my hand up to my face to plug my nose, leaning my head against the side of the building. I listen for something, anything, but the walls are too thick to make anything out.

The stone behind me vibrates with the sound of the familiar bell, and I know that someone is leaving. The slam of the door shutting comes next, followed by intense but quiet voices flowing on the wind, stretching toward my ears. I scooch further toward the corner, as far as I can go while still remaining hidden.

"Jo," Lucia's saying. "Don't. That's not an option."

"It absolutely is, and probably a better one."

"I'll go," Lucia cuts her off, and the sounds of their steps halt in the parking lot. "You... you stay here, okay? Or go home, but..."

"Lucia."

"You can't stop me," she snaps. "You have to let me handle this."

"Lucia," Jo says again, but she doesn't get another word. Lucia enters my vision first, striding with a purpose down the road. Jo starts to follow before holding herself back, hands covering her mouth. I can't quite tell if she's crying, but she seems to come to a decision, because she turns on her heel and marches back into the diner.

I roll away from the dumpster, air rushing back into my lungs as I allow myself my first full breath in ten minutes. I lean forward, peering around the side of the building, but Lucia has already disappeared from view.

I fall back against the wall, trying to steady the breathing that spiraled out of control as I eavesdropped. I lay my hand flat across my chest, counting the rises and falls in my head until I lose count, until it's something near normal again.

It's only once the pounding inside my skull has eased that the conversation I heard dawns over me, the reality of what it might mean, where she might be going.

Oh, God. Where is she going?

Where is she going where is she going where is she going-

Reyna's words echo in the back of my head from earlier, when she spat them in Lucia's face. *You know where I'll be tonight.*

All of a sudden, I know, too, and I take off towards the other side of town once more, following the invisible tracks Lucia dropped behind her.

I DON'T KNOW WHICH quarry she's heading to.

I speed walk through the deserted town, trying not to look overwhelmingly suspicious, even though the way I keep looking behind me *definitely* does. I can take a breath once I forge into the trees but freeze when I go to pull out the flashlight on my phone. The image of the device dropping onto the concrete, where I left it, flashes behind my eyes, and I curse.

Okay. I've done this quite a few times now. I know the path.

Slowing my pace and feeling around for the space between the clusters of trees, I operate by scattered moonlight, following the sliver of light that drips along the trail. God, in New York I'd be screwed (as Luna would say, the light pollution would fuck me over), but here the stars act as my guide, pulling me towards where they found Anthony's body.

I stop just shy of the tree line, listening for any voices, but there's nothing. Animal sounds and rustling rise up around me, but when I get a good look of the clearing through the branches, no one is there.

I spin around, finding that I'm not all that surprised. If Reyna wanted to draw Lucia out, she wouldn't bring her to the scene of Anthony's death.

She'd bring her to Carlos's.

I hear them before I see them when I reach The Ledge, the voices bouncing through the trees. They have no reason to be quiet right now, no reason to think anyone else would be crazy enough to come out here at night alone, especially these days.

God, I think as I step carefully over a twig, shimmying between two narrow trees. I *must* be crazy.

Each breath I take feels too loud, every step I take monstrous. The ground seems to shake beneath me as I approach, but they're so loud and wrapped up in each other that I shouldn't even be worried.

"Reyna," Lucia is saying, voice strained as she tries to stay calm. "I know you're upset-"

"*Upset?*" Reyna shouts incredulously. "*Upset?* Lucia, that's the understatement of the *year*, I'm *furious*."

"And you have the right to be," Lucia says. "But I don't know why this anger is directed at me."

"Stop playing dumb! You know exactly what you did!" Reyna's voice is raw and hoarse, and I wonder how long she's been screaming, pleading with Lucia to tell the truth.

I shift forward, until only a few layers of trees keep me out of sight, and they finally drop into view. Reyna jabs a finger at Lucia's chest, backing her up toward the railing, until she's leaning back against it.

"Reyna," Lucia warns, gripping the metal pole behind her. "I need you to calm down."

"*Calm down?*" Reyna takes another step forward, but Lucia has nowhere to go. "Look at what you've done, and you have the *audacity* to tell *me* to calm down. I don't owe you anything. You owe me *everything*."

The last thing I'm expecting is for Reyna to lunge forward the way she does, but before I can even blink, they've both tumbled over the railing and into the water.

"No!" The sound tears from my throat before I can stop it, but it's overshadowed by the voice behind me, a body sprinting past me, knocking me sideways in the process.

"*MOM!*"

Luna tears through the forest, faster than I've ever seen a human move, ducking under the railing and following where her mom and Reyna disappeared before I can even take a step. I start after her, but then I'm shoved aside by another body, a sturdier body, bolting after Luna. I shake myself out of my stupor, racing after her, the sounds of yells, splashes, and shouts clogging my ears the closer and closer I get.

I bend under the railing, trying to make out the shapes thrashing in the water. I make out Luna first, inserting herself between Reyna and the other two. The third woman's face shifts just slightly, and I make out Jo's features as her arms wrap around Lucia. But Reyna is relentless, trying to kick and elbow her way through the barrier.

"*Alex*," Luna gurgles, snapping my attention back to her, water splashing across her face. "Help!"

"Damnit," I mutter, because those two words are all it takes, and without another thought I'm slipping into the fray. The cool water washes over me, ripping the air from my lungs and the thoughts from my head. The only one left is *swim. You need to swim.*

My head breaks through the surface, where noise crowds around me once more. Shooting myself forward, I pick out Reyna, who's still ferociously attacking the others, barely remaining above the surface, devoting her limbs solely to her assault. I hesitate, unsure where to start, how to insert myself into the flying limbs. I'm right to be wary, because as soon as I swim within range, her elbow tears back, clocking me in the jaw, and I propel backwards. Blood from my lips washes into the water, but it's so dark I can't distinguish the red from the inky black.

"Son of a bitch," I mumble, spitting out water, and an idea comes into my mind. Bracing myself, and giving myself as much air and courage as possible, I dive beneath the water.

The water may look murky from above, but that's only because it goes so deep. In reality, the water is clearer than I expected when I open my eyes, and I can make out the shape of Reyna's legs, kicking to keep herself afloat, and to cause as much damage to her enemy as possible. But she's not kicking backward, so I swim forward. In one swoop, I wrap my arms around her legs, and using all my limited strength, I tug her underwater with me.

The sound of someone screaming under water is terrifying, quite possibly worse than my own screams that I heard the last time I found myself submerged. I can't see Reyna's face, because she's facing away from me, but the cluster of tiny bubbles that she screams out propel toward the surface, carrying her fear with them.

I count in my head. I count until my lungs burn, until Reyna has stopped screaming and waving her arms, and started reaching toward the surface again. Once her hands are nowhere near my body, I kick up, tugging her with me.

When she breaks the surface after me, gasping and sputtering for air, I push her roughly against the wall of the quarry, pinning her arms above her and over the edge, wrapping one of my legs around hers to keep them still, using the other to keep us afloat

"*Stop. Moving!*" I scream in her face.

She blinks away water, and she's so surprised by who she sees that she momentarily stops struggling. "Alex, what-"

"Shut up," I say. "And if you move, I swear to god I'll pull you under again."

Reyna swallows, eyes wide, because she clearly hadn't expected this fight to be three against one.

There shouldn't have even been a fight at all.

I glance to my left as quickly as possible, not wanting to tear my eyes from Reyna for more than a few seconds. I look just long enough to see Luna, her arms still wrapped around her mother, who clings to the two women on either side of her like a lifeline.

"Alex," she breathes, and the way she says it compared to how Reyna said it makes the water seem less tight, less claustrophobic. "Jesus."

"We have to stop meeting like this," I respond, straining to keep my mouth above the water, before jerking my head in the other direction, toward the path she'd used to get me to land. "Get out of the water. Now. Before I lose my grip."

But it doesn't matter, because Reyna has stopped struggling. In fact, she's stopped moving completely, and the only reason she's not falling beneath the surface is because I keep my body pinned to her.

"Reyna," I whisper, listening as the water splashes made by Luna, Lucia, and Jo grow fainter as they paddle across the way. "Reyna, can you hear me?"

"I can hear you," she says, voice dull and flat.

"Can you tread water?" I ask, panting with the effort of keeping two humans afloat. I've never been a great swimmer, I struggle to keep *myself* up on a good day. "Can you do that?"

Reyna just shakes her head, mouth sealed shut. I hate to think about the five stages of grief right now, but she seems to still be progressing through them. All at once, as soon as her lips part, the anger and bargaining seep out of her, replaced by the heavy depression, the misery of the loss of her brother. That weight snaps something within her, and she lets out a strangled cry as her tears mingle with the lingering water dripping from her hair, until I can't tell which is which.

"Reyna," I say again, louder. "I need you to swim, I'm not that strong. I need you to help me."

"You should just let me go," she sobs, fighting against the restraint on her arms, but her heart clearly isn't in it. "You were gonna drown me anyway, you should just finish the job."

"I was never gonna drown you," I say harshly, nausea sweeping over me at the very thought. "I just did that to get you to chill, so you'd stop hitting me in the face."

Her face crumples. "I hit you."

"Just once," I say, running a tongue along my lip, the metallic taste of blood spreading around my mouth. Reyna moans, starting to kick again, and I just shake her against the rocks. "Stop it. You are *not* drowning on my watch."

She looks up at me, eyes slits in the night, no light peeking through. "I deserve it."

"No," I say, voice hard and final. "That was your whole point, right? That no one who's lost their lives here has deserved it? That's why you came tonight."

She barely has enough energy to nod, and I can barely make it out because of how hard she's shaking.

"Good," I say, not entirely satisfied but figuring that's good enough for now. "No one else is drowning in this goddamn quarry."

Testing to see what she'll do, I ease my grip around her legs, although my hands stay around her arms like iron. I stiffen when I feel her legs start to move, afraid I might get pummeled in the shins, but she moves slowly and delicately, kicking the water to bring her chin fully out of the water. I breathe a sigh of relief, finally using both my own legs to keep myself up as well.

Satisfied that she won't lash out as soon as I take my eyes off of her, I whip my head from side to side, frantic, searching for Luna in the dark water. I follow the path they would have taken, the one she guided me down, but find it deserted, not a molecule of water out of place outside the rings coming from Reyna and me.

"Alex!"

I jerk my head up to see Luna falling to her knees above us, grabbing onto Reyna's arms. Jo and Lucia join her soon after, looking haggard and wide eyed and a little banged up, but otherwise unharmed. It's only when I see them up on dry land that I sag, exhaustion and ticks of pain coursing through my limbs, unsure of how much longer I'll be able to hold myself up, let alone Reyna.

"Pull her out," I beg, releasing my death grip now that Luna holds her. My fingers come away stiff and stark white, curled in on themselves from holding something so aggressively for so long. I plunge them into the water, trying to shake them out, but my arms' mobility is decreasing moment by moment.

I cling to the edge, watching Reyna's limp body rise above me, water torrents tumbling from her skin and clothes. Luna flings her onto the land, and Reyna rolls onto her back, sputtering.

"Can you get to the edge?" Lucia asks now, placing a hand over mine where I grip the rocks to make sure I don't slip.

"No," Luna says immediately, reading the anguish on my face, the way I'm starting to drop under. "She can't." Lunging forward, Luna grabs me beneath my shoulders just before my nose goes under the surface, pulling me up and towards her. Jo seems to get the idea, because two other sturdy hands grab me, and the water falls away, replaced by a warm night breeze and tiny pebbles.

I collapse into Luna's lap, and she doesn't push me off like I'm half expecting her to. Instead, she bows around me, resting her head against my chest as she holds me.

When she doesn't say anything, I cough out, "You have to stop saving me. It's doing nothing for my ego."

Luna's shoulders rumble around me, a weak laugh erupting from her lips as she sits up. I can gaze at her now, perched above me, head wreathed with a circle of stars. She runs a hand down my forearm. "Your ego doesn't need my help." She pauses, and then asks, "Did he do it, then?"

I know what she means, eyes welling up. "I don't know. He has his secrets, but I just…" I shake my head, tears spilling onto my cheeks. "I don't think so." Though every muscle screams at me not to, I sit up in realization, pushing my hands against the solid ground. I might never go swimming again. "Were you following me?"

She tucks a strand of wet hair behind her ear, nodding. "If you've shown me anything, it's that you're persistent. I knew you'd go off and do… something." She glances at her mom, who stands with Jo a few feet away. "It's a good thing you did."

"It's a better thing *you* did," I say, breathless, glancing at Lucia. "Are you okay?"

She doesn't take her eyes off Reyna. "Fine. Are you?"

"I've had better hours, but nobody drowned."

"That's not true," Reyna whispers from her spot on her back. She hasn't moved since getting pulled out. "A lot of people have drowned."

Luna sucks in a harsh breath, and I shift my eyes between Reyna and Lucia, who's pulling Jo further and further away, toward the edge of the clearing. "Hey!" I call out, stumbling to my feet. "Going somewhere?"

I don't miss the way she steps in front of Jo, positioning herself between her and the rest of us. "What are you thinking?" Lucia asks, sounding exhausted.

I take a few steps toward her, and hear Luna stand behind me. "Honestly? At this point? Not a fucking clue."

She sighs. "Let me make things a little clearer. Ask me."

I shift uncomfortably, eyes flickering to Luna, whose head is going back and forth like she's at a tennis match. "I'm not sure I want to."

"You won't take your eyes off me until you do."

I stare at her, looking at Luna to ask for permission. She doesn't do anything, so I just say, "Fine. Did you do it?"

"No," Luna says without missing a beat.

"Luna-"

"No," she says again, sharp. "I listened to you before, now you listen to me. She didn't do it." She stares at me desperately. "I believe you about Parker. Believe me about her."

I stare at her, eyes narrowed. "I believe you." I jerk my head towards Lucia. "Now let me hear it from her."

Lucia's mouth is a thin line, but she doesn't look angry. "I didn't," she says softly. "As most people who lose loved ones to violence will tell you, it's best to avoid violence at all costs."

Jo flinches behind her, an expression flitting over her expression that's familiar, but impossible to recognize in the dark.

But Luna seems to recognize it, because her hand touches mine at my side. "Alex-"

Lucia moves further in front of her friend, or *little sister*, as Jo has described their old dynamic. She's taking a defensive stand, which doesn't make sense, because what does Jo need protecting from?

I find my hands raising into the air, taking a step back as my heart jumps into my throat. *Why are you so afraid, Alex? You know these people, and Lucia just said-*

My shoddy attempts at reassuring myself are blasted open when I see a hand reach toward a waistband, toward a lump I hadn't noticed before. How hadn't I noticed? Isn't my job to notice what others can't, to put the pieces together?

Fear suffocates Luna's voice as she repeats, "*Alex.*"

Lucia's not protecting Jo, I realize all at once, as Luna's mom shifts in front of the other woman even more. She's putting herself in her path, protecting *us* from *her*.

Lucia just has time to shriek, "*Run!*" before she's pushed aside. But we don't run, because the weapon's been drawn before we can move, and we're left staring down the barrel of a gun, Jo's sorrowful face waiting behind it.

Chapter Twenty-Five

MY HANDS WON'T STOP trembling. They're held up in front of my face, so I'm acutely aware of it. But I'd rather focus on that than the weapon pointed directly at my forehead, only a few feet of space in between. The people here are so nice, I'd almost forgotten this is a hunting town. And therefore, a gun town.

I glance at Lucia, who's landed on her stomach to the left of Jo, unharmed. Jo hadn't pushed to hurt, she'd pushed to get her out of the way. Because if there's one thing that I'm coming to realize, is that she might do just about anything to protect the Morgan family.

"Jo," I find myself saying, even though I have absolutely no control over my mouth. "What are you doing?"

She doesn't even look like she knows. Panic spreads across her features, and she's shaking as much as I am, which makes my pulse jump at the sight of her finger hovering over the trigger. "You're a reporter."

My eyes widen, because, *oh*. Word gets around in this town, jumping from Luna, to Lucia, to... "I'm not," I say, because technically, that's true.

"You are," she says. "That's why you came, to *investigate*."

I'm not a reporter. I'm a journalist. It's my job to do whatever I can for the story, the article, the truth. I've gone all over the place, with all kinds of people to write everything under the sun, but one thing I swore I'd never do was put my life on the line for a *job*.

You're not putting your life on the line for a story, I remind myself. *You're putting your life on the line for* her.

"Don't move," I murmur to Luna, and she's close enough that I can tap her foot with mine. She doesn't say anything, but she's shaking so much that I don't think she could follow me if she wanted to.

I shift, moving to the right, away from the water and towards the center of the clearing, and to my relief the gun follows me. I have no idea where Reyna is, but I know she hasn't moved, because no sounds come from behind me. "I did. I did do that, that's what my bosses told me to do."

Jo's breath hitches. "So that's why you were always coming into the diner? Because you knew?"

I shake my head, too quickly. Not because it's a lie, but because I'm afraid if I stay quiet for too long, she might accidentally shoot me. "No, no, I came in because your food is delicious, and I can't cook for shit. And I liked you, and the other people I met there."

Her lip wobbles, the hand not holding the gun squeezing into a fist at her side. "I don't believe you."

"You don't have to," I say. "It doesn't matter, because I never knew. I never knew until just now. Didn't you just see me accuse Lucia? I thought it was her, because only the immediate family and his closest friends could have known exactly who threw Carlos into the water, because they were the only ones who saw him in the hospital those first few days. I accused my own *brother*, Jo, because he could have been there that night. I had no idea."

Her next words surprised me, choked up and full of voice cracks. "Parker. As if he would ever hurt Xavier." I don't move an inch as she gazes over my shoulder, lost. "Xavier. I didn't want to hurt him."

I stare at her, because, what? "I don't-"

Tears spill down her cheeks. "He was there, that night at the party but he wasn't *there*. He was off with his boyfriend, they were always sneaking off, as if I didn't see them flirting during Parker's shifts at the diner. The reputations of small towns precede themselves, and those boys were so *scared*, even though it would have been *fine*, everyone would have been *fine*. But they were *sneaking around*, and Xavier got there first-"

"Xavier saw you," I exhale in realization. I can almost see it, Xavier waiting on bouncing feet in the woods by the quarry for his boyfriend to arrive, but Parker was late because his mom wouldn't let him out of the house, or his shift ran late. Relaxing against a tree, Xavier could see through the brush, a screaming match between a woman and a boy, the fury in her voice, the pleading in his.

The eventual silence of them both, the silence of death.

Xavier trying to run, to tell someone, but the crunching leaves beneath his feet boomed over the night, and Jo couldn't let him go, her mission wasn't done, there were more boys who hurt Carlos-

It clicks in my head all at once. Parker's grief, his lies, the disdain on Anthony's face. The secrets that piled up on my brother's shoulders, the ones that would stay there forever. Parker must know. He must have known what the boys were dying for, perhaps knowing from the beginning exactly what happened to Carlos.

Keep your mouth shut.

One secret exchanged for another.

"He didn't deserve it," Jo whispers, sounding like a wreck. "But the others... what they did..." She swallows, gathering herself. "I went. I went to the hospital that night, even before the family got there. Do you know how fast news can travel between high school students? A quick text from someone at the party, to someone getting a late dinner at the diner?"

I don't answer, unsure whether it's a rhetorical question, and not wanting to talk more than I have to for fear of saying the wrong thing.

"Fast," Jo says. "Faster than the time it took the cops and doctors to figure out who Carlos was, to contact Lucia. One of my workers got a text, and I was out the door in a matter of seconds."

Jo glances at Lucia, who's staring up at Jo with wide eyes. Lucia had known *something*, that's clear enough, but she evidently didn't know this. Jo goes on, "He was drifting in and out of consciousness when they brought him in. I guess it took a while for his body to enter the state of shock and damage that it ended up in."

Luna whimpers a few feet away, gasping through the tears that have started to fall. Every instinct in my body tells me to run to her, to comfort and hold her, but if Jo is going to pull that trigger, the only one in its path will be me.

But I can't look away from Jo, who says, "They let me in. It was so chaotic, I said I was his aunt, that his mom was out of town, and they just… let me in. Rutland City, they don't know any of us over here, they never second guessed me for a second." She swallows hard. "It wasn't a particularly long conversation. He told me who threw him in, four boys from that soccer camp, and I told him he would be just fine." Jo swallowed roughly. "It turned out only one of us was telling the truth. He was gone before I even left the room."

"So you *killed* them?" Luna moans. "You… you-"

"I had to." Jo's full-on sobbing now, and it'd be distracting if I weren't so worried about how carelessly she's holding that damn weapon. "You and Lucia, you became *ghosts*. I watched it happen, you evaporated in front of my very eyes."

"And *more death* was supposed to fix that?"

"It worked," Jo says desperately. "I watched you come alive again, with the distraction of a different tragedy, how it distanced you from your own."

"I didn't come alive because of the people dying," Luna says brokenly. "That was because of Alex."

I don't have time to overthink her words, or to even recognize the aching in my heart. Jo's taken a step toward me, and that same heart stops completely.

I hold my hands up higher, fingers and legs trembling so much I fear I might just collapse and let her shoot me. But I keep my voice steady and strong, fighting through the fear closing up my throat. "Jo, please. It's enough. This town, it's seen enough."

She just shakes her head, tears turning into rivers of moonlight slipping down her cheeks. "It will never be enough. Not for her."

My mind jumps to Luna, who still stands with her hands over her mouth a few yards away from me, body racking with sobs. "For who?" I plead. The thought that she's doing this for Luna of all people makes me woozy.

"*For Lucia*," she cries, voice ripping and tearing with the effort and grief of the past eight months. The gun trembles in her hands, and I wonder why she never used it before, on her other victims. Why she's using it on me now.

Except I do know. I didn't drown Carlos, so she doesn't need to drown me.

Trying not to sound too incredulous, I ask, "And you really think she *wants* this?"

"Of course not," she sobs. "She didn't want any of this. She didn't want to lose her sister, or her boy-" She cuts herself off, barely able to speak through her tears.

"But the man that killed her sister went to prison," I say. "Don't you think that would have been a worse sentence for what they did to Carlos?"

"They were minors," she spits out bitterly. "And since they didn't go in with the intent to harm… the sentence would have been bullshit."

"Maybe. But please," I plead again. "You did what you had to do, you can stop this now. Do you really want to see this town crash and burn?"

Her eyes harden, and so does her grip on the gun. "No, I don't. I love this town, these people. But if the town doesn't burn then something is going to crumble in its place." Her throat bobs with the effort of talking, of speaking through the lump in her windpipe. "It won't be me, and it won't be Lucia, and it won't be Luna."

I tear my eyes from the tip of the gun just in time to see Luna's horrified face. I can read the thought all over her face. *She did this partly because of me.*

I whip my head back to Jo, waving my hand towards Luna. "Don't you see? She's crumbling anyway! Because of *you!*"

Jo takes another step toward me, and all the air flies from my lungs. "Don't say that. Don't-"

I try to stumble backward, to get further away from the gun that's now only a meter or two away, but my feet are rooted to the ground. I'm thrown back to a conversation with Luna, about how I'd taken root here. But, God, I really need to move right now, I need to-

"Why do you need to hurt me?" I breathe out, the strength behind my voice diminishing to almost nothing, until I'm cowering before someone I thought to be my friend. "Haven't you done your job? Why- why do you n-need to hurt me?"

Jo jerks her head toward Luna. "Because you hurt her."

Luna squeals in objection because I can't. It's like I used up every ounce of courage I have. That one step she took, it made the gun come into focus with my blurry, glassesless vision. And I can't look anywhere else.

"That's not true," Luna is saying. "She didn't hurt me, she did nothing but help me—"

"She lied to you," Jo croaks out. "Just like she lied to me, but she did you worse."

"No," Luna sobs. "No, no, no, it doesn't matter—"

"Your mother had to listen to you cry in your room for *hours*."

Hysterical, Luna backtracks, "Yeah, yeah, I was pissed, but that doesn't mean that I don't still *love* her."

The words are enough to start my heart up again, to make me tear my gaze from my death sentence to Luna. I'd moved further away from her than I thought, but I can make out the way she's holding her head in her hands, tugging at her hair, desperation leaking from every pore.

It happens quickly after that, and I don't see it because I'm too busy staring at Luna. My eyes fly back to Jo as she hollers out, tumbling to the ground with the weight of the body thrown into her. Except Reyna wasn't aiming to knock her over, because as they both fall, her fingers wrap around the gun, tighter than Jo, twisting it.

"*You bitch*," I hear Reyna shout, the words caught up in the scuffle, the sounds of two bodies wrestling together. "Did you even think about the families of *your* victims? Carlos had a mother and a sister, but *so did Anthony.*"

I don't even think she means to pull the trigger, at least not yet. The gunshot rings out in time with their bodies hitting the ground, and I stumble back, hands flying to my ears, eyes open with horror. They're both so still afterward I can't tell which of them is dead, or if it's both.

The world is still for only a few seconds, as though all five of us have reached that space between life and death. I'm so woozy, I almost convince myself that the bullet hit *me*.

Luna's scream makes its way past the fog clouding around my brain, and I have just enough awareness to abandon my gaze on the bodies. I sprint toward her, where she's already falling, and I just feel my hand graze hers before I fall, too.

Chapter Twenty-Six

THE SEVENTH AND FINAL body is found at approximately nine forty seven in the evening, ten minutes after we saw it happen. We watch them take her away on a stretcher, performing CPR and everything they can, but I know it's too late. I felt the life leave her, and all I can do is watch as two women are taken from my life forever.

Jo, taken by the police. And Reyna, just… taken.

Luna and I sit huddled by the edge of the forest, watching the police take Lucia's statement. They'd already taken ours, giving us towels and blankets to dry ourselves with. It feels like so long since we were in the water, I almost forget we're wet.

Luna's blanket slips from her shoulder, but she doesn't seem to notice, too focused on her chattering teeth and watching the lights of the ambulance disappear through the trees. Flashlights wave across the ground, police and crime scene investigators surveying the area, marking it. I don't see why, it's not like they need evidence. Jo told the truth.

The blood, the anguish on Reyna's face in her last moments flash before my eyes, and I wince. I'd tried to stop it, the blood, once I realized she shot herself instead of Jo. But the bullet went clean through her, and the blood coated my fingers, and her entire torso, until the dirt beneath her turned crimson, too. It turned into an unstoppable waterfall, bleeding first through her shirt, and then *my* shirt.

I look down, surveying my fingers in the dim light offered by the flashlights and lanterns. Flecks of red remain scattered across my knuckles, dried into the creases of my skin, and I pick them away, breathing a little easier as each bit is scratched free. I washed most of the lingering blood off in the water, but I must have missed some in my haste. I scrubbed as fast as possible, running from the quarry as fast as I could. Even now, I stare at it, into the water disappearing over the edge, and I can feel it staring back at me.

Ducking my head, I fix my focus onto Luna instead, anything to make the pounding in my chest go away. Or at least diminish. Just for a moment or two. Leaning over, I pull Luna's blanket back up into place, tucking it firmly around her shoulders.

She glances at me. "Thanks."

All I can do is stare at her, and marvel at the fact that it hadn't been us. Neither of us got taken.

"There's still…" she mutters, and then it's her turn to lean over, using her finger nail to scratch a trail down the side of my cheek. More blood, I can presume, as the flakes drift down from my skin. I resist the urge to gag, and just let her get it off of me.

When she's done, she rubs her hands on the ground beside her, and it makes me wince. Even dried, the blood just keeps spreading, and spreading. It's *everywhere*.

I don't think I'll ever be able to get it all off. Not completely, not those lingering traces, the ghost of it on my skin.

I stare at that pool of blood, the center of it all where it's only spread since. "Do you think she meant to do it?" I ask. "What she did?"

Luna chews on the words as she replies, and I get it. Just saying it aloud is unsettling. "Shooting herself?"

I nod slowly. I can't move much faster than slow motion, it's like my body can't catch up with what happened. Although, to be fair, my mind isn't doing a great job, either. "I mean, do you think she meant to shoot Jo when she grabbed the gun?"

To my surprise, Luna merely gives a tired shrug. "Could've been either, could've been both. I don't…" She sighs. "I'm not gonna speculate. I can't."

"I might spend the rest of my life wondering." Numbness spreads through me, stemming from that leftover blood, and I scrub harder against my skin. It needs to go away, I need it *gone*.

"Stop," Luna murmurs, resting her hand on top of mine, settling them back down into my lap. To my horror, I can't stop her when she stands, striding away from me, toward that awaiting water. I know it's waiting, that's all it ever does, just waits until someone gets close enough for it to swallow. A strangled garble of sounds fall from my mouth, indecipherable as I shake my head, and I start to stand, to go after her, but my legs won't hold me-

And then she's back, putting both hands on my shoulders, easing me back against the tree. I stare at her, almost weeping in relief now that she's touching me again, her fingers digging into my collarbones.

"Sit," she shushes me, lowering herself back to the ground in front of me. She dangles her towel, now damp, in front of my nose. "This might work better."

Wordless, I offer her my hands, and she drags the cloth along them, washing away the last remaining traces of Reyna's blood, until nothing but skin remains. She moves to my face, washing down my cheeks, chin, then my forehead. I close my eyes, allowing her to cleanse me until she sits back, nodding. She pushes the towel into my fingers. "Better?"

I breathe out, steadier than I have in hours as I wrap the cloth around my hands, not wanting to look at them quite yet, because that red is still clinging to my eyelids. It's still there, but at least it's not *there* there. "Better."

She sighs, sitting up a little straighter. Like the ease of my burden is the ease of hers. "When do you think we can leave?" she whispers.

"Now." I nearly jump out of my skin at the unexpected voice. After everything, I'd tried to block everything out besides Luna.

Luna spins around, looking up at her mom. "They said we can?"

Lucia leans down, patting her daughter's cheek. "No reason for us to stay, a million reasons for us to leave and never come back again."

Luna springs to her feet, probably ready to run through the forest and never look back, but I sag further into the dirt. The knowledge of my destination settles into me, of who won't be there. Who I'll never see there again. How do I just walk into that place and go to sleep? How do I *live* there?

Luna leans down to tap me on the chin, and I look up. "I know what you're thinking about, and stop thinking it immediately." She straightens, extending her hand out to me. "You're not going back to your apartment. Not after…"

After seeing my roommate shoot herself.

Luna swallows her words, and wiggles her fingers. "You're coming home with me."

I inhale, nodding. Reaching out to clasp her hand, I rise to my feet.

SLEEP DOESN'T COME ANY easier in Luna's room than it would have in mine. The air mattress blown up on her floor is uneven and deflating steadily by the minute, pushing into my back as I sink further and further toward the wood beneath.

I flop over on my side, shoving my head into the pillow, wondering if I could just knock myself out cold against the floor.

Luna's raw voice drifts down to me, and she shifts in bed at the sound of me tossing and turning. "Alex?" She leans over the edge, propping herself up on her elbow.

"Sorry," I whisper. Air mattresses are like bubble wrap. They don't know how to not make noise. "Can't sleep."

"That makes two of us."

Looking at her is waking me up even more, so I gaze past her, up toward the ceiling. She has one of those popcorn ceilings, and

I've never really understood the point of those. I grew up with them, too.

Luna seems to notice I'm avoiding her eye, because she twists in bed, following my eyeline. "What are you looking at?"

"Your ceiling," I say honestly. "Wondering what the hell the point of ceilings having lumps on them is."

Gazing up, Luna tilts her head. "I think it's a matter of convenience more than anything, it's a type of spray and it covers up any cracks or discolored spots there might be. That's what my dad said, at least."

"That's disappointing," I murmur, and I hear her turn her body toward me again. "When I was little, I thought they were supposed to be stars. Once when my parents weren't home, I put black paint around the white dots, so it looked more like a night sky. It just ended up looking like a four year old painted it."

"Well, were you four?"

"Eleven, but I think we've already covered that I don't have an artistic bone in my body."

Luna huffs, snuggling into the edge of the bed, not tearing her eyes off of me. "Is that what's keeping you up? Thoughts about my cheap ceiling?"

"Of course not. There are a million and one things keeping me up right now, and I can't form a coherent thought about a single one of them."

"My brain feels like mush," she says, and the dulled glint in her eyes shows it. "I think it's trying to protect me, like… if I can't think, I might stop hurting."

I rub my neck. "I wish my brain was that nice to me." I shift again, because my arm is pushing into something hard, and I might just be making full contact with the floor at this point. "Also, I think this thing has a hole."

"I think it does, too," she says. "That's why I told you to just sleep in the bed."

I shift awkwardly. "I didn't think you'd want me to."

"I *literally* told you to."

The thoughts and memories swim to the surface. Over and over, I've tried to decipher that desperate look on her face, those shouted words that led to Reyna being able to take the gun. Maybe if I think about *that* enough, I'll stop seeing blood everywhere.

"Saying it doesn't equate to actually meaning it," I blurt out, without thinking, immediately regretting it as soon as the words have passed into the space between us.

Luna's head slips off her hand in surprise, and to my never-ending shock she tumbles from the bed, landing nearly on top of me with an *oof.*

"Jesus," I groan, dislodging her elbow from my gut, both of our limbs all over the place as we get tangled in the air mattress and within each other.

"I'm sorry," she breathes out, brushing away the hair falling into her face. She shifts until she's lying beside me, scrutinizing me through the dark. "I just... what?"

I try not to blush, but if the way my face is burning is any indication, I don't think I succeed. Trying to backtrack, I say, "Nothing, it's nothing, I just wasn't sure if you'd be comfortable-"

"If I'd be *comfortable?*" She pulls her body back up, fighting against the deflating mass beneath her. "Alex, you put yourself in front of a *gun* for me not *four hours ago*. I think you might be the only person I feel safe around right now."

"But you don't trust me," I say weakly, staring at the ceiling. "I mean, it's not like I blame you."

"Who said I don't trust you?"

I look at her incredulously. "Um. You did."

She closes her eyes, breathing in deeply. "Honestly, that whole... whatever, I sort of forgot about it. It feels like a million years ago."

"It was yesterday," I say through a burning throat. "You hated me."

She rubs a hand down her face. "Alex, I swear to everything holy, didn't you hear me?"

My heart is pounding so hard against my ribs I wonder if she can hear it. Is it possible to hear someone's heartbeat if you're not right up against their chest? The thought that you can't is almost comforting, that some information you can keep to yourself. "I heard you."

Luna stares at me like I'm about to chop off my own hand. "So, if you *heard* me, what are you talking about?"

The question plaguing me falls from my lips, even though I almost don't want to hear the answer. "Did you mean it?"

"What?"

"When you said you love me? Did you *mean* it?" I plead, still refusing to look at her, because if I see her face I might just crumble on the spot. "Or was it just a Hail Mary, to distract her?"

I glance over at her just in time to see a flicker of realization dawn over her features. I try to look away again, but Luna's hand shoots out to hold my face still. Her eyes are so dark in the dim light of the room, her pupils bleeding into her irises. "I wasn't trying to distract her, Alex. It was a hail Mary, but not because it was a *lie*. Because it was the *truth*. She was coming at you with a gun, Alex, I thought if she knew... if she knew how I *felt-*"

I can't take it anymore. Her voice grows panicky again, too much like it sounded all day yesterday, like it did when I showed up at her house, or when she told me to leave. My cheek tingles where it still rests beneath her fingers. Her grip eased as she talked, no longer holding me as though her life depends on it, but rather just holding me for the sake of holding. I raise my hand, placing it over hers, and her voice trickles into silence.

"You looked so... terrified..." I choke out. "I thought you'd say anything."

"I would have. But the truth happened to work out alright."

I don't mean to brush my lips against her, but it feels like the most natural thing in the world, just the softest whisper of a kiss. And when I murmur that I love her, too, that I would have shouted the same thing had I thought it would make a difference, that feels as natural as breathing, too.

"I think I'll be able to brag about that for the rest of my life," I say into her ear once we've both sunk back down, somehow both fitting our heads onto one pillow. "That a girl's love *literally* saved my life. Like, from a weapon."

Luna actually lets out a small laugh, probably the first one I've heard in nearly twenty four hours, and I nearly sob at the sound. It's soft, and breathy, and over as quick as it started, but her lips are curving up on the edges, and the view can tide me over until I get a real smile. "You totally should. None of your friends in New York will believe you though."

"I don't even care. It's very poetic, you can't change my mind."

"You know what else is poetic?" Luna asks.

"Tell me."

"Everyone's talking about how when they're with their person, their heart can't stop racing."

My heart starts racing at those two words. *My person.*

"And that's totally true, don't get me wrong, but it's not *always* true. Like right now, you're the only thing that's keeping my heart under control, keeping it steady."

Any other time, I might joke about how that feels like an insult, but it doesn't. I know exactly what she means, because for the first time since yesterday, my heart beats in time with hers, too.

"Definitely poetic," I agree, voice hoarse, unsure whether it's from emotion or exhaustion. Now that I have one less thought, one less worry, I think I might actually be able to close my eyes and see nothing.

Luna looks the same, eyelids drooping down, muscles giving out as she falls completely into the mattress, even though it's barely even a mattress anymore.

"This really doesn't have any air in it," she mumbles into my ear, but neither of us want to move, and we both manage to fall asleep, anyway.

Chapter Twenty-Seven

THE MORGANS HAVE NO choice but to close the sculpture center for the rest of summer, because none of them could stomach walking through it. Luna tried to walk down that path, toward the awaiting ticket booth and paths that lead to where we were that night. We got halfway there before she froze, running into an invisible wall, unable to get past whatever mental block she's built around this path that we took. I couldn't help but feel a little relieved when she stopped, because I wanted nothing more than to turn around, too. So, I just grabbed her arm, steered her into the other direction, and we walked back home.

Lucia never even bothered trying to go, sending Roger to pack up and close down instead. I can't say I blame her.

"We'll open back up next year," Luna tells me from the other side of the picnic table, but there's no art supplies around her. I don't think she's painted at all in the past two months. "It's just that, now…"

"It's too fresh," I nod. She doesn't need to explain herself to me. If it were my decision, I'd encourage her to never go back there. That's sort of my plan.

"Yeah. And it's not like we'll get any customers anyway, right? Who would want to go there, right after…"

She trails off, and she's right. The sculpture center might be a small hike away from the quarries, but they're inherently connected. Half the statues there are built out of pieces of those quarries, pulled from the holes in the days before they were relentlessly filled with water.

"Not me," I say with rigor, and we fall into silence. I play with the words in my mouth, before asking what I've been wondering for the past four times we've sat out here. "Where's all your supplies?"

"What supplies?"

"Your painting stuff. Usually when we sit out here, you're painting."

She flushes, looking down, picking at her cuticles because she doesn't have a paintbrush to occupy her hand with. "I don't know. I guess I haven't been feeling very inspired lately."

I can't argue with that. "Because of…?"

"Yeah," she says quickly. "I don't know, I've tried a few times, but every time… it's like I can't think of anything beautiful. It starts off alright, but then I lose my train of thought, and it veers into something ugly that I end up throwing away halfway through."

I try to imagine her producing something ugly, and it just doesn't make sense in my brain. And then I think about all the ugly things she's seen, and how easy memories can muddle a person's thoughts. I'm not an artist, but I imagine when your brain is all churned up like that, the painting you produce might be a little churned up, too. "Maybe you should finish it," I suggest after a moment.

She looks up. "What?"

"Yeah," I say. "You said you always give up halfway through, but maybe if you finish something shitty, you can get past… whatever it is. Is there an artist's version of writer's block?"

She nods. "Some people call it painter's block, but it doesn't have nearly the same ring to it."

"Right, painter's block. Except you're not really *blocked*, your body just wants to paint something different than your mind. So if you let your body do its thing, maybe your mind can take over."

Luna lets out a small laugh. "I think you're seriously overthinking it."

"I'm doing that on purpose," I joke. "I'm solving *your* overthinking with more overthinking on my end. It's foolproof."

She stares at me for a long moment before pushing away from the table and jogging to the house. She comes back with her arms laden with supplies, spreading them across the table.

I grin. "This feels more normal." It clearly does for her, too, because the tension in her muscles eases, and she sets up with smooth, fluid motions. Unscrewing paint bottles, opening the mason jar of water she uses to clean her brush, settling a towel over her lap. It's sort of a long process, setting up to paint, and by the time she pulls the canvas toward her, an idea must have sprung up, because she immediately tackles the white with color.

"Talk to me while I paint," she says, making wide strokes with watered down paint. She's doing something called an underpainting. "Maybe that'll help, too. Distract me."

"You do know that *telling* someone to talk is the best possible way to get every single thought and possible conversation starter to fly out of their brain, right?"

She chuckles, swirling the olive green paint around in the previously clear water, and I watch as the jar steadily fills with pigment. "I'm sure you'll think of something."

For several moments, I don't, too mesmerized by watching her hands move fluidly around the canvas, making something that I can't recognize yet. It's a fascinating process, really, how several layers of paint will look like absolutely nothing, and then you'll reach a tipping point, and shapes begin to form.

"You're staring," she says, reminding me of how she'd called me out for it after she pulled me from the water.

"I can't help it," I tease. "You've already got paint on your cheek."

She scowls, using the towel on her lap to wipe it away, only partially successful. "Okay, besides that, what are you thinking about?"

I drum my fingers against the table. "Mostly how beautiful you look, but I'll try to think of something else."

Luna blushes furiously, smiling, but doesn't look up.

So I look elsewhere, around at the surrounding trees. "I'm starting to get what you were saying," I say slowly, looking around. "When I first moved here, and you were so baffled. There really is *nothing* to do here."

She laughs. "I tried to warn you."

"You did, although I'm glad I didn't listen." I don't add that leaving wasn't really an option.

She seems to be thinking it, though, because she glances up at me. "No wonder you were never bored, never complained, you were too wrapped up in researching, or whatever it is you did."

"Researching was part of it," I say. "Mostly I was wrapped up in you."

Her cheeks warm again. "Don't change the subject."

I hold up my hands. "I'm not changing the subject. Just stating how I had more than one effective distraction."

"So you *did* spend a lot of time researching?"

"At first," I nod. "Until I ran out of stuff to research. And then at the end, that's how I found that picture."

She knows the one, and she presses her lips in a thin line, jerking up to face me. I panic for a second, eyes flitting to make sure her hand hadn't moved in the same way, but it's perfectly poised over her palette. "Did you ever research me?"

I hesitate, because how do you tell someone, yes, I looked into every nook and cranny of your life because every person in this town was on my list as a potential murderer? But she doesn't look like she'll be upset by my answer, so I brace myself. "Don't take it personally. I delved into the lives of everyone I met."

To my surprise, she actually laughs. "Was there anything interesting? I can't imagine you found much, I'm not super into social media."

"I saw that," I say dryly. "I found... frustratingly little."

She brushes her hair off her shoulder, letting it drop down across her back. "Good. Glad to know I kept up my mysterious facade." The gears behind her eyes shift, and she squints, all humor dissipating. "So, if you researched me, you already knew about Carlos when I told you…"

I nearly fall off the bench. "No," I scramble to say, waving my hands, remembering how broken she sounded telling me about him, how she had to tear every word from her throat. "No, no, actually I had no idea about that. Afterwards, I figured it's because he has a different last name than you, so nothing about him came up."

Her muscles ease. "That's reassuring. I couldn't figure out if you were *actually* shocked when I told you that story, or just… a really good actress."

I huff. "I'm a terrible liar, believe it or not."

"Your whole job for the last month has been lying. Not that I hold it against you," she adds when my movement stills. "But, like… wasn't it?"

I shrug. "Actually, no. I had to lie about why I moved, and my job, but everything else…" My words trickle into silence, and I reach out, tapping under her chin to make her stop painting, to make her look at me. "You have to know that I lied as little as possible. Especially to you."

She smiles softly. "I believe you. You did look surprised, that day, and… angry."

"And if I'd known, I'm pretty sure I never would have jumped into the quarry in the first place," I say seriously, shivering at the memory, the feeling of water in my windpipe.

Luna presses her lips together. "My mom agreed to sign the papers, you know."

My forehead creases. "Papers...?"

She scratches her neck with the back of her paintbrush. "Yeah, um, the... release papers."

My breath catches in my throat, and my legs take me up and around the picnic table, until I'm sitting sideways on her bench. "She did?"

Luna nods, not looking up from her work. Shapes are beginning to take form now, the image bleeding from her paintbrush in soft, blended tones and sharp angles. "I think everything that happened, with the revenge, and all the pain we've dragged out since the fall. It's like you said. Enough is enough."

"I'm sorry," I whisper. "I know you were hoping-"

"I wasn't," she cuts me off brokenly, choked up. "Not really. I knew. You don't come back from that long in a coma. I mean, it wasn't even a coma I don't think, because a coma's a temporary state. What he was, he just... became."

I wonder if she's spent the last two weeks thinking over how the last people to speak to Carlos hadn't been his killers, or his friends, but Jo. I know I haven't been able to get that out of my mind.

"He deserves to be somewhere else," I agree. "Someplace better."

She wipes her eyes before a single tear can escape. "So do we."

Several hours later, colors have filled her canvas: an image of a young boy caught in the clouds, torn between heaven and earth.

I FIND LUCIA IN the garage, where she's moved all her equipment now that she's avoiding the center. Except unlike the first time encountering her like this, she's not leaned over her work, dutifully chipping away until stone somehow looks soft. Instead, she's fallen into a chair in the corner, gripping one of her tools. staring at the block of untouched marble in the center of the concrete floor.

"This doesn't look productive," I say, tucking my hands into my pockets as I enter. I'm doing my best to always announce myself when I come into the room, increasingly aware by the day of how jumpy everyone in this town is. I made that mistake in the kitchen once, of being too quiet, and she spilled an entire pot of coffee on the counter.

Lucia glances at me, turning the tool over in her hand. Two lessons, and I still can't remember any of the names or technical terms. "That's probably because it's not."

"I didn't think you had an unproductive bone in your body," I say. "You crank out sculptures like no one's business. Are you having artist's block, too? Luna's been having the same problem. Like mother, like daughter."

She smiles, but it's frail. "It's not my mind, it's my body. My arms are tired, feels like all the time. I can barely hold them up for longer than two minutes."

I don't say aloud that it probably *is* her mind, and that the two are more linked than most think. "I can't say I blame you. I'm pretty sure I've developed a permanent crook in the neck from when Reyna punched me in the face."

My voice stumbles over her name, the syllables coming out in broken fragments. It still feels wrong, saying her name in common conversation, like it's normal. Like she's still here. I lift a phantom touch to my lip, where the cut that has since faded into a scar pushes against my fingers.

"It's a nice piece of marble," I say to steer my mind away, running my fingers along what looks to be a two by five block. "What's your plan?"

"I don't have a plan," she says honestly, leaning further back into her chair and tossing whatever she held onto the table to her side. "I'm actually more interested in *your* plans."

Pressing my hand into the cool stone to steady myself, I peer over it and ask, "*My* plans? What plans?"

She spreads her hands out wide. "You tell me."

I narrow my eyes. "Is this the whole, *what are your intentions with my daughter,* talk? Because I sort of thought we were past that."

"Sort of," Lucia says. "It's more like… what are your intentions with… where you plan on living."

"Where I… oh," I trail off as I realize the conversation I've entered. I'd honestly been hoping to push it out a few more weeks. "I, um, I haven't really thought about it. I can't say I've had a spare moment."

Lies. It's sort of all I've been thinking about.

I'm fairly sure Lucia can tell, because she sighs. "I know that you came here planning on returning to your old life in New York."

"Lucia," I stop her. "I'm not breaking up with your daughter. If that means I stay here, then I stay." It comes out a lot more confident than I had expected.

She smiles. "Again, I hadn't doubted that. It's just…" she presses her lips together, swallowing. "Do you know how short term memory and long term memory works?"

"In, like, the *vaguest* way possible, but yes."

"I can't say I'm an expert," she says, "but I do know that the capacity of long term memory is essentially unlimited, and once a short term memory gets converted into long term, it can stay there in the brain for quite a while."

It certainly can. For the good and for the bad.

Lucia goes on. "Luna has good long term memories here, and so do I. But the only ones she can see right now are the bad ones." She pauses. "Things are bad here right now. And I imagine they're about to get a whole lot worse."

I know what she's talking about. "Luna told me," I whisper, voice reverberating throughout the stone room. "I'm sorry for your loss."

She glances up at me, a flicker of pain passing over her features before disappearing. "He's not dead yet, Alex, it's a… little bit of a process."

I swallow. "I know. But you've still lost plenty, and I'm still sorry."

"Thank you," she murmurs. "So has she, and… I think she needs to make some new memories. Better ones."

"Lucia," I say slowly. "That's great, and I totally agree, but I can't just *make* her leave here. This is her home."

Lucia holds up a hand. "Did you know she planned on moving to New York?"

"No. She mentioned it in passing once, I think, but it seemed more like she wondered distantly about it, rather than actually wanting to go."

"She always wanted it," she sighs, "Vermont isn't exactly the artist's hub of the country. I've made it work because of my specific art form, but painting is a considerably more urban medium. She had an apartment lined up and everything." She holds up her hand, displaying the smallest of spaces between her thumb and index finger. "She was *this* close to signing the lease and getting out of here, at least for a little while."

But then…

"After it happened, there was no way she was leaving. She barely left the house, other than to go to the hospital." She leans forward, rubbing her temples, then her burning eyes. "She stopped painting, stopped… dreaming."

I suppose it's the only thing she could do. How do you keep on dreaming, when your life has turned into a living nightmare?

"It's my fault she stayed as long as she did," she mutters, almost as if she's speaking to herself instead of me. "After it happened, I wouldn't let either of them go."

"You shouldn't have had to," I say gently, walking over to sit in the chair beside her. My heart wrenches as I gaze at the woman who, since meeting her, I've almost only ever seen smiling. Silver lines her eyes, face red and splotchy from the effort of holding in the emotion. "You still shouldn't have to."

She looks back up at me, looking suddenly so old. "Yes, I do. After they're fully grown, that might just be a parent's *only* job. Letting them go. It also happens to be the hardest."

Neither of us say how Carlos isn't fully grown, and she has to let him go anyway.

Not entirely sure why I'm feeling choked up, I say, "I'll bet you were an incredible mom."

"I tried my best," she sighs. "I could only take them so far."

I rub my jaw, staring down at my feet. "But if she didn't want to go then, do you really think she'll want to go now?"

Lucia smiles. "She wanted to go then. She just couldn't."

"My question still stands."

Lucia takes a deep breath, before smacking her hand on the table beside her and scooping up her tools. "I suggest you talk to her, but I'll say this for certain. She needs you more than she once needed to stay here. I don't think she needs or wants this town at all anymore."

Chapter Twenty-Eight

I HAVE ONE MORE matter of business before I can even think about leaving. Before I can consider the *after* of all of this. And it's not writing that damn article. I've already told Elise that I'm never writing that article. With Luna's blessing, I shipped all my notes and research off to the office and washed my hands of it. It's another journalist's problem, and whatever they churn out, neither of us will ever read.

Instead, I find myself outside Parker's home once more, at a time when I know Parker is at work, so I can speak to Sadie again.

"Alex," she says softly. "Hi."

"Hi," I whisper, fingers fidgeting with the envelope I hold. "Don't worry, I'm not here to see Parker, I'm here to see you, and then- then I'll be out of your hair."

Her body relaxes, and I can't imagine how these past couple of days have been for this family, finding out exactly who took Xavier from them. *Why* she took him from them. "I didn't mean for you-"

"I know," I assure her, even though my last spark of hope is extinguished. At least for now. "I didn't come here to cause more pain. I won't do that, because enough has happened to this town. To the people of this town."

Sadie's eyes well with tears, and she says the last thing I expect. "Your father did a good job raising you. I'm glad to see it, that Parker came from something good."

I swallow roughly. "Yeah. He did his best." Hands shaking, I hold out the envelope, holding only my contact information without a note that I know Parker doesn't want. "Let him know… Let him know, when he's ready, that I tried to come. And if he's never ready… Then at least you know that I tried."

CARLOS'S OFFICIAL TIME OF death is two thirty seven in the afternoon, on an otherwise uneventful Tuesday. He flatlined as soon as they unplugged the machines, because they were the only thing keeping him alive. Luna says it was almost relieving, that he couldn't hold on for even a second, because that means they made the right choice. But I still hold her as she cries, through the funeral and the weeks following, as she adjusts to losing him for good. To doing something different on Sundays, instead of visiting the hospital to speak to a boy who wouldn't answer.

The rest of the summer comes and goes, and Luna brings me back to the bridge because we can't go to the quarry anymore, and the lingering days of warmth are growing fewer and fewer. I watch from my perch at her side as the leaves begin to shift from their normal green into a colorful frenzy, painting the mountains in warm autumn hues. I can somehow note the change even now that the sun has set, the silhouette not as dark, not as ominous.

"It's crazy how beautiful we think it is when the leaves change," Luna murmurs. "People come to Vermont from all over in the fall just to watch them shrivel up and die."

"I don't like to think about that when looking at foliage," I say. "Because in their defense, it's really freaking pretty."

Luna cracks a smile. "That's one thing we've got going for us right now."

The unspoken words sit heavily between us, the topic I've been allowing her to build up to for the past month.

To my surprise, she takes a deep breath. "I've been thinking about what you were saying the other day..." she trails off.

Not wanting to pressure her, I say, "You're definitely gonna have to be more specific, because I say *a lot* of things. Elise is always going on and on about how I never stop talking, which I personally found ironic."

Luna's brows furrow. "Who's Elise?"

I pull up short with a startled laugh. "Ah, yes, I keep forgetting about the intense separation between this new life, and the one I left behind, and how you don't know much about that other one."

Luna hesitates. "Is Elise your ex-girlfriend?"

I burst out laughing, baffled at the mere thought. *"Definitely* not. She's my best friend, we work together back in New York."

After hearing about... everything that went down here because of what I came to investigate, my boss was shockingly eager to give me some paid time off, to wrap up here and deal with the mess they threw me into. Except it doesn't feel like a mess, not anymore.

Luna tilts her head. "That's actually what I wanted to talk about."

My thoughts shut off, breath hitching in my chest. "Okay..."

Luna presses her lips together before blurting out those four words. "What if we left?"

I turn to her fully, lifting my brows. "You want to leave?"

"Oh, don't act so surprised, I know my mom played mediator."

I sigh. "I'm sorry I didn't bring it up, I didn't want you to feel pressured, or like I wouldn't stay here if that's what you wanted."

She jumps, eyes sparkling in surprise and awe. "You would?"

"Luna," I say softly. "I'm offended that you thought anything else."

She exhales, a strand of hair blowing up in front of her face in the breeze. "That's nice to hear, but what my mom told you wasn't wrong." She pauses, throat bobbing. "I had two things keeping me here. Carlos, and my parents. One of those is gone."

"I know," I whisper.

"And my parents were urging me to just *leave* last year," she goes on through a stuttered breath. "I think it'd hurt them more if I stayed, like... they were holding me back. Like I was ignoring what I wanted."

I press myself back against my hands, the heels of my palms digging into the worn wood of the roof. How old is this thing? How many storms has it weathered? Buildings and bridges don't get enough credit for how long they stay standing. "So, what *do* you want?"

Luna looks around, tugging her knees up to her chest. The cream cardigan enveloping her shoulders flows over her skin like milk, holding her in, keeping her warm. I always forget how quickly the warmth of summer sweeps away. Instead of answering, she asks, "Are there places like this in New York?"

I gaze over at her, back lit by the moon, features fading into a soft silhouette. "Like what, exactly?" This feels like a test.

She lifts a shoulder. "Beautiful, I guess? But not just that. Places you go to make you feel… whole."

I breathe out of my nose, and it's not quite cold enough for the air to materialize in front of me. I can take comfort in that, in something so simple that we won't freeze up here. "I don't know. I think New York can make you feel whole in a different way, you don't need to go anywhere in particular."

"Did it make *you* feel whole?"

I brush my hair aside, regretting it when the breeze nips at the tip of my ear. "Sure, at times. Not so much recently, though, but maybe that's just because you've always been here."

Luna lets out a breath of laughter. "Something can only make you feel whole if you let it."

"I think time away from it was good," I agree. "I'd never had that before, it always… was what it was. Maybe it held me together more than I thought."

"You looked like you needed a break when you first got here," Luna says, gazing out over the mountains. "I think I need one, too."

"Stagnancy goes against human nature," I say. "It's not a break, it's… allowing yourself to breathe again."

"I can't breathe here right now," she whispers, resting her chin on the knees she hugs. "And neither can you."

I don't bother agreeing, because she knows, and I know. "To answer your other question," I say into the space between us, "yeah, it's beautiful there. In a monumentally different way than this, but I'd never call New York anything other than magnificent."

Luna turns back to me, eyes twinkling. "Even though you can't see the stars?"

I roll my eyes, huffing, "You can see the stars. What do you think a city is, a bubble filled with smoke from cars and factories or something?"

Luna grins. "Sort of. Like you didn't have assumptions about Vermont before coming here."

"I totally did, except half of those assumptions still stand."

She laughs, the sound brushing over my skin and making me shiver. "Tell me what the sky looks like, then, from your bubble of pollution."

I gaze up above us, at the galaxies always watching over us, waiting for us to look back. "It's less," I admit. "You can only see the stars that are really bright, that are closer to Earth. The ones that are far away sort of… fade away into black. Dulled."

"I can fill in the blanks for us," Luna murmurs, eyes turning toward the sky. "I've been looking at this long enough, I've got it memorized."

"Good," I say with a slow smile. "Because I could use some distance from here, from…" I cut myself off, but she knows the place I'm talking about. The place filled with blood and near suffocation that still plagues my nightmares.

She nods, eyes crinkling in understanding. "I know, at this point you hate… there… almost as much as I do."

I scratch my jaw, "Almost dying there twice will do that to you. I must say, despite the crime statistics, I've never almost died in New York."

"You almost died here," she chokes out, almost a realization. As if it truly set in. Both that I almost did, and that I didn't.

I nod slowly, cringing at the memory. "But I didn't, thanks to you."

"You still jumped in after me," she whispers, referencing the same thing I'd asked incredulously back then, sprawled soaking wet next to Luna under the sun. "The second time."

My eyes shine. "I'll always jump in after you. Besides, You followed me in first." I lean in to brush my lips against hers, blocking her from the cold. "Come to New York with me?"

She reaches out, takes my hand, and makes me feel whole again. "I'll follow you there, too."

Acknowledgements

I feel like this has been a 12-year long journey, from the day I wrote my first book in sixth grade to now. For a long time, it was hard to imagine that I would ever write something like this at the end of my debut novel, that I would get to thank the people that helped me get here.

Hansen House, thank you for taking a shot on this book and helping me develop it into something more. The fact that Parker didn't exist in the manuscript I initially submitted is baffling, but you still saw something in the story. My editors, Cate and Mercy, gave me the outside perspective that Fifty Feet Down needed, transforming my mind soup into something ready to be perceived by the outside world.

Elizabeth, thank you for starting this publishing house in the first place. This home for queer stories made me and Fifty Feet Down feel beyond welcome, and I couldn't imagine a better place for my debut. Thank you for helping me through the process, answering my endless questions, and being so patient when I started freaking out toward the end.

To my family, whose existence laid the groundwork for this book to begin with.

One of my core memories of the carving studio was on Father's Day, when my Dad wanted to walk around and look at all the sculptures. Mom and Grandma, I'd know nothing about the hidden quirks of West Rutland without you. I may have grown up in Rutland, but I spent enough time at Grandma's on Sundays, and heard enough of Mom's stories, that I could write this story.

Grandma, I got the idea for this book Junior year of college when I was home for winter break. It was a Sunday, and we'd gone to your house for the day, and I don't know why, but someone brought up the quarries and the carving studio. That night, I wrote the first scene, where Alex almost drowns and Luna saves her. But while at your house, I started writing in my notes all these ideas about quarries and West Rutland and mystery and family. Fifty Feet Down truly started when I was sitting on that recliner in your living room, so thank you for that.

About the Author

Sophie Tanen started writing books when she was 10, and never stopped. She grew up in Vermont, loving books for as long as she can remember. It wasn't until high school that she read her first sapphic book and decided that she wanted more for people like her, even if she had to write them herself. For college, she moved to New Orleans to study computer science but wrote in her spare time. With a love of solving puzzles and finding the right answer, Sophie fell down a hole of reading, and eventually writing, mysteries. When she can't get her hands on a book or her laptop, Sophie spends her time playing rugby, painting, or watching Criminal Minds on repeat. Sophie now lives in Chicago, where she has covered her walls in books and made a perfect booknook for writing.

Printed in the USA
CPSIA information can be obtained
at www.ICGtesting.com
LVHW041955061023
760217LV00029B/529/J